Copyright © 2025 by Paul Baldwin

All rights reserved

hardcover ISBN: 979-8-9884730-9-1

paperback ISBN: 979-8-9884730-7-7

e-book ISBN: 979-8-9884730-8-4

Scripture quotation marked as New Living Translation are taken from the Holy Bible, New Living Translation, copyright 1996, 2004, Tyndale House Publishers, Inc., Wheaton, Illinois 60189.

No part of this publication may be reproduced, distributed, or transmitted in any form or by any means, including photocopying, recording, or other electronic or mechanical methods, without the prior written permission of the publisher, except as permitted by U.S. copyright law. For permission requests, contact DJBaldwinBooks@gmail.com

The story, character names, characters, and incidents portrayed in this production are fictitious. No identification with actual persons (living or deceased) is intended or should be inferred. Business names are used for the purpose of Northern Virginia authenticity and storytelling only. No ownership decisions or happenings within and around businesses are factual. No endorsement implied.

Cover, logo, and illustrations by Adam Hay

Second Edition

Syndrome
Paul Baldwin

DJ Baldwin Books

Contents

I dedicate this second book, which completes the series, to my wife and soulmate Michelle. I'll love you forever. And to my niece, Brianna Salo, who left us too soon from spinal muscular atrophy. A portion of royalties goes to Cure SMA.

For our dying bodies must be transformed into bodies that will never die.
1 Corinthians 15:53

Prologue

Unity

E xistence was not a heavy blanket; it was a lead apron, the kind used in radiology, pressing the breath out of Unity's fragile body. It bore down on her chest, a suffocating weight that made every inhalation a conscious, agonizing effort.

Lying in the clinical starkness of her sickbed, she stared at the ceiling tiles, counting the perforated dots until they blurred. She clenched the thin, starched sheets with trembling hands. Her muscles, dormant for two decades, screamed in a chorus of fiery protests after another brutal physical therapy session. They were trying to jumpstart an engine that had sat rusting in a garage for twenty years.

"I'm sick of three-a-days!" she shouted.

Her voice was brittle, unfamiliar to her own ears. It slapped against the drab, bare walls of her containment unit, echoing in the aggressively antiseptic silence. The air conditioner hummed its monotonous monotone, indifferent to her misery. No one witnessed the outburst. The solitude only mocked her.

She wasn't a screamer by nature—the old Unity, the teenage Unity, had been the quiet one, the shadow to Mia's bright light. But eighteen months of this routine—wake in a panic, endure physical torture, choke down sludge, return to the void of sleep—had eroded her filter. It had stripped away the soft parts of her humanity, leaving only exposed nerves and a simmering, volcanic rage.

The Romanos called it rehabilitation. They spoke of muscle atrophy and synaptic pathways in hushed, reverent tones. Unity called it what it was: manufacturing. They weren't trying to heal a person; they were trying to refurbish a weapon. They were polishing up leverage to use against the sister she hadn't seen since there was peace between Russia and Ukraine.

Outside her heavy, reinforced door, the muffled murmur of animated chatter drifted from the hallway. The sound grew louder, sharp consonants bouncing off the linoleum floor.

Unity stiffened. A wave of apprehension washed over her, chilling the sweat that had pooled at the base of her spine during therapy. It hit her just seconds before the wretched aroma of dinner seeped through the ventilation grate near the floor.

"Oh, God. Not that same nasty shit." She pulled the sheet up over her nose, inhaling the scent of industrial bleach detergent instead.

The stench—scorched cow dung mixed with oxidized garlic and something distressingly sour, like old pickles—was unmistakable. The family's nutritionists, severe men in expensive suits, claimed the protein-heavy, microbiome-stuffed sludge was medically necessary to counter decades of intravenous feeding. Unity suspected they just enjoyed watching her gag. It was a small, petty torture, a daily reminder of who controlled even the most basic functions of her body.

The voices outside sharpened, rising in pitch. For the first few months of her captivity, after waking from the long dark, the noise outside her room had been nothing but a wall of irritating sound. A meaningless cadence. Now, like oil separating from water, the syllables clicked into rigid place. She could distinguish the rhythm of the conversation, the specific rolling dialect of the region.

Italian.

It had taken her a month to realize she wasn't just guessing at the meaning based on tone; she was translating it in real-time. The miracle serum Mia had injected her with—the stuff that had dragged her back from the edge of brain death—hadn't just woken her up. It had uploaded data. She was fluent in a language she had never studied. It was alienating, feeling foreign words assemble themselves into coherent thoughts in her own mind, but it was also power.

She knew exactly what the clones outside were whispering about: troop movements, supply lines, and the looming, inevitable shadow of war.

The heavy electronic deadbolt slid back with a loud, metallic *clack* that made her jump, despite knowing it was coming.

Unity dropped her hands from her face, arranging her features into a mask of boredom. The lock was overkill. Where was she going to go? Her legs were still wasted stems, her balance nonexistent. If she sat up too fast, the room spun till she vomited.

The door swung inward on silent hinges. Jon stood framed in the doorway, holding a stainless steel tray and a digital clipboard. His pristine white scrubs contrasted sharply with his dark skin, and a practiced, plastic smile was plastered across his face like a decal.

Unity didn't return it. She stared dead at him and slowly flipped him the middle finger, putting every ounce of her limited energy into the gesture.

Jon didn't flinch. He didn't check his watch or sigh or show any ripple of annoyance. He just stepped inside, kicking the heavy door shut with his heel, sealing them back in the pressurized silence.

"You did exceptionally well today on the parallel bars,"

he said, his tone infuriatingly conversational, as if he were talking about the weather and not her imprisonment. "Your weight-bearing capacity is up four percent. But the screaming... it reminds them you're a problem."

"I *am* a problem. I intend to remain a problem."

"We're back to this again?" With a swift, clinical motion, he stripped the blanket off her legs, exposing her shins to the cool air. "I need to measure your improvements before nutrients."

Unity huffed, crossing her arms over her chest, feeling the shallow rise and fall of her ribs. At least she was wearing a sports bra and compression shorts beneath the humiliating hospital gown. "You already see everything when you sponge-bathe the parts I can't reach. Just write down 'still crippled' on your little pad and give me the slop."

"Your skin continues to improve," Jon murmured, ignoring her jab. He set the tray down on the rolling table and began his examination. He pressed his cool fingers into her calf muscle, then her thigh, checking density and tone. His touch was completely devoid of warmth; he handled her like a mechanic inspecting a faulty carburetor. "It's... irregular by today's medical standards. The cellular regeneration rate is off the charts. The boss is going to be pleased."

"The boss can choke on a chicken bone."

Jon paused, pulling a penlight from his pocket. He leaned in, invading her personal space, and shone the beam into her pupils. "Your muscle tone is phenomenal considering the time frame, Unity. You'll be mobile in no time."

Mobile. A wheelchair was the best she dared to hope for in the next six months. But she kept her mouth shut. When she'd first woken from the twenty-year coma, screaming and thrashing in a body that didn't feel like hers, she had spit food at him. She had raged at his betrayal. He had been her caretaker for years at the facility back home, the nice man who changed her IVs and read to her while she slept, all while reporting back to the

Italian mob that enabled the creation of her sister. But rage took energy she didn't have in reserve tonight.

He clicked off the light and handed her the dinner tray. The gray mound quivered slightly.

"It's always the same," she said, her stomach rolling as she stared at it. "I want actual food. I want a cheeseburger. I want real clothes that don't tie in the back."

"We all make our own choices." Jon leaned in closer, his voice dropping to a barely audible whisper, defying the room's hidden microphones. He gripped the metal bed rail, his knuckles tight. "Listen to me. Give Mother what she asks for today. Please. Trust me on this one thing. Do not be obstinate."

Unity paused, the plastic spoon hovering halfway to her mouth. The air in the room shifted, thickening. Jon's banter usually had a predictable rhythm—cajoling, clinical, vaguely condescending. This was different. There was genuine tension in the set of his jaw, a new pattern of coarse gray in his curly black hair that hadn't been there a month ago. He smelled faintly of nervous sweat beneath his deodorant.

"What does she want?" Unity asked, lowering the spoon.

"Compliance."

"Why do you help them, Jon? You seem decent. Is the pay really that good that you can sleep at night?"

His face flushed, a muscle twitching in his cheek. But before he could answer, the sharp, staccato click of hard heels on the tile floor echoed from the corridor outside.

"Give it to her," he hissed, stepping back from the bed as if burned.

The door swung inward again, harder this time. Caterina entered first, surveying the room like someone checking for vermin. Then came the devil herself—Mother Sophia—followed by her battalion of copies.

The matriarch swept into the room, sucking the oxygen out of the space. She wore a sculpted green wool blazer that probably cost more than Unity's pre-coma life insurance policy. Her midnight hair was pulled into a severe, architectural bun, pulling the skin of her face tight, emphasizing the sharp cheekbones and predatory eyes.

Behind her, the *Animae* assembled.

A wall of identical faces stared back at Unity. It was like looking into a fractured mirror.

"You look healthy, child," Mother said. Her voice was smooth, cultured stone. She didn't blink. "Jon tells me you're improving rapidly. You've been eating?"

"Yes, ma'am," Jon answered instantly, straightening his spine like a cadet under review.

Unity bit her tongue hard on the word *child*. She was thirty-eight years old, according to the calendar, even if she had lost over two decades to the dark and still felt eighteen inside. She surveyed the clones standing shoulder-to-shoulder. External distinctions were minimal—a slightly shorter haircut here, a younger tilt to the jaw there—but the biological redundancy was nauseating. It was an assembly line of humanity. Every single one of them bore the small tattoo on their forearm, a mirror image of the strawberry birthmark Mia had.

A red envelope appeared in Mother's hand like a magic trick.

"You told me she can write legibly now," Mother said to Jon, never taking her eyes off Unity.

He nodded. "Her fine motor skills in the dominant hand have returned to ninety percent."

The woman tossed the envelope onto Unity's lap. It felt heavy, heavier than paper should, landing with the weight of a judgment. "Write something. A proof of life. Something only Mia will recognize."

Unity picked it up. Her fingers, still clumsy and thick-feeling, brushed the expensive paper. The room fell into a suffocating silence. Twenty pairs of identical eyes fixated on her, waiting for a mistake. Unity realized this wasn't just a test of her motor skills; it was bait. They were finally making their move on Mia.

She uncapped the black pen Jon offered her. She needed something specific. Something that would prove beyond a doubt that the real Unity was awake, but also something that would signal the profound danger of the situation.

A memory surfaced from the haze of her awakening. The hallucinations. The shared dreamspace she and Mia had occupied when Mia was dying. The baseball game where the score was a tally of Mia's bodily injuries.

Unity pressed the pen to the paper. Her hand shook, fighting the resistance of her own nerves. She wrote three words and two sets of numbers. It took immense concentration to keep the letters from sprawling. She capped the pen with a snap that sounded like a gunshot in the quiet room and held the paper out, her arm trembling with the effort of holding it steady.

Mother snatched it, her dark, intelligent eyes scanning the brief text. Her brow furrowed slightly, a crack in the porcelain facade. "What does it mean? This is nonsense."

Unity forced a hollow, scratching laugh that hurt her throat. "You wanted something only Mia would recognize? Trust me. That will get the bitch's attention better than a tear-stained letter."

Mother hesitated. For a split second, the veil of absolute authority slipped, revealing genuine confusion and a flicker of unease. Then she snapped her jaw shut, restoring the mask.

"Is this her handwriting?" Mother asked, thrusting the paper at Jon.

Jon squinted at the note. The words stared back at him: *The Angels won 37-36.*

He stared at Unity, and she saw a flicker of recognition in his eyes. He knew. He knew the story. "Yes. It matches her childhood records perfectly."

Mother turned to her soldiers. "Caterina. Livia."

Two clones stepped forward from the phalanx. Caterina, the "Daughter-in-Waiting," moved with an arrogant, fluid grace, already acting like the heir apparent. Livia moved with the jagged, kinetic energy of a coiled spring.

"Take this to the girl," Mother commanded, handing the letter to Livia, who tucked it into a tactical vest. "Ensure she wears the gi. It'll be a good distraction; she's sentimental. Secure the target, then get out. Nothing more. Do not engage in unnecessary heroics. Understood?"

"Yes, Mother," they said in unison, their voices a chilling harmony.

"Cat, you maintain observation perimeter. Report in at the usual time."

"Of course."

"Everyone out," Mother said, turning on her expensive heel, dismissing Unity as if she were a piece of furniture. "Jon, prep her for transport. We're leaving within the hour. The Americans are getting too close."

The room emptied as quickly as it had filled, the oppressive energy receding like a tide, leaving a vacuum of silence in its wake.

Jon let out a long, shaky exhale and pulled a prepared syringe from his breast pocket.

"Good job, Unity," he said softly, his eyes seeming sad. "You played that right. No resistance."

"I can't wait to see my next dungeon," she muttered, offering her arm without being asked. The fight had drained the last of her strength.

The Romanos moved her every week, sometimes twice, to stay ahead of the Feds and Mia's private hunters. Unity watched the needle pierce her pale skin, the clear liquid swirling into her vein. She didn't fight it. She welcomed the oblivion. The darkness was the only place she didn't have to look at identical faces.

But as the room began to spin and the edges of her vision grayed out into fuzz, Unity didn't just let go. She held onto the image of the note she had just written in her shaky script. She had just handed the Romanos a live grenade, and they were marching it straight to her sister.

Come and get me, Mia, she thought, the words echoing in the closing trap of her mind.

Ceremony

Mia

T he Shenandoah wind snapped the flags atop the new facility, the sound like pistol cracks in the crisp autumn air.

Mia sat in a folding chair on the dais, smoothing the fabric of her dress. Her hands were sweating. The tremors were there, a subtle vibration in her fingers that no amount of therapy had fixed, but she clasped her hands together in her lap to hide it.

To her right, Chris squeezed her knee. He looked good in his new suit—better than he ever had in his regular courtroom attire. He leaned in, his breath warm against her ear.

"Breathe, Dr. Peers. You've faced down missiles. You can handle a ribbon cutting."

Mia forced a smile, the tension in her chest loosening.

It had been a whirlwind year. The wedding had been small—just them, the justice of the peace, and the mountains. The construction of the lab, however, had been a spectacle. She had burned through her bank accounts, and stacks of cash from near-endless donors, to get it done, bypassing government oversight with sheer financial brute force.

She glanced up at the glass-and-steel monolith rising behind them. Four floors. Forty-five of the world's best minds. And on the top floor, a penthouse apartment where she and Chris lived, because old habits died hard. She still liked a fortress.

In the front row, Chuck from the homeless shelter waved. He wore a new jacket, his face beaming. Behind him, Brian Carter sat with his arms crossed. He was the head of R&D now, though he still scanned the perimeter like he expected a black SUV to crash through the gate.

Mia stood up.

The applause rolled over her, a physical wave. She walked to the podium, the wood smooth under her shaking hands.

"Thank you," she said. The microphone whined slightly, then settled. "Standing here today... it's the only finish line I ever really wanted to cross."

The crowd cheered. Cameras flashed in a blinding strobe.

"We built this place on a promise," Mia continued, her voice strengthening. "To eradicate the diseases that steal our families. Cancer. Parkinson's. Spinal Muscular Atrophy."

She paused, letting the weight of the last one hang in the air.

"We are open. And we are ready to work."

The applause thundered again. Mia stepped back, reaching for the giant pair of ceremonial scissors Chris held out.

Movement flickered in her periphery.

At the edge of the press pit, a young girl in a white gi slipped past the velvet rope. She moved with an eerie grace, ghosting toward the security detail. She handed an envelope to the lead guard, stared directly at Mia, and smiled.

Mia's heart hammered a warning against her ribs.

The girl seemed to have Mia's eyes. And Unity's chin. A secret triplet?

Before the guard could react, the girl turned and melted into the crowd, vanishing like smoke.

The guard frowned, staring at the envelope, then up at Mia.

"Bring it to me," Mia commanded, her voice cutting through the applause.

Chris stepped forward, his smile fading. "Mia? What is it?"

The guard handed the envelope over the railing. Mia snatched it. Her name was scrawled on the front in elegant, old-world cursive.

On the back: *The Angels won 37-36.*

A code. The baseball game from her near-death experience. The score of her life.

The world went gray at the edges. The sounds of the crowd—the clapping, the camera shutters—dulled to a roar of static. Mia tore the envelope open.

Dear Mia,

You killed my children. Sophia, Alessia, Gabriele. You think you have won because you buried the pawns, but you have forgotten the Queen.

Nowhere you go will be safe. Not this fortress. Not your husband's arms.

As for Unity... congratulations. You are as bright as Jeffrey designed you to be. Yes, my dear, I know the secret of your father's arrogance. But our scientists understood his mistake years ago. When he cloned you and programmed you to protect her, he didn't just copy the body. He unwittingly split the soul.

You are one person in two vessels.

If you want Unity to live, you must find her. But know this: your life has an expiration date. My calculations give you less than two years before the meltdown. We call it the Syndrome. That's what your serum was meant to fix. By the look of your shaking hands, you've failed. And if your half of Unity's soul dies, so does Unity.

Tick tock, little experiment.

— The Matriarch

The paper slipped from Mia's numb fingers, fluttering to the stage.

"Mia?" Chris was at her side, gripping her shoulders. "Mia, you're pale. What's wrong?"

Mia stared out at the sea of faces—smiling, oblivious people cheering for a future she might never see. She stared at the mountains in the distance, vast and empty.

She grabbed the microphone stand to keep from falling. She turned to Chris, her eyes wide with a horror that went deeper than bone.

"She's alive," Mia whispered, her voice trembling violently. "Unity is alive."

"That's good," Chris said, keeping his voice low, urgent. "We knew that. We'll find her."

"No, Chris. You don't understand." Mia stared at the letter on the ground. The clock had started. "We share a soul. And if I die... so does she."

A scream tore through the air near the parked media vans, sharp and terrified.

The ceremony dissolved into instant chaos. The crowd parted like water as people shoved backward, screaming, creating a clearing shaped like an arrowhead.

Crack.

The first gunshot shook Mia to her core. She knew the sound—she had lived with it for months, dreamed of it—but here, in this place of healing and hope, it paralyzed her.

Boom.

A deafening explosion sent a shockwave through the ground, shaking the dais violently. It hurled Mia and Chris to the hard concrete. Chris scrambled on top of her, covering her body with his own, shielding her.

Mia's mind reeled, stuck on the image of the blonde girl in the gi, the letter, the words *Tick tock*. It was a trick. A distraction.

She needed to move. Her physiology, designed for war, should have propelled her into action instantly. Yet a strange hesitancy anchored her to the concrete, a insidious voice in her head whispering that she was fragile, that her soul was damaged, that she was already broken.

She stared up at Chris. His gaze met hers, terrified but

resolute. He was human, frail flesh and bone. She was the one with the ultrahuman power coursing through her veins. It should have been her diving on him.

She shoved him off with a grunt of effort.

"Mia! It's okay. You're not the person you were at Cabela's. Get up and stop whoever's doing this!"

His words rebooted her mind. The fog cleared.

Mia hopped to her feet, kicking off her heels in one fluid motion. She scanned the lawn, her vision sharpening, processing threats. Her security team was screaming for people to get down, weapons drawn. Journalists scrambled behind chairs and equipment cases. In the grass, Chuck was already applying pressure to a guest's shoulder wound.

Seven assailants. Maybe more. They weren't spraying bullets randomly into the crowd; they were moving with precision, suppressing the security detail with controlled bursts of fire. They were clearing a path.

Directly to the dais.

A woman to Mia's right blurred into her peripheral vision, moving impossibly fast—someone who looked shockingly like Sophia. But Sophia was dead. Mia had watched her die.

A clone. Another goddamn clone.

"Mia!" Chris screamed, pointing. "Look out!"

The woman crashed into Mia like a battering ram, pinning her against the steel podium with bone-crushing force. Concrete sprayed as the heavy anchor bolts ripped free from the floor. The woman was destruction incarnate, a blur of fists and knees. Mia was too shocked to block the first three strikes, each one feeling like a sledgehammer.

Pain encased Mia, sharp and hot, but it was short-lived. Her body knit itself back together in real-time, the damage vanishing almost as soon as it was inflicted. With a roar of frustration, she leveled the woman with a devastating hook, sending her sprawling across the grass.

The clone inched to her feet, cracking her neck to the side with a sickening pop. She grinned, blood staining her teeth.

One of Mia's security guards rushed forward, leveling his pistol. He fired two rounds into the clone's back from close range.

The woman didn't fall. She spun, eyes wide and furious, and charged the guard. He backed away, firing again, but the clone moved with a phantom speed Mia recognized from her own reflection.

"Please!" the guard shouted, falling to his knees, throwing his hands up. "I have a family!"

The clone didn't hesitate. She snapped his neck with a brutal, efficient twist.

Mia gagged. The eighteen months of peace had softened her edges. She had stood there frozen, a soldier with battle fatigue, and watched a good man die. The guilt overrode her adrenaline, a suffocating weight. The ceremony vanished—along with her consciousness.

Mia opened her eyes to a jerky, bouncing view of the sky. Baby-blue atmosphere. Cottony clouds. The smell of exhaust fumes and the taste of copper.

Her senses slammed back into place. She was being dragged by her ankles across the lawn, the grass rough against her bare legs.

To her left, attendees crawled through the grass, weeping. To her right, a young woman lay motionless in a spreading pool of blood. The clone dragging Mia held a stolen news camera in her free hand, filming herself with a manic grin as she hauled Mia toward a waiting black van.

Mia struggled to focus. Her head felt like it was packed with wet sand. Was this the Syndrome? Was her brain failing her now, when she needed it most? *Tick tock, little experiment.*

The despair threatened to suffocate her. She was a cracked mirror of Unity. A failed copy. A battery running on empty.

The van door slid open ahead. The screaming continued, mingling with gunshot blasts and the screech of tires. Mia felt pain blossoming in her ankles as the clone gripped them tighter, accelerating her pace.

Mia dug her fingers into the grass, leaving deep ruts in the sod, trying to anchor herself.

The clone noticed the resistance. In a flash, the woman let go of Mia's legs, grabbed her by the throat with one hand, and threw her toward the open van door like a ragdoll.

Time slowed. Mia soared through the air. Her upper body crashed into the fiberglass paneling of the van; her lower half swung through the open door. The sickening sound of bone crunching filled her ears as her spine fractured against the metal frame.

Men with greedy hands grabbed her legs, pulling her deeper into the cargo bay.

Darkness pressed in at the edges of her vision. She had survived falling from a jet; she could survive a broken back. But captivity? Being a lab rat again? That she wouldn't survive.

A tingling sensation radiated from her toes upward—electricity charging every nerve ending, knitting bone and sinew back together. The healing factor. It wasn't just repairing her; it was arming her.

Mia stopped fighting the sadness. She fed it to the rage that was coiling in her gut.

She grabbed the door frame, anchoring herself against the pull. As the men pulled harder, she retracted a leg and kicked with all her strength. The boot connected with a wet crunch. The man holding her foot dropped without a sound.

Mia rolled, bracing herself between the door and the frame. She whipped her legs upward in a reverse crunch, scissoring her thighs around another man's neck and flinging him out onto the asphalt.

The remaining men attacked. Their strength was pitifully human. Mia was a hurricane in a confined space. Bones snapped. Guttural cries were cut short. With a twist, she broke one man's neck. An uppercut silenced the next. A forceful kick to the sternum caved in the chest of the last man standing.

Her sixth sense screamed a warning.

Mia dove to the floor just as the female clone—the one who had dragged her—slammed into the side of the van, ripping the sliding door off its hinges with a screech of metal.

Mia sprang out of the vehicle, landing in a crouch. She rolled her neck, feeling the vertebrae click back into alignment. The pain vanished. She felt light as helium, buzzing with power.

The two women stood frozen on the bloodstained grass, staring at one another, mirror images, monsters, separated by a lifetime of different choices.

"One way or another, you come with me," the clone said. Her accent was thick, European. "We have work for you."

Sirens blared in the distance, getting louder. Blue lights flashed against the trees.

"Didn't your family learn anything?" Mia spat, her voice low and dangerous. "I don't work well with others."

The woman attacked without warning.

Mia retreated, dodging left and right, evading swings that cracked the air like whips. This clone was fast—faster than Sophia had been, more refined.

"You've only got... two years," the clone grunted, throwing a punch that grazed Mia's ear, drawing blood that healed instantly. "The shaking. It worsens."

Mia stumbled backward. They knew. They knew everything. The letter was true.

The sirens were louder now. The police would be here in seconds. If they saw this fight, if they saw what Mia was about to do, there would be no going back to the life she had built. She needed to end this now.

Mia baited a left hook, leaving herself open. The clone took it.

Mia ducked under the blow, stepping inside the woman's guard. She grabbed the clone's extended arm by the wrist with one hand and gripped her shoulder with the other. She planted her foot firmly against the woman's ribcage.

And she pulled.

She channeled every ounce of the serum's power into her back and legs. Wet, tearing sounds sickened the air. Ligaments popped like rifle shots. Muscle fibers shredded.

The clone screamed—a sound that wasn't human, a primal shriek of agony.

Mia stumbled backward, the sudden lack of resistance sending her sprawling onto the grass. She glanced down. She was holding the arm.

The clone fell to her knees, eyes wide with shock and pain, gaping at the ragged, bleeding hole at her shoulder joint, blood pulsing onto the ground.

Mia stood up, gripping the severed limb like a club. She breathed heavily, scanning her property. Her beautiful ceremony was a ruin. The field was a slaughterhouse.

The Romanos had taken her peace. They had taken her sister. Now, they had come to her home, to the sanctuary she had built.

Mia walked over to the screaming woman, her shadow falling over her. She grabbed the clone by the remaining arm and hauled her up to her feet.

"You have work for me?" Mia whispered, her voice cold as the grave. "You're right. We have a lot to talk about."

Checking to ensure the chaos and the arriving police shielded them from the immediate view of the press, Mia dragged the wailing woman toward the service entrance of the lab. She had built a soundproof room in the basement for testing, and she intended to use it. The interrogation would begin now.

Farmhouse

Lethabo

Major Lethabo Washington, call sign "DC," crouched in the elongated shadow of the tactical SUV, the mid-day sun a physical weight beating against his black fatigues. He spat his gum into the dust. The flavor was long gone, replaced by the gritty taste of the Virginia soil. He hated day ops. Sunlight was for parades and ribbon cuttings. He needed darkness, shadows, the psychological edge of being a phantom in the periphery.

Instead, he got bright sunshine, chirping birds, and a dilapidated farmhouse ninety minutes west of Washington that smelled of dry rot and neglect.

The structure was a rotting molar in a field of vibrant green. Peeling white paint curled off the siding like dead skin, and the aluminum storm door banged against the frame in the wind—*squeak, bang, squeak, bang*—a metronome counting down the seconds to violence.

Thermal scans from the drone had cleared the house of human heat signatures, but the storm shelter entrance fifty feet away was glowing like a Christmas tree on the infrared spectrum. Intelligence blueprints suggested the underground footprint was massive—too big for a root cellar, too expensive and complex for a simple farmer.

"Comms check," Lethabo muttered, tapping the small implant behind his ear. The device was a decade old, itching to be replaced, a constant low-grade irritation against his skull. He refused to let the military carve him up again until it was absolutely necessary, a small rebellion against the system that owned him.

"All clear, Alpha One," Kristin whispered, her voice a cool breeze over the secure channel.

"All clear, Alpha Two," Peyton followed, steady as a rock.

"All clear, Alpha Three," Tony said. His voice carried a thick, syrupy Southern twang that hadn't been there at breakfast. Tony treated every op like an improv class; today, apparently, he was playing the role of a hillbilly sharpshooter. It was his way of managing the stress, but today it grated on Lethabo's nerves.

"Alpha Leader is green," Lethabo said, pushing down the unease that had settled in his gut. "Let's crack it open."

He signaled the advance. The squad moved with the fluid synchronization of a single organism, four parts of one machine. Two years together in the field. They were family. Command tried to rotate teams to prevent emotional attachment, but Lethabo had buried enough paperwork and pulled enough strings to keep them together. They were better this way. Lethal.

Kristin and Peyton ghosted toward the shelter doors, their movements silent on the packed earth. Kristin jammed a glob of thermal putty into the heavy padlock's keyhole.

"Burning in three, two, one."

Smoke spiraled from the handle, smelling acridly of burning metal. The putty liquefied the tumblers in seconds. Kristin kicked the door hard. It swung inward with a groan of rusty hinges, revealing a maw of darkness and cobwebs.

Peyton didn't hesitate. She pulled the pin on a flashbang and tossed it into the void.

Bang.

The concussive blast shook the ground. Lethabo blinked through the whiteout, his ocular implants adjusting instantly to the sudden shift in light. "Clear. Move in."

He and Tony joined them at the breach, swapping their heavier rifles for laser-sighted pistols for the close quarters. They descended the concrete stairs into the gloom. The air grew cooler with each step, smelling of damp earth, mold, and something else—something metallic and coppery, like old blood.

"Main level clear," Kristin reported, her weapon sweeping the shadows. "One interior door. Looks undisturbed."

Lethabo took point, stepping past her. The floorboards above were silent, but the ground beneath his boots felt wrong. It vibrated, a subtle tremor that traveled up his legs.

He stopped, holding up a fist. His audio enhancers picked up a sound—not the wind, not the settling structure.

Click. Hiss.

"Hold," Lethabo signaled, freezing. "You hear that?"

"I don't hear—"

Thump.

It came from below the floor. Deep. Then a scrape of metal on concrete. Then a chorus of clicks, like a thousand deadbolts tumbling into place simultaneously.

A cold dread washed over him. This wasn't a hideout. It was a barracks.

"Back," Lethabo ordered, his voice low, urgent. "Everyone out. Now."

"But DC, we haven't even—"

"That's an order! Move!"

The team scrambled back up the stairs, bursting into the blinding sunlight. They took defensive positions behind the rusted hulk of an old tractor and a chest-high woodpile. Lethabo was the last one out, his boots skidding on the loose dirt as the shelter door behind him exploded outward with a roar.

They didn't come out like men. They came out like a geyser of flesh.

A horde of naked, pale bodies erupted from the earth, climbing over one another in a frantic, insectile swarm. Their eyes were wide and vacant, their movements jerky and synchronized. Some held pistols; others held combat knives; most just clawed at the air with bare hands.

"Contact! Contact!" Kristin screamed, opening fire.

Lethabo squeezed the trigger. His rifle bucked against his shoulder, spraying rounds into the mass of humanity. The male clones didn't scream when they were hit; they just fell, becoming stepping stones for the ones behind them, who didn't even slow down.

"How many are there?" Tony yelled, his Southern accent vanishing in the chaos.

"Too many! Keep firing!"

Lethabo emptied a magazine, the hot brass casings chiming on the gravel around his boots. He reloaded in a blur of practiced motion. The smell hit him then—not sweat, not fear, but something chemical. Like ozone and burning plastic, a scent that didn't belong in a human body.

The wave of bodies crested the lip of the shelter, spilling out onto the grass. They were pasty, hairless, and terrifyingly identical. A factory-made army.

"Frag out!" Peyton yelled.

The grenade arc was perfect. It landed in the center of the crush. The explosion was a dull *whump* of pressure that threw bodies into the air like ragdolls.

Lethabo didn't stop shooting until the bolt of his rifle locked back on an empty chamber.

Silence slammed back down on the farm, heavy and sudden.

Smoke drifted across the field. The pile of bodies at the

shelter entrance was motionless. Lethabo's breath hissed through his teeth. He scanned the carnage, waiting for a twitch, a groan, any sign of life.

"Status?" he barked, his voice rough.

"Alpha One, green."

"Two, green."

"Three... I'm good," Tony said, sounding breathless. "That was... a lot of naked dudes."

"Eyes on the target," Peyton said, her voice tightening. "Ten o'clock. Look at the bodies."

Lethabo scanned the pile. "Which one?"

"All of them."

Lethabo stepped closer, keeping his pistol raised. A chill that had nothing to do with the receding adrenaline spider-webbed down his spine.

The bodies were moving. Not reviving—*dissolving*.

The flesh of the nearest corpse bubbled like cheese under a broiler. The structure of the face collapsed inward, skin sliding off bone in wet sheets. A gray, viscous fluid pooled beneath them, steaming faintly in the cool air. The chemical smell intensified, becoming sickeningly sweet.

"What the hell is that?" Kristin whispered, her weapon lowering slightly.

"Chemical self-destruct," Lethabo theorized, though he'd never seen anything this rapid or thorough. "They're erasing the evidence."

Movement at the shelter door snapped their weapons back up.

One survivor stumbled out from the smoky entrance. He was naked, his skin pale and smooth. But his arms...

Lethabo nearly gagged. The man had no arms. Just weeping, raw sockets where shoulders should be. He took two faltering steps, his eyes wide and vacant, then fell to his knees in the dirt.

As the team watched in horrified silence, the man's torso

began to liquefy. He opened his mouth to scream, but his jaw unhinged and sloughed off, dissolving before it hit the ground. He collapsed into a puddle of sludge, leaving nothing behind but the memory of a man.

"I want this recorded," Lethabo commanded, his voice steady despite the bile rising in his throat. "Command needs to see this. Every second."

"We clearing the basement?" Tony asked, his voice tight.

Lethabo stared at the dissolving soup blocking the entrance. "Yeah. But watch your step. Don't get that stuff on you."

It took fifteen minutes to clear a narrow path through the gelatinous remains, using shovels from the barn. They descended into the bunker, boots squelching in the residue.

The space below was massive—a cathedral of concrete and steel that stretched half the length of a football field. It was pristine, lit by humming LED strips that cast a clinical white light.

To the left, rows upon rows of empty glass pods stood like silent sentinels. To the right, intricate machinery that looked like high-end medical equipment crossed with a server farm hummed with power.

"Stasis transports," Kristin murmured, running a gloved hand over a console. "This is high-end tech. Romano family signatures all over it."

Lethabo moved deeper into the room, his boots echoing on the polished concrete. The silence was heavy, oppressive.

"Rear of the room," Peyton called out. "We got a straggler."

Lethabo joined her at the far end of the row. One pod was still active. Amber lights blinked rapidly on its console. Inside, a man floated in a clear suspension fluid, naked and identical to the ones outside.

"Can we open it?" Tony asked.

"Don't touch it," Lethabo warned. He leaned in, peering at the digital display. It was scrolling Italian text too fast to read.

He blinked his translator overlay into existence.

ERROR. SEQUENCE FAILURE. PURGE IMMINENT.

The man inside opened his eyes.

He slammed his hands against the glass, his mouth opening in a silent roar of terror. He stared directly at Lethabo, his eyes pleading for help.

Then, he began to boil.

Steam filled the pod, obscuring the view. The man's skin rippled and detached from his muscle.

Tony turned away, retching dryly.

"Okay," Lethabo said, his voice flat. "We're done here. Everyone out. Now."

They retreated to the surface, the smell of death and chemicals clinging to their fatigues. Lethabo keyed his comms as soon as they hit the sunlight.

"Green Tail Ops, Alpha Leader. Sitrep."

Static hissed in his ear. Then, "Alpha Leader, stand by."

Lethabo frowned, his patience fraying. "Negative, Green Tail. I have a priority one discovery. Mass casualties. Advanced biological weaponry. I need a clean-up crew and a hazmat team yesterday."

"Stand by, Alpha Leader." The voice was dismissive.

Lethabo kicked a loose stone, sending it skittering across the driveway. *Stand by* was operator speak for *shut up and wait*. He paced the perimeter, watching the farmhouse rot, the adrenaline souring in his veins.

Ten minutes passed. Then twenty. The silence from Command was deafening.

"Green Tail, what is the hold-up?" Lethabo snapped into the mic. "I have unsecured foreign tech out here and a field full of melting bodies."

"Alpha Leader," the voice crackled back, tight and urgent now. "We are diverting all support assets. We have a Situation Red at the Shenandoah site."

Lethabo froze. Shenandoah. The new lab. Mia's lab.

"Subject M.1.A. is under attack," the operator continued, the professionalism cracking. "Hostiles confirmed. Advanced human combatants on site. Multiple casualties."

Lethabo glanced at the mess soaking into the dirt at his feet. *Advanced human combatants.*

"Is she alive?" Lethabo asked, his voice a low growl.

"Unknown. We have reports of mass casualties at the ceremony. We are retasking your extraction chopper to the Shenandoah site. You are grounded until further notice. Dig in and hold your position."

The line clicked dead.

Lethabo peered at his team. They were watching him, faces pale under the grime and sweat.

"What is it, DC?" Kristin asked, her voice soft. "Is it Dr. Peers?"

Lethabo looked at the liquefying clones, the empty bunker, then back at his squad. The connection was impossible to ignore. This wasn't a random raid. This was a coordinated strike.

"Pack it up," he said grimly, shouldering his rifle. "We're not going home. The war just started."

Axe Throwing

Caterina

C aterina's frustration was a physical heat, a rolling boil beneath her skin that made her palms slick with sweat. She paced the length of the marble corridor, her rubber-soled Converse sneakers squeaking faintly against the polished stone—a sharp, rhythmic counterpoint to the muffled silence of the safehouse. She clenched her fists, knuckles turning white, and held them out, checking for the tremor.

Her hands remained steady.

Not yet.

She wasn't shaking from the Syndrome—the inevitable cellular meltdown that claimed every *Animae* near forty, dissolving them into muck. She was shaking from the suffocating weight of waiting. The waiting was a poison, slowly corroding her composure. She checked her watch, a utilitarian digital model that looked absurd against her delicate wrist. Twenty minutes past the appointment time.

She was the anomaly in this hallway. While her sisters drifted through the house like ghosts in Italian silk and stilettos, mimicking the Matriarch's outdated elegance, Caterina wore distressed jeans and a loose cashmere sweater. The others called it disrespectful, a rejection of their heritage. Caterina called it tactical. You couldn't blend into an American crowd wearing a tailored skirt suit, and you certainly couldn't run for your life in four-inch heels. She was prepared for the reality of their existence, not the fantasy Mother tried to maintain.

Housekeepers bustled in and out of the ornate double doors at the end of the corridor, heads bowed in subservience, carrying piles of fresh linens. Caterina glared at them, her jaw tight. As the Daughter-in-Waiting, the designated successor to the Matriarch, she should have had unrestricted access. She should have been in that room twenty minutes ago.

But the rules had changed since the disaster at the hangar. Mother Sophia was paranoid. And rightfully so. The world was closing in on them.

Caterina shoved her hands deep into her pockets, her fingers brushing against the cold, smooth glass of the vial hidden deep in the lining of her jeans. A vial filled with contradictions.

It was the only one left. Sophia had stolen it from Mia's lab before she died, and Livia had used hers in a desperate bid for power. That left Caterina holding the last of the serum in existence. It wasn't just a drug; it was her insurance policy, her golden ticket to possibly surviving Mother's recently bizarre decision-making. If Mother knew she had it, Caterina wouldn't just lose her title; she'd lose her head, and probably not quickly.

The double doors opened with a heavy groan. Two maids scurried out, eyes wide with terror, looking like they'd just escaped a cage with a starving tiger. They didn't even look at Caterina as they fled down the hall.

"Daughter," Mother's voice boomed from inside, resonant and commanding. "Enter."

Caterina took a steadying breath, composed her face into a mask of filial obedience, and stepped through the doors into the lion's den.

The suite was expansive, stripped of the usual plush hotel furniture to accommodate Mother's singular obsession. A massive target wall made of thick, unfinished pine beams had been erected on the far side of the room, dominating the space. A high-definition projector mounted on the ceiling cast a life-sized, glowing image of Mia Peers onto the wood.

Thunk.

A bearded axe, its head gleaming steel, buried itself with a sickening crunch deep in Mia's chest. The projected image flickered for a moment around the steel.

Mother Sophia stood at the throwing line, dressed in a sharp wool blazer and trousers, her back to the door. She didn't turn around. She marched to the wall, wrenched the axe free with a grunt of exertion, and retreated to the line, her movements precise and practiced.

"I have eyes everywhere, Cat," Mother said, her voice low, testing the weight of the weapon in her hand, adjusting her grip on the leather-wrapped handle. "Don't sugarcoat it. Livia hasn't checked in."

Caterina bowed, though she kept it shallow, a small act of defiance. "No, Mother. Her feed cut out shortly after the attack began. We have nothing."

"Failed," Mother spat, the word dripping with venom. She wound up and threw again in one fluid motion. The axe cartwheeled through the air, a silver blur, striking the projected image of Mia squarely in the throat. Wood chips sprayed onto the expensive carpet. "Despite her assurances. Despite her arrogance. She failed."

"Are you surprised?" Caterina asked, keeping her voice carefully neutral, watching the Matriarch's back. "We all inherited your ambition. Livia wanted to prove she was worthy, to step out of your shadow. If you had the choice to become... more, would you not have taken it?"

Mother spun around, her dark eyes flashing with dangerous energy. "I built this family from nothing. From the ashes of your grandfather's incompetence. I am the original. Do not presume to know what I would do."

She stalked toward Caterina, the axe hanging loosely by her side, a dormant threat. Caterina forced herself not to flinch, to hold her ground.

"I wouldn't have risked my life on an untested drug like Sophia and Livia did," Mother hissed, stopping inches from Caterina's face. "The world has gone mad. My own daughters, poisoning themselves with that witch's science, desperate for a shortcut. A shortcut that doesn't work!"

"Apologies, Mother. I only meant that we desire what you want: the longevity of the family. The survival of our legacy."

"Longevity," Mother mocked, a cruel smile twisting her lips. "As long as you're at the top, I presume?" She gestured to a velvet armchair positioned uncomfortably close to the throwing lane. "Sit."

Caterina sat, the velvet soft beneath her fingers. She tucked her feet beneath her chair, acutely aware of the glass vial pressing against her thigh, a cold reminder of her own ambition. The serum might not counter the Syndrome, but it *would* give Caterina the power she needed until Mia created a cure.

"Tell me what happened," Mother commanded, returning to the line, her back to Caterina once more. "Leave nothing out. I want the truth, not your spin."

"There's little to tell beyond the news feeds," Caterina said, trying to keep the frustration out of her voice. "Livia went off-script. She grandstanded at the ceremony. She exposed our numbers to the cameras. The police will trace the dead mercenaries back to our shell companies up north within days."

Whack. The axe slammed into the wall, inches from Mia's face.

"And Livia?" Mother asked, walking to retrieve the weapon, her voice dangerously quiet. "Is she alive? Captured? Or did she run?"

Caterina wiped a bead of cold sweat from her hairline. The air in the room felt thin. "The feed cut instantly. Mia... Mia ripped her arm off, Mother. The biometric implants aren't designed to withstand that kind of trauma. It's likely the shock killed the signal. Or Livia is dead."

Mother turned slowly, grinning, a predatory baring of teeth that was terrifying in its intensity. "You'd like that, wouldn't you?"

"I want a family to lead when it's my turn," Caterina snapped, her patience finally fraying. "Sisters are dying left and right. Livia is gone. Sophia is dead. The rest of us are ticking clocks waiting for the Syndrome to melt our brains at forty. Why are we still playing games? Why can't our scientists operate at the same level as Dr. Peers?"

Mother glared at her, her eyes pools of darkness. She threw the axe without looking. It missed the target completely, burying itself in the drywall with a hollow, dusty crunch.

Silence stretched in the room, heavy and dangerous.

"Watch your tone," Mother said softly, almost gently. She walked to the wall and ripped the axe free, showering plaster dust onto the floor. "The answer starts with Jeffrey. Mia's father was brilliant, in his own limited way. He didn't just clone Unity; he programmed Mia. He tweaked her DNA to drive her toward science, toward a... different cure. But ultimately, he made her a weapon."

"In your own lab. As you and grandfather made simple copies of yourselves," Caterina muttered, unable to stop herself.

"Clones are yesterday's news." Mother inspected the blade of her axe, wiping drywall dust from the steel. "What is the point of recreating the body if you cannot recreate the soul? That is what we are striving for. That is the legacy."

"A legacy built on selling our brothers to terrorists?"

"Enough," Mother snapped, her voice like a whip crack. "We fund our research however we must. Which brings me to the update." She turned to face Caterina fully, her expression hardening. "The Americans found the farmhouse."

Caterina froze. The blood drained from her face. "The stasis bunker?"

"Yes. They raided it an hour ago. The Sentry Blade squad found the storage unit." Mother smiled, but there was zero warmth in it. "It was an older batch of males. Expired product. They dissolved on contact with the air."

"But the exposure—the government knows what we are now."

"It is irrelevant," Mother interrupted, waving a hand dismissively. "Because we are escalating. Livia failed to capture the target. You are not getting any younger, Cat. I see you checking your hands for tremors when you think I'm not looking. Do you want to end up like the brothers in that farmhouse? Melting into a puddle?"

Caterina's hand twitched toward her pocket, toward the vial. "No."

"Then we stop playing in the shadows." Mother walked to the window, looking out at the Virginia tree line, her silhouette stark against the afternoon light. "I am reclaiming assets. I have sent the signal to wake the reserves."

"Reserves?" Caterina stood up, her chair scraping loudly on the marble. "You mean the combat units? The unstable ones? Mother, that's suicide."

"We need soldiers, not diplomats," Mother said, not turning around. "We will take Mia by force. We will drag her back to the lab and flay her mind until she creates a cure for us. And to do that, we must break the system protecting her."

"You're going to start a war on American soil," Caterina whispered, horrified by the scale of the ambition.

Mother turned back slowly, her eyes gleaming with a terrifying, unwavering resolve. She raised the axe, pointing the handle directly at Caterina's chest.

"The war, my daughter, has already begun."

Twenty-Two Years Earlier

Unity

The bedroom door opened without a knock, the latch clicking open with the subtle, terrifying precision of a loaded weapon being taken off safety.

Unity froze. Her paintbrush, heavy with a glob of alizarin crimson, hovered inches from the canvas. She didn't turn around. She didn't need to. The architecture of the house broadcast her mother's movements; the floorboards in the hallway always groaned under Theresa Peers's nervous, pacing energy. But Theresa had a way of entering a room that defied her own anxiety—silent, tense, and immediately suffocating, like all the oxygen had been sucked out through the vents.

"Theresa?" her father's voice drifted from the living room, muffled by distance and the hum of the television. "Our show is starting. You coming?"

"Just pause it, Jeff!" Theresa called back over her shoulder, her voice tight, a violin string wound to the snapping point. She stepped fully into the room, closing the door behind her until it clicked shut, sealing them in. "I'll be right there."

Unity sighed, the sound loud in the sudden quiet. She lowered the brush, resting it on the palette smeared with violent reds and muddy blacks. The smell of turpentine and linseed oil was thick in the room, an aroma that usually comforted her, but now felt tiresome.

"Sorry to disturb you, honey," Theresa said. Her heels clicked sharply on the hardwood floor, a disordered rhythm that set Unity's teeth on edge.

Unity's mother was still wearing her lab coat over her silk blouse, even though it was nearly eight o'clock at night. Neither of her parents ever really stopped working. They just brought the science home, dragged it through the front door, and applied its rigid methodologies to their children. Mia got the academic pressure cooker; Unity got the physical experimentation.

"What are you drawing?" her mother asked, moving closer. Her presence was a physical weight in the room, a cold draft displacing the warm air.

"Painting, Mom. It's paint. Oil paint."

"Painting, drawing... it's all the same creative output." Theresa began her inspection. She moved around the perimeter of the room, her eyes scanning the walls like a building inspector looking for code violations.

The bedroom walls were a chaotic gallery of Unity's latest obsession. Dozens of canvases cluttered the space, tacked up with blue painter's tape or leaning in precarious stacks against the baseboards. The imagery was repetitive, almost compulsive—swirling helices, mirrored faces, bodies pulled apart by unseen forces. Her high school art teachers called it "prodigious talent" and "emotionally mature." Her parents called it a "nice hobby" in public, then immediately pivoted to asking about her karate forms or her resting heart rate.

Theresa stopped behind Unity's chair. Unity could feel her mother's body heat, smell the sterile scent of her anti-bacterial soap and the underlying metallic tang of high-end vitamins.

"You seem to have latched on to this twin theme pretty hard," Theresa murmured, her voice devoid of artistic appreciation.

It was clinical curiosity. She leaned over Unity's shoulder, pointing a perfectly manicured, coral-colored nail at the wet canvas on the easel. "It looks like you and Mia again. Like you're split down the middle."

Unity stared at the image she had been wrestling with for three hours. It was messy, raw. Two androgyne figures were entangled in a dark void. One painted in high-key whites and yellows, the other in deep indigo and charcoal. They were connected at the chest by a thin, shimmering silver thread that looked impossibly fragile.

"It's not me and Mia," Unity lied, though she knew it was. It was always them. "It's just an idea. A study in contrast."

"You're getting really good at anatomy," Theresa continued, ignoring the deflection. Her tone remained detached, analytical. "Those deltoids, the trapezius muscles... they look biologically accurate. But careful with the posture, honey."

Theresa's hand landed on Unity's shoulder. It wasn't a caress; it was a calibration. Her fingers dug in slightly, checking the muscle density near the neck.

"You're slouching over the easel. You don't want a secretary's spread before you're twenty. If you sit too long, your hip flexors tighten, and it throws off your kicking center of gravity."

Unity rolled her eyes so hard it made her temples throb. A wave of hot resentment washed over her. "God, Mom. Stop. I'm just sitting."

"I'm just saying, athleticism is a perishable skill, Unity. It requires constant maintenance. You have the regional tournament tomorrow. You can't afford tight hips."

"I'm not quitting karate to become a painter, if that's what you're worried about."

"We're not worried about that," Theresa lied smoothly. Her grip on Unity's shoulder tightened just a fraction—a warning squeeze. "We just want you to reach your full potential. We've invested so much in... your development. Coach says you're a natural. A perfect physical specimen."

Specimen.

They always used words like that when they forgot she was a person. Optimal. Robust. Resilient. It made Unity feel less like a daughter and more like a prize heifer being prepped for the county fair blue ribbon. Meanwhile, Mia was in the other room, probably reading advanced biochemistry textbooks, getting completely ignored despite having the highest GPA in the state. Mia was the brain; Unity was the body. That was the deal.

"I'm ready for tomorrow," Unity said, putting on her best obedient-daughter smile. It was a defense mechanism she'd perfected by age twelve—give them what they want so they leave. "I'm tapered, I'm hydrated. I'm going to crush it."

"Are you nervous? Your cortisol levels seemed high this morning."

"Who wouldn't be nervous? Most of the girls in my bracket have been sparring since they were toddlers. I've only been doing this for six months."

Theresa didn't answer. Her hand had slipped from Unity's shoulder, the pressure gone. She wasn't looking at Unity anymore. The silence in the room stretched, thin and taut.

Unity turned in her chair.

Her mother was standing in the corner near the closet, frozen. She was staring at a canvas that was drying on a portable easel.

Unity followed her gaze, and a strange coldness settled in her gut.

It was a piece she'd finished last week in a fugue state, waking up the next morning with paint under her nails and no clear memory of executing the brushstrokes. It was strange, even for her morbid fascinations. It depicted two arms intertwined in a desperate grasp. One arm was healthy—muscular, vibrant, glowing with golden undertones. The other was horrific—shriveled, gray, and decaying. The skin was sloughing off the bone in wet, necrotic flakes, dissolving into a charcoal mist.

But it wasn't the gore that had caught Theresa's eye. It was the background.

Behind the wrestling arms, rendered in broad, aggressive strokes of a palette knife, was a flag. Vertical stripes of green, white, and red.

Theresa's face had gone dead pale. The blood had drained right out of her lips, leaving them looking like wax. Her breathing was shallow, rapid.

"Where did you see this?" Theresa whispered. Her voice trembled so badly the words barely formed.

"See what?" Unity asked, genuine confusion warring with the sudden, radiating panic coming from her mother.

"This imagery. The flag. The... the arm." Theresa pointed a shaking finger at the decaying limb. "Where did you see an arm like that?"

"I didn't see it anywhere, Mom. I made it up."

"Don't lie to me, Unity." Theresa spun around, her eyes wide and frantic, searching Unity's face for something—deceit, or perhaps infection. "Did someone talk to you? Did you receive a package? An email?"

"No! What are you talking about? I just... I felt it. I don't know. We're studying Europe in history class. I guess the Italian flag stuck in my head. The arm is just... symbolism. For betrayal, or revenge. I don't know."

"Italy," Theresa whispered, as if the word itself was a curse. She looked like she'd seen a ghost rising from the canvas.

"Yeah. Italy. Why are you freaking out? It's just paint."

Theresa blinked rapidly, several times, as if trying to reboot her brain. Slowly, agonizingly, her mask slid back into place. The color didn't return to her cheeks, but the trembling stopped. The scientist took back control.

"Nothing. It's nothing. Just... vivid imagination. It's striking,

Unity. Very striking technique." She backed toward the door, her movements jerky, robotic. "I need to go. Your father is waiting for his show."

"Mom? Are you okay?"

Theresa paused in the doorway, her hand gripping the frame until her knuckles turned stark white. She glanced back at the painting one last time—a look of pure, unadulterated terror that Unity had never seen directed at anything, ever.

"I love you," Theresa said.

"I love you too," Unity replied instinctively.

But Theresa's words were automatic, hollow things. She wasn't looking at her daughter; she was looking at a nightmare painted in oil. She closed the door quickly, cutting off the view.

Unity sat in the sudden silence. The smell of turpentine seemed thicker now, almost choking. Her heart was thumping a strange rhythm against her ribs, a slow, heavy dread.

She got up, her legs feeling unsteady, and walked to the painting of the shriveled arm and the Italian flag. She tilted her head, staring at her own work as if a ghost had put it there.

She didn't know why she'd painted it. She didn't know why, when she closed her eyes at night, she saw flashes of places she'd never been—a mountain with a fake-looking goat, running on a white-sand beach with Chris Holden, speeding around Washington, D.C. in an unfamiliar red sports car.

She just knew it didn't feel like imagination. It felt like a memory she hadn't made yet.

A sudden, irrational surge of panic pierced her. Her mother's fear was contagious. Unity grabbed the wet canvas, smearing gray paint onto her palms. She felt an overwhelming urge to hide it, to bury it, to protect whatever dangerous secret she had accidentally spilled out of her subconscious and onto the fabric.

She ripped the painting off the easel with a violent jerk and shoved it face-down into the large metal trash can in the corner, covering it with crumpled sketches until the green, white, and red were buried in the dark.

Abstract Art

Mia

In the center of the lab, surrounded by the low, industrious hum of forty-five of the world's brightest minds, Mia Peers was trying to paint a sunset.

She had set up her easel in the middle of the main research floor, a calculated move to remain visible, a captain refusing to abandon the bridge even as the ship took on water. At least, that's what she told Chris. Her real motive was to show the Syndrome, and its tremors, who the boss was. But five weeks after the attack, the captain was falling apart, piece by piece. The Syndrome was clearly master and commander.

The air in the lab, usually crisp with optimism and expensive filtration, felt thick with paranoia to her today.

Mia dipped the brush into the dollop of cadmium red acrylic. The paint was thick, heavy on the bristles. She aimed for the horizon line she had sketched on the canvas, a simple, straight line that felt miles away.

Her hand betrayed her.

The tremor started in her wrist, a fine, high-frequency vibration that hummed down the length of her forearm and traveled like an electric current into the wooden brush handle. The tip skittered uncontrollably across the canvas, missing its mark entirely. Instead of a smooth, glowing orb, the sun became a jagged, bloody smear that bled into the painted ocean below.

Mia cursed under her breath, the sound harsh in the quiet room. She dropped her hand to her lap, clenching it into a fist, fighting the involuntary movement. The tremors were getting worse. The Parkinson's medication Brian had synthesized wasn't touching them; it was like trying to put out a forest fire with a squirt gun.

She picked up a rag stained with a rainbow of previous failures and wiped the canvas, smearing the crimson into a muddy bruise. She wasn't painting sunsets. She was painting her own deterioration in real-time.

"Time," a flat, monotonous voice said from behind her.

Mia didn't look up. She didn't need to. Brian Carter stood beside her, his presence as constant and unobtrusive as the lab's air scrubbers. He extended his hand into her peripheral vision. In his palm lay two small, pale yellow pills.

"It's been three hours already?" Mia asked, her voice rough. Time was dissolving, slipping through her shaking fingers.

Brian nodded once. He was a vision of calculated eccentricity in the ultra-modern lab. He wore wide-leg bell-bottom jeans that swished when he walked and a vintage, threadbare blue work shirt with a faded yellow flower stitched crookedly on the shoulder. His feet were encased in neon green Crocs—a blinding replacement for the red pair that had finally disintegrated after years of abuse. He looked like a time traveler from Woodstock who had taken a wrong turn south near Baltimore and ended up in a high-tech bio-research facility in Virginia.

Mia popped the pills dry, swallowing hard against the bitter taste that coated her tongue. She hated them. She hated needing them.

"Don't say it," she warned, picking up the brush again.

"I wasn't going to say anything." Brian tilted his head, his shaggy hair falling over his eyes as he studied the ruined canvas. "Though, strictly speaking, from an astronomical and optical perspective, sunsets are spherical. That looks... agricultural. Like a crime scene involving heavy machinery."

"It's abstract, Brian. It's about feeling, not accuracy."

"It's angry," he corrected, his voice devoid of judgment. He pulled up a metal rolling stool and sat down, his knees knocking against the easel. "You're chewing the meds again. The manufacturer explicitly warns against that. It alters the absorption rate."

"I'm not the manufacturer's target demographic," Mia snapped. "I'm an outlier. A glitch." She willed her hand to still, focusing all her mental energy on the simple act of holding the brush steady. *Just be steady. For one second.*

"I need results, Brian. The tremors are... distracting. They're interfering with my work."

"Distracting," Brian echoed, the word sounding alien in his flat delivery. He leaned in closer, invading her personal space, smelling faintly of solder and stale coffee. "Your eyes are bloodshot, Mia. The capillaries are bursting. You're not sleeping more than two hours a night. And you're kicking easels when you think no one is looking. I fixed the leg on this one yesterday."

Mia froze. The brush hovered over the canvas, trembling violently now. She hadn't realized he'd seen that moment of pure, childish frustration.

"I'm fine," she lied, the words tasting like ash.

"You're not fine. You're spiraling. And you're hunting." Brian lowered his voice further, barely a whisper now, though the nearest scientists were engrossed in the rhythmic *whir-clack* of a centrifuge. "The private investigators called the secure line again this morning. I saw the encrypted log on the server."

Mia shot him a glare that could cut glass. "I told you to stay out of those logs."

"I run the servers, Mia. I built the encryption. I see everything that comes in and out of this building." He leaned in even closer, his eyes dark and unreadable. "Does Chris know you're still paying them fifty thousand a week? Or does he still think we're just focusing all our resources on a Syndrome cure and spinal muscular atrophy, like we agreed?"

Mia slammed the brush down onto the easel's tray. The sharp *crack* cut through the quiet hum of the lab like a gunshot. Heads turned at adjacent benches, eyes wide over safety goggles.

"This isn't a debate, Brian," she hissed, leaning in to meet his gaze, her voice trembling with fury. "Every day that goes by is a day closer to the deadline. The Matriarch wasn't lying. My hands are shaking. My brain feels like it's tilting inside my skull. If I don't find Unity in eighteen months, I die. And when I die, so does she. We are linked."

She stood up abruptly, the stool screeching backward on the polished concrete floor. She began to pace the small, confined circle of her workspace, like a caged animal.

"So no, I'm not taking a vacation to the Bahamas to relax. I'm not resting. I'm going to find my sister, even if I have to burn this whole world down to do it. And I will use every resource I have, including my own money, to make that happen."

Brian didn't flinch at her outburst. He just sat there, watching her with that unnerving, blank stare, like he was observing a particularly interesting bacterial culture under a microscope.

"You're letting fear drive the bus," he said calmly. "You need to let the professionals handle the search. You need to focus on the science. That's how you save her."

"I am the professional! I'm the only one who—"

Her phone buzzed violently in her pocket against her hip, cutting off her tirade.

Mia snatched it out, her heart leaping into her throat. The screen glowed with an unfamiliar area code. *Unknown*

Number.

"What?" she snapped into the receiver, her patience gone.

"Dr. Peers?" The voice on the other end was male, scratchy with static, and clipped with military authority. "This is Agent Flowers. Sentry Blade liaison."

The air left the room. The lab noises faded into a distant hum. Mia pressed the phone tighter to her ear, turning her back to Brian and the rest of the room, hunching over to create a private space.

"Did you find her?" she whispered, the words scraping her throat.

"We... can't discuss specifics over an open line, Doctor."

"This is a secure, encrypted phone, Agent. Do you have my sister or not?"

"It's not that simple," Flowers said, his voice tight. "We found... something. A facility. There are... complications. Massive ones. Things you need to see for yourself to understand."

Mia's grip on the phone tightened until her plastic case creaked. "What kind of complications?"

"We also need your scientific assessment on some... interesting hardware we recovered on site."

Mia's heart hammered against her ribs, a frantic bird trapped in a cage. Hardware. That meant Romano tech. Advanced tech.

"When?" Mia asked, her voice steadier now.

"Now. Immediately. Is your helipad operational and clear?"

"Yes."

"Bird is five minutes out. We're already inbound. Bring your tech lead, the hippie. We might need him to interface with the hardware."

The line clicked dead before she could ask another question.

Mia slowly lowered the phone, pocketing it with a hand that was still shaking, but the chaotic, frantic anger was gone. It had been replaced by a cold, sharp, razor-edged focus. The waiting was over.

"Who was that?" Brian asked, standing up slowly, seeming to sense the shift in the atmosphere.

"The government," Mia whispered, turning to face him. Her eyes were wide, the pupils dilated. "Sentry Blade. They found something. A Romano facility."

Brian's stoic mask cracked for a fraction of a second. "Unity?"

"They wouldn't say. They dodged the question. But they want us there. Both of us. Now." Mia grabbed her leather jacket from the back of the chair, the movement sharp and decisive. "They're sending a chopper. It's five minutes out."

"Where are we going?" Brian asked, already moving toward his bench to pack.

"They didn't say that either. Just that it's bad." Mia buttoned her jacket rapidly, her fingers fumbling slightly with the stiff material. She reached to the small of her back, checking the comforting weight of the ceramic knife she now kept sheathed there at all times. Old habits from the last few weeks of paranoia.

"Go grab your field kit. The big one with the interface cables. Meet me on the roof in three minutes."

Brian hesitated, looking toward the glass-walled conference room near the entrance. "Mia... Chris is in a meeting with the new investors downstairs. The Japanese firm. Should we—"

"No time for goodbyes." Mia was already moving toward the private elevator that led to the penthouse and the roof, walking with a purpose she hadn't felt in weeks. "Text him from the bird. Tell him we're going hunting."

She hit the call button for the roof. As the brushed steel doors slid shut, cutting off the view of her unfinished, bloody sunset, she caught her reflection in the metal. The bloodshot eyes, the pale skin, the tension etched into her jawline. Brian was right. She looked like a woman on the edge of a complete breakdown.

But for the first time in five agonizing weeks, she didn't feel helpless. She didn't feel like a victim waiting for the inevitable collapse.

She felt dangerous.

Bunker

Mia

The helicopter ride was short in miles, but it felt interminable as the ghosts of the past caught up to Mia. The rhythmic thrum of the rotors acted as a sensory trigger, pulling Mia back to the worst moment of her life. The wind screaming past her ears was the same wind that had ripped at her clothes as she fell from Sophia's jet. The cold air biting her skin was the same high-altitude chill that had numbed her fingers as she let go of the fuselage. The terrifying weightlessness was the same gut-dropping plunge she had experienced just seconds before a heat-seeking missile turned her nemesis—her tormentor—into a cloud of metallic mist and fire over the Virginia landscape.

Mia gripped the armrest, her breath shallowing in the confined cabin.

"Dr. Peers?" the crew chief asked, his voice crackling over the noise-canceling headset. He was watching her in the reflection of his visor, his eyes narrow with professional concern. He'd seen people break on rides like this.

Mia nodded sharply, forcing her jaw to unclench, swallowing the bile that rose in her throat. "I'm fine. Just turbulence."

He didn't look convinced, but he didn't press. He handed

her a rugged iPad and a digital stylus, the motion practiced. "Standard NDAs. Sign at the bottom. Then press play. Command wants you briefed before we touch down."

Mia signed, her hand shaking so badly the signature was an illegible scrawl. Beside her, Brian did the same, his face pressed against the thick plexiglass window, watching the Virginia countryside roll by in a blur of green and brown. His foot tapped a frantic rhythm on the metal floor of the chopper.

The video feed opened. It was shaky body-cam footage, the time stamp indicating five weeks ago—the same day as the attack on her lab.

Daylight. A farmhouse in a field of overgrown grass. The camera moved toward a storm shelter entrance. And then, the swarm.

Mia watched in horrified fascination as the wooden doors exploded outward. Dozens of naked, identical men erupted from the earth like a geyser of pale flesh. They climbed over one another in a frantic, swarm, their movements jerky and unified. Clones. *Animae.* They were male, all of them, copies of a face she remembered from old photographs—Cesaro Romano, the original patriarch. But it wasn't the fighting, or the sheer number of them, that made her breath hitch in her throat.

It was the dying.

On the small, backlit screen, the camera focused on a pile of bodies left behind after a grenade blast. They began to steam in the cool air. The flesh bubbled like crust in the oven, the structure of faces collapsing inward, skin sloughing off bone in slimy, taupe sheets. In seconds, the corpses were nothing but puddles of viscous, steaming sludge soaking into the dirt.

Brian glanced at the screen, then quickly looked away, his face paling. He seemed to have fixed his gaze on the horizon in possible denial of what he had seen.

Mia couldn't look away. She watched it three times.

Tick tock, little experiment. The Matriarch wasn't bluffing. This wasn't a threat; it was a forecast. This was her future. This was the Syndrome. This was what was happening to her cells right now, a slow-motion dissolution that would end in a gooey puddle.

The helicopter banked hard, the G-force pressing her against the seatbelt as it descended toward a field of tall, windswept grass. As the skids touched down with a jolt, Mia shut off the iPad. Her hands were shaking so badly she had to shove them deep into her jacket pockets to hide them.

A group of heavily armed operatives waited near the tree line, their silhouettes stark against the setting sun. Mia recognized the leader immediately—Major Lethabo Washington. She'd met him briefly in the chaotic, blood-soaked aftermath of the ceremony attack, a calm presence in a storm of violence.

He approached as they ducked under the still-spinning rotors, the wind whipping her hair around her face. His expression was grim, his eyes tired. "Dr. Peers. Mr. Carter. Welcome to the farm."

"The video," Mia shouted over the whining down engine, her voice raw. "This happened the same day as the attack on my lab?"

Lethabo nodded, not breaking stride. "Synchronized. Not coincidental. Let's talk inside. The bunker is shielded."

He led them past the farmhouse—now just a rotted shell, the smell of mold clinging to it—to a heavy steel door set into the side of a hill. Three other operatives flanked the entrance, their posture alert, weapons held at the low ready. Mia recognized the two women and the man with the British accent from the brief introductions at the lab. They were walking arsenals, bristling with more weaponry and tactical gear than Mia had seen on entire SWAT teams.

"You think we're being watched right now?" Brian asked, eyeing the dense tree line with renewed suspicion.

"Always assume someone is listening," the woman with

the tactical shotgun, Kristin, said, her voice flat. Her eyes constantly scanned the perimeter.

"Ignore Kristin," the other woman, Peyton, said, rolling her eyes beneath her helmet. "She's paranoid. You can't imagine the joy of working with someone who believes there are ninjas in every shadow."

"It keeps us alive," Kristin shot back, not looking at her teammate.

"I'm a fan of the paranoia," the British man, Tony, added with a grin. "Keeps things spicy. Keeps the blood pumping."

They descended a long flight of concrete stairs into the gloom. The air grew cool and damp, smelling of cleaner, decay, and the faint, sickeningly sweet scent of the chemical reaction Mia had seen on the video.

The bunker was a cavernous space, half-emptied of its secrets. Rows of tall glass stasis pods stood like silent sentinels in the gloom, all of them now empty and dark. At a folding table near the center of the room, under the harsh glare of a portable work light, a thin man with a tapered military haircut and a pressed suit was arranging plastic-bagged evidence with meticulous care.

"Dr. Peers," the man said, extending a hand without looking up from his task. "Agent Peter Flowers. Thanks for coming on such short notice."

"Mia," she offered automatically, shaking his hand briefly. His grip was dry and firm. "And this is Brian Carter, my head of R&D."

Brian ignored the pleasantries completely. He drifted toward the nearest stasis pod, his eyes wide with professional curiosity, fingers seemingly itching to touch the glass, to understand the machinery that had held an army in suspended animation.

"We're on a timeline," Flowers said, checking his watch, which looked expensive. "Transport trucks are five minutes out. We're scrubbing this site clean."

"Why are we here, Agent Flowers?" Mia cut straight to the chase, her patience fraying. "The deal on the phone was simple: find Unity, get my help. You haven't found her."

Flowers tightened his lips, a flash of irritation crossing his face. "We thought you might see the light, Mia. After the attack at your lab, where your people died... and after seeing the video. You watched it?"

"I watched people melt," Mia said, her voice cold as ice. "Is that your leverage? Showing me my future? Hoping I'll be scared enough to cooperate?"

"It's a reality check. We are dealing with an existential threat. We need to stop these people, Mia. These clones were expired product—copies of Cesaro Romano, the family patriarch. But the next batch... they might be younger. Faster. More stable. And if they have your serum..."

"I don't make clones," Mia said, her voice rising. "I just happen to be one. I can't help you fix them or stop them."

"We don't want to fix them," Flowers said, stepping closer. "Although, I'm sure *you* do. We want to understand them. And we want to know why they attacked when they did. We want to know how they were controlled." He gestured to the table, to a small, anti-static bag. "We recovered these from the skulls of the few who didn't fully dissolve before we could get to them."

He held up the bag. Inside was a small, incredibly complex microchip, its design unlike anything Mia had ever seen.

"Brain implants," Brian said from across the room, his voice echoing in the cavern. He walked back to the table, his eyes locked on the tech. "Similar to military spec in function, but the architecture is... remarkable. You can't hack them with standard protocols. The encryption is biometric."

Flowers looked impressed, a flicker of respect in his eyes. "Exactly. Our cyber warfare division is stumped. They're brute-forcing it and getting nowhere. We don't know if they received a command signal to attack, or if it was automated coding that triggered on waking. We need to know if these chips can lead us to the source. To the broadcast signal. To Sophia Romano."

"Sophia is dead," Mia said flatly. "I watched her die."

"The original Sophia," Flowers corrected, his voice dropping. "The Matriarch. The one who wrote you that letter."

Mia crossed her arms over her chest, hugging herself against the chill and the truth. This was it. They were desperate. Their own experts were failing, so they needed the only scientists on the planet who understood the Romano biology and technology from the inside out.

"Find Unity," Mia said, holding his gaze. "Then we talk about the serum. Then we talk about decoding your chips."

"Mia, be reasonable—"

"I am being reasonable. You want access to my brain? To my life's work? I want my sister back."

Brian stepped up beside her, a silent show of solidarity. "We want the video file," he said flatly, his voice devoid of emotion. "The raw footage. And we want two of each device you recovered. The implants, the stasis machine controllers, and those incubator units I saw in the back of the room."

Mia suppressed a smile. *Good boy, Brian.* He was already thinking three steps ahead.

Flowers laughed, a dry, humorless sound that bounced off the concrete walls. "You want classified military evidence? Hardware that doesn't officially exist?"

"You want us to decode it," Mia countered, her voice hard. "We can't do that without the hardware to test against. Brian inspects the equipment. I study the biology and the neural interface. That's the offer. Take it or leave it, and scrub the site without knowing what you found."

Flowers seemed to hesitate. He glanced at the bag in his hand, at the stubborn woman standing in front of him, practically glowing with a desperate energy.

"And," Mia added, sensing his weakness, pressing her advantage, "I want protection."

"You have private security. You hired the best."

"My security team is dead or in the hospital," Mia snapped, the memory of the attack raw and painful. "And they weren't ready for a super-soldier that moved like the wind and snapped necks like twigs. I want them." She pointed to Lethabo and his squad, who were standing passively near the entrance, listening. "I want Sentry Blade. At my lab. 24/7. You need me alive to solve your puzzle, Agent. They're the only ones who can guarantee that against what's coming."

She saw the calculation behind Flowers' eyes. Placing a black-ops squad inside her lab would give the government unprecedented eyes and ears on her operation. It was a Trojan horse, a way to monitor her as much as protect her.

But it was a Trojan horse she needed. She was out of options.

"Fine," Flowers said, extending his hand again, his expression sour. "You get the hardware. You get the squad. They deploy immediately. But the serum discussion isn't over, Mia. Not by a long shot."

Mia took his hand. Her grip was firm, even if her fingers trembled against his skin.

"Find my sister," she said, her voice a vow, "and we can discuss whatever you want."

Press Conference

Mia

The teachers' lounge of the rented high school smelled like the ghosts of a thousand anxieties—stale coffee that had sat on a burner since dawn, the whiff of floor wax, and the faint, underlying odor of adolescent sweat from the adjacent locker rooms. It was an oppressive atmosphere, heavy and clinging, perfectly matching the storm raging inside Mia Peers's body.

Mia gripped the porcelain rim of the toilet. The cool ceramic was an anchor in a spinning world. She retched violently, her body convulsing with the force of it, until there was nothing left but bitter yellow bile and the taste of acid in her throat.

She flushed, the sound loud and violent in the small, tiled space. She leaned her forehead against the cool stall door for a moment, breathing raggedly, before forcing herself to stand up. She spat the acrid taste into the sink and rinsed her mouth, watching the water swirl away. Her face in the smudged mirror looked gray, her eyes bright and feverish, the pupils blown wide.

She ripped a rough brown paper towel from the dispenser and wiped her mouth, the texture abrasive against her sensitive skin. Her hands were shaking. Nothing new there. It wasn't the adrenaline flutter of nerves. It was a deep, cellular vibration, a bone-deep tremor that started in her marrow and radiated outward. It was the Syndrome.

"Do you want to cancel?"

Mia spun around, her heart lurching. Chris stood in the open doorway, his handsome face etched with deep concern. He was wearing his "media suit," a sharp navy number that usually made him look invincible, but right now he just looked scared. He held out a plastic bottle of water.

"No," Mia said, snatching the bottle, her voice rough and raspy from vomiting. "We're not canceling."

"Mia, look at yourself. You're sick." He took a step into the lounge, reaching for her arm.

Mia flinched back, dodging his touch. "It's just a bug, Chris. Or nerves. Probably that rubbery chicken at lunch yesterday." She forced a smile onto her face, feeling the muscles strain. It felt brittle, like old plaster that might crack and crumble at any moment.

She wasn't sick with a bug. She was melting. She was dissolving from the inside out, just like the clones in the video from the farmhouse, the ones that had turned into pools of warm sludge in seconds. She hadn't told Chris about the video. She hadn't told him that the "bug" was actually a genetic self-destruct sequence with a countdown clock that was ticking louder every day. He wasn't aware of *how* the Sydrome ended clones. He had already buried one wife; the guilt of putting him through that again was a heavier weight than the Syndrome itself.

"We can delay," Chris pressed, his voice gentle but firm. "An hour. A day. The media will wait. This is too important to screw up because you're not feeling well."

"The media is a shark tank, Chris. You know that better than anyone." Mia leaned against the sink, using it to support her weight. "If we bleed in the water, they don't wait. They frenzy. They control the narrative. We do this now, while we have the momentum."

She straightened her blazer, smoothing the fabric over her roiling stomach. She checked her reflection one last time. The face looking back was pale, but the eyes were sharp, focused. It was the face of a woman who had survived two collisions with industrial-sized trucks. She could survive a press conference.

"How's the house?" she asked, her voice steadier now.

"Packed. Standing room only. Every major outlet from CNN to the Post is out there, plus a dozen streamers. We gave them twelve hours' notice on a Saturday, and they still showed up in droves. They smell blood in the water, Mia."

"Good. Let's go give them something else to chew on. Let's go make history."

The auditorium was a cavern of noise and heat. The high school's aged air conditioning system was fighting a losing battle against the body heat of three hundred people and the blazing television lights that baked the sweat onto Mia's forehead the moment she stepped onto the stage.

She sat in a metal folding chair center stage, flanking the podium. To her left and right sat twelve people who owed her their lives. Her "Ghost Trial" participants. They were dressed in their Sunday best—ill-fitting suits, dresses that smelled faintly of mothballs—but their discomfort was palpable. They shifted in their seats, eyes darting nervously as the photographers' cameras flashed like a relentless strobe light, capturing every twitch and bead of sweat.

Mia didn't blame them. Twelve years ago, she had pulled them from the darkest corners of the medical system—hospices, long-term care facilities, homeless shelters. They were the forgotten ones, the cases deemed hopeless by conventional medicine. She had experimented on them with an early, unstable version of her Neuro-Regen serum, created for Unity, without FDA approval, without oversight, operating entirely in the gray zones of ethics and legality.

Today, she was parading them in front of the world like prize poodles to save her reputation and leverage the government. It was a cynical, desperate move. It felt exploitative. But desperation was the only fuel she had left in the tank.

Chris gave her the signal from the wings. Mia stood up, her legs feeling unsteady on the risers. She stepped to the podium. The microphone whined with feedback before settling.

"Thank you all for coming on such short notice," Mia said, her voice amplified, echoing slightly through the cavernous hall. "We're here today to discuss the future of regenerative medicine. Specifically, a compound my lab has developed called Neuro-Regen."

A reporter from the front row, a man with a face like a bulldog and a reputation to match, stood up without waiting to be called on. "Dr. Peers, let's cut to the chase. Isn't it true that you conducted human trials with this compound a decade ago without any FDA oversight? Isn't it true that you put these people at risk, treating them like lab rats?"

The crowd murmured, a low wave of sound. The sharks were circling, sensing weakness.

"We've admitted that protocols in the early stages of research were... unconventional," Mia said, gripping the sides of the podium to steady her hands, which were vibrating against the wood. "But the results we achieved—"

"Unconventional?" another reporter shouted from the aisle, waving a recorder. "You broke the law! You operated an illegal clinic outside the United States! How can we trust a scientist who operates in the shadows, Dr. Peers? How do we know these people are safe?"

"Dr. Peers is a danger to the medical community!" someone yelled from the back of the room. "She's a cowboy, not a scientist!"

Mia's chest tightened. The air in the room felt thin. A full-blown panic attack was clawing at her throat, making it hard to breathe. The lights were too bright, the noise too loud. The faces in the crowd blurred into a hostile mass. She peered toward the wings for Chris. He was standing there, pale, chewing his lip. He looked helpless.

This was a mistake. A massive, arrogant mistake. She was going to lose them. The narrative was slipping away, spinning out of control. The Syndrome buzzed beneath her skin, a physical manifestation of her loss of control.

"Stop."

The voice wasn't loud, but it had a quality that cut right through the rising clamor of the room. It was sharp, clear, and commanding.

Ginger Matthews stood up from her chair at the end of the row.

She was small, almost birdlike, dressed in a thrift-store suit that was two sizes too big in the shoulders. Her gray hair was pulled back in a severe bun that emphasized the sharp angles of her face. She walked to the podium, her steps measured and steady on the hardwood stage.

Mia stepped aside automatically, her heart hammering against her ribs. Chris had explicitly said no unscripted speeches. This was wildly off-script.

Ginger adjusted the microphone, lowering it significantly. She didn't look at Mia. She stared straight out at the hostile crowd, her eyes clear and piercing under the bright lights.

"My name is Ginger Matthews. Fifteen years ago, I was a senior analyst on Wall Street. I had a condo in Manhattan overlooking the park and a portfolio worth millions. I ran marathons. I had a life."

The room went quiet. The shouting died down. The cameras focused on the small woman at the microphone.

"Then a taxi jumped the curb on 5th Avenue. I hit my head on the pavement. Traumatic brain injury. I was in a coma for six weeks. When I woke up, I had lost my job. I lost my condo. I lost my ability to remember my own mother's name or how to tie my shoes. Six months later, I was living in a shelter in Queens, waiting to die."

Ginger paused, letting the silence stretch. She turned her head slowly and looked at Mia, a look of profound gratitude and fierce loyalty.

"Then I met Dr. Peers. She found me. She didn't promise me a cure. She promised me a chance. She paid for my hotel room out of her own pocket. She bought me food. She sat with me for hours, talking to me like I was a human being when the rest of the world just saw a crazy homeless woman muttering to herself."

Ginger turned back to the cameras, her voice gaining strength. "Was what she did legal? I don't know. I didn't care. When you're drowning in the middle of the ocean, you don't ask the lifeguard for his certification before you grab the life preserver. You just grab the damn hand."

She swept her arm dramatically toward the row of people seated behind her.

"Look at them. Look at John. He was in a persistent vegetative state for three years. His family had signed the DNR. Sarah couldn't speak a coherent sentence without slurring. David had early-onset dementia at thirty and didn't know his own wife. Look at them now."

One by one, as if on cue, the subjects stood up. John waved awkwardly. Sarah smiled, tears streaming down her face. David stood tall, his eyes clear and present. They were living, breathing proof of the impossible.

"We heard the FDA wants to shut Dr. Peers down," Ginger said, her voice rising with passion. "They say she moves too fast. They say she's reckless. Well, guess what? Death is fast. Disease is reckless. It doesn't follow protocols. We needed someone who could outrun them, someone who wasn't afraid to break the rules to save a life."

She pointed a bony finger directly at the bank of reporters.

"Dr. Peers gave us our lives back. She gave us our memories, our futures. If that's a crime, then lock us all up. Because we're the evidence. And we're not going anywhere."

Ginger stepped back from the podium and took the hand of the woman next to her. The subjects linked hands down the line, a human chain of defiance and solidarity on the stage.

For a second, there was absolute silence. Then, the auditorium erupted.

Not with questions, but with applause. It started slow, a few isolated claps, then swelled rapidly into a thunderous roar that shook the walls. Even the cynical press corps, the sharks who had smelled blood minutes ago, were standing up, clapping, caught up in the raw emotional power of the moment.

Mia felt hot tears prick her eyes. The relief was so intense it made her knees weak. She glanced at Chris in the wings. He was grinning from ear to ear, giving her a thumbs-up, tears shining in his own eyes.

Ginger had saved them. She had taken the narrative and rewritten it in a language everyone understood: survival.

Mia stepped back to the microphone, waiting for the noise to die down. It took a full minute.

"You have their medical records in your press kits," Mia said, her voice rock-steady now, amplified by the energy in the room. "You have their stories. The drug works. And we are submitting it for fast-track FDA approval effective immediately."

Chris stepped out onto the stage, waving his arms, playing the role of the busy handler. "That's all the time we have today! Thank you all for coming! Dr. Peers will not be taking further questions at this time!"

He ushered Mia and the subjects off the stage and behind the heavy velvet curtain as the reporters shouted follow-up questions that went unanswered.

Back in the relative safety of the dimly lit wings, Mia leaned against the cool brick wall, exhaling a shaky breath she felt like she'd been holding for an hour. The adrenaline crashed hard, leaving her lightheaded.

"We did it," Chris said, grabbing her shoulders and pulling her into a fierce hug. "Mia, that was incredible. You were perfect."

"Ginger was perfect," Mia corrected, pulling back, her eyes searching the shadows backstage.

She peered past him, toward the rear exit door where Major Lethabo Washington was standing. He was speaking quietly into his wrist comms, his face grim. He caught her eye across the backstage clutter and nodded once, slowly. It wasn't a celebratory nod; it was an acknowledgment.

The public battle was won. The narrative was secure. But the private war was just heating up. Now the government had their cover story. Unity's drug was public; the demand would be immense. Not exactly the superhero drug they wanted, but they had no excuse to delay their end of the bargain.

Mia straightened up, pushing off the wall, the tremor in her hands swallowed by a renewed sense of purpose.

"Get the car, Chris," she said, her voice hard. "We have a drug to file with the FDA. And then I have a phone call to make to Agent Flowers. He owes me a sister."

Playland

Mia

The meeting place smelled like a middle school gym desperately trying to mask its odor with artificial grape flavoring and bleach. It was a thick, humid scent.

Mia pushed through the heavy glass double doors of the Manassas Mall Playland, immediately assaulted by the climate—ten degrees warmer than the rest of the mall and thick with the exhalations of a hundred over-sugared children. She pulled the brim of her Washington Nationals baseball cap lower, shadowing her eyes. The red fabric felt hot against her forehead. The curly 'W' logo was a cruel irony, a physical manifestation of the shared hallucination—the baseball game where injuries were runs—that she and Unity had experienced on the threshold of death. It was the easiest hat to purchase on her way there, and wearing it felt like pressing on a bruise.

Inside, the noise wasn't just sound; it was a physical architecture. The high-pitched, joyous screams of toddlers, the manic, synthesized jingle of a dozen different arcade games, and the relentless thrum of Top 40 pop music bass created a chaotic sonic shield. It was overwhelming, relentless, and perfect. It was the last place on earth the sophisticated, marble-dwelling Romanos would look for a world-class geneticist, and the only place loud enough to ensure a conversation couldn't be recorded by a parabolic microphone.

Mia waded through the sea of primary colors, careful not to trip over a miniature human. Toddlers zigzagged across the sticky patterned carpet like drunk pilots, fueled by juice boxes and adrenaline. Their parents sat slumped on vinyl benches along the perimeter, eyes glazed and glued to smartphone screens, mentally checking out of their own reality.

Mia spotted her team at a corner table bolted to the floor near the massive, multi-colored ball pit. They blended in perfectly, a tableau of suburban exhaustion. Everyday clothes. Tired expressions. Just three more adults waiting for the sugar crash.

Sydney, the lead investigator and former FBI manhunt specialist, sat with her back to the wall, her eyes constantly scanning the exits over the top of a coffee cup. Roger, the hacker whose fingernails were chewed to the quick, wore an oversized Bengals hoodie and nursed a soda, looking like an overgrown teenager. Cynthia, the former CIA Intel analyst, completed the domestic camouflage with an empty stroller parked beside her and a Ziploc bag of Cheerios open on the table, though her eyes held none of the softness of a grandmother.

Mia took the empty plastic chair opposite Sydney. It was tacky with spilled soda residue. She kept her hands in her jacket pockets to hide the tremor that was worse today—a fine, mumbling hum in her bones that spoke of her cellular expiration date.

"Tell me you have something, because the government sucks," Mia said, her voice low, barely audible even to herself over the shrieking of a child going down the spiral slide.

Sydney didn't waste time with pleasantries. She set her coffee cup down with a soft *tap*. "We found a safehouse. Falls Church area. Vacated two weeks ago."

"Clean?" Mia asked, her stomach tightening.

"Pro level. Like ghosts," Sydney said. Her voice was a flat monotone, designed to carry no emotion. She slid a glossy 4x6 photo across the sticky table face down, then flipped it. It showed a nondescript suburban rental house, beige siding, tidy lawn. Totally anonymous. "Bleached counters, vacuumed carpets. No fingerprints, no stray fibers on the furniture. They even took the trash bags with them."

"But?" Mia pressed, sensing the 'but' hanging in the air.

"But nobody is perfect, not even them. The cleaning crew missed the HVAC intake." Sydney tapped the photo with a manicured nail. "We found a single strand of blonde hair caught in the filter mesh."

Mia's heart kicked against her ribs, a hard, painful thump. *Unity*. She pictured her sister's hair, that specific shade of pale gold, so like her own.

"DNA match?" Mia whispered.

"Partial. The root was damaged. But it's enough," Sydney confirmed, her dark eyes locking onto Mia's. "It's her. She was there."

Mia closed her eyes for a second, letting the mixture of relief and terror wash over her. Alive. She was alive. But two weeks was an eternity.

"They're still in Virginia, Mia," Sydney continued, pulling the photo back. "They're moving during satellite blackouts, likely hopping between short-term rentals, paying cash, using burner identities. They aren't leaving a digital exhaust trail."

"So we're chasing ghosts in the machine," Roger added, his voice cracking slightly. He crushed his empty soda can in one hand, the aluminum shrieking. "They stay ahead of the grid. Every time we get a ping, they're gone."

"We know they're here," Mia said, opening her eyes. The noise of the playland seemed to recede, replaced by a cold ringing in her ears. She gripped the edge of the plastic table, using the pressure to steady the shaking. "And we know they're watching the lab. They're not running, Sydney. They're circling. They're waiting for an opening."

"We found something else," Sydney said. Her tone shifted, dropping an octave, losing its professional detachment. It became heavy. "Roger went down a rabbit hole on the personnel records you gave us from the facility where Unity received care."

Mia frowned. "The care staff? I interviewed them all years ago."

Roger leaned in, pushing his glasses up his nose. "Jon Turner. Unity's primary caretaker."

Mia stiffened. The name brought an instant image to her mind: a gentle man with a soothing baritone voice and infinite patience. She remembered Jon's kindness, the way he had brushed Unity's hair when she was comatose, the way he read her classic novels out loud. She remembered the way he seemingly flirted with Mia during her early visits, before he got married, a harmless warmth that had made the sterile facility feel a little less cold. He had been a fixture in Unity's tragic life. A soft spot.

"What about him?" Mia asked, her throat suddenly dry.

"He didn't quit," Roger said, glancing nervously at Sydney before continuing. "He vanished. His employment file was terminated the exact same day as the military operation at the hangar where Sophia died. No two weeks' notice. No forwarding address. His bank accounts were closed simultaneously. He just walked out the door and deleted his entire digital footprint."

The betrayal hit Mia like a physical blow to the solar plexus, stealing her breath. Jon. The man she had trusted to sponge-bathe her helpless sister. The man she had brought coffee to at Christmas. He wasn't just a bystander caught up in the Romanos' web. He was the inside man. He had been feeding intel to the Romanos for years, maybe decades. Every visit Mia had made, every tear she had shed over Unity's unresponsive body, Jon had been there, watching, reporting back to the Matriarch.

"His social security number was a synthetic identity," Cynthia added softly, speaking for the first time, her eyes on the bag of Cheerios as if they held the secrets of the universe. "Top-tier forgery. He never existed before he took that job. The Romanos planted him there."

Mia stared at the ball pit, watching a small boy laugh as he buried himself completely in the multi-colored plastic spheres, disappearing from view. A mole. A deep-cover sleeper agent. The Romanos hadn't just reacted to Mia's human enhancement serum; they had been managing the situation, playing a long game. The violation felt intimate, oily.

"Can we find him?" Mia asked, her voice devoid of inflection.

"I found his sister. Or maybe the woman who posed as his sister for his emergency contact info," Sydney said. "She's real. Lives in Baltimore. We have eyes on her house. If he makes contact, we'll know."

Mia nodded slowly, her mind racing, recalibrating the entire board. The game had changed. The government was involved now. Major Washington's squad was guarding the lab, turning her home into a fortress. But the government was stuck. They had the hardware from the bunker—the mysterious implants, the stasis pods—but they couldn't crack the foreign architecture of the code. They were blunt instruments trying to pick a lock designed by geniuses.

She looked at Roger and Cynthia. She was paying them a fortune to chase shadows in the suburbs, utilizing only a fraction of their skill sets.

"Change of plans," Mia said, the quiver in her voice replaced by cold steel.

Sydney raised an eyebrow.

"Sydney, you stay on the hunt. Keep tracking the safehouses.

Burn down every lead."

"And us?" Roger asked, fidgeting with his hoodie strings.

"You're coming inside," Mia said.

Roger blinked. "Inside the lab?"

"The government recovered Romano tech from that bunker in Virginia. Advanced brain implants. Biometric stasis pod controllers. Their cyber warfare division is hitting a wall. They don't understand the biological interface."

Roger's eyes lit up behind his thick glasses. The tired teenager vanished, replaced by a predator sensing prey. "You want me to hack alien-level tech that stumped the NSA?"

"I don't want you to just hack it. I want you to break it wide open," Mia said, leaning forward, ignoring the sticky table. "I want to know how they communicate, how they track their units, and how we can turn their own technology against them. And Cynthia, I need you on the AI patterning. If these implants are networking, they're talking to a central hub. We need to know where that hub is."

"When do we start?" Cynthia asked, already sealing the bag of Cheerios with a decisive *zip*.

"Now," Mia said, shoving her chair back. It scraped loudly against the floor, momentarily drowning out the pop music. "Report to the lab in an hour. I'll have security badges waiting at the front desk."

She turned and walked away without looking back, leaving the screaming chaos of the playland behind. Jon Turner was out there, perhaps still with Unity, thinking he had gotten away clean. She was going to make him regret the day he ever learned to spell the name Peers.

Trapped

Jon

The latest house smelled of aggressive lemon—a scent so potent it tickled the nose, trying and failing to mask the underlying odor of damp drywall and dread.

Jon Turner stood in the narrow upstairs hallway, waiting. He hated the waiting most of all. It gave him time to think, time for the decades of lies to compost in his gut. The Romanos moved every week, sometimes sooner if the wind changed direction, and every house was identically soulless: stripped bare of personality, scrubbed raw by silent cleaning crews, and utterly devoid of life.

There were no pictures on the beige walls, only slightly lighter rectangles where frames had once hung, ghostly reminders of previous inhabitants. There were no rugs to muffle footsteps on the cheap laminate flooring. Just echoes. Every sound in the house—a closing door, a flushed toilet, a cough—reverberated, amplifying the tension.

Jon shifted his weight. His cheap suit, bought off the rack at a strip mall three towns over, itched at the collar. He was sweating, a cold, oily sheen that made his shirt stick to his lower back. He wasn't suffering from the Syndrome—he was just a regular human, disposable—but he was suffering from two decades of looking over his shoulder, of being a cipher in someone else's grand design.

"Enter," Mother Sophia's voice called from behind the closed door at the end of the hall. It wasn't a shout, but it carried the undisputed weight of command, cutting through the frigid silence.

Jon swallowed dryly, wiped his palms on his trousers, and pushed the door open.

The room was meant to be a bedroom, but like the rest of the house, it had been repurposed for war. It was empty save for a heavy oak desk that looked out of place on the scarred subfloor, and a large wooden target board hung on the far wall, splintered from repeated abuse.

Thunk.

The sound was deep and heavy. A bearded tactical axe was buried in the projected red bullseye, its handle vibrating almost imperceptibly from the force of the impact.

Mother Sophia stood at the makeshift throwing line. She didn't turn when he entered. She wore a charcoal gray silk blouse and trousers, an incongruous vision of old-world elegance against the paint of the suburban bedroom. She walked to the target with a fluid, predatory grace, wrenched the weapon free with a grunt of exertion that sounded terrifyingly masculine, and turned.

She held the axe loosely at her side, but her eyes were tight. "Sit," she commanded, gesturing with her free hand to a metal folding chair positioned opposite the desk.

Jon took the seat. The metal was cold against his legs through the thin fabric of his slacks. He placed his hands deliberately on his knees, pressing down to hide his nerves. He needed to appear useful, stable. Always. Not like a loose thread waiting to be snipped.

Mother walked behind the desk, placing the axe on the polished wood surface with a deliberate *clack*. The metal gleamed under the harsh light of the naked ceiling bulb.

"They took the bait," she said calmly, as if discussing the weather.

Jon's stomach dropped, a sensation like falling in a dream. "Mia?"

"Mia. And her new friends in the government. They have the hardware from the farmhouse bunker. They have the video footage of the melting clones. The seed has been planted in fertile ground."

She leaned back in her leather chair, steepled her fingers, and admired the trap she had sprung. The faint scent of her perfume—expensive jasmine and something metallic, like cold steel—drifted across the desk, overpowering the Pine-Sol.

"We are stringing her along, Jon, feeding her breadcrumbs that lead straight to the oven. Mia needs to believe she is dying. Not just intellectually—she needs to feel the panic in her marrow. She needs to believe that she is the one driving this investigation, that she is finding us." Mother's lips curled into a humorless smile. "If she thinks she has a choice, a chance, she will fight with that stubborn Peers arrogance. But if she thinks the sand is running out of her hourglass, she will beg. And when she begs, she will give us what we want."

Jon felt sick. The farmhouse. "So the raid... the clones in the bunker... it was all planned? You knew they were coming?"

"It was a calculated sacrifice," Mother said dismissively. "Old inventory. Unstable units destined for liquidation anyway. The Sentry Blade squad needed a win to feel confident, to feel justified in partnering with Mia. And Mia needed a demonstration of her future. I gave them both what they required."

Jon nodded slowly, keeping his eyes on the axe resting between them. He had spent years playing a role—the kindly, gentle caretaker with the soft spot for literature. He had wiped soap from Unity's skin, read her Dickens while she stared at the back of her eyelids, and brought Mia coffee during her agonizing visits. He had invented a wife, pregnancy, a nonexistent past, an entire backstory to make himself trustworthy, invisible.

He had almost convinced himself the lie was real. He had genuinely liked Mia. He had felt a protective warmth for the silent, broken girl in the bed.

And all the while, he had been sending weekly encrypted reports to this woman. He was just another pawn, sacrificing pieces of his own soul for Mother's game.

"What's the next move?" Jon asked, his voice rough.

"We wait." Mother picked up a silver letter opener and tapped it rhythmically against the desk. *Tap. Tap. Tap.* "Mia is stubborn. The programming Jeffrey put into her is deep. She needs to exhaust every other option. She needs to realize that her money, her brilliance, and her government friends with their guns cannot save her from biology. But when she breaks... and she will break... you need to be ready to receive her."

Mother stood up abruptly. The chair scraped loudly against the floor. She walked around the desk, closing the distance between them. Jon had to fight the urge to recoil as she stopped inches from his chair, looming over him.

"There is no going back to your old life, Jon. The mask is off now. You understand that, yes?"

He glanced up, meeting her obsidian eyes. There was no warmth there, only calculation. "I understand. There was never really an old life anyway."

"Good. Because I sense hesitation in you, Jonathan. I sense the milky residue of guilt." She placed a hand on his shoulder. The weight of it was shocking, heavy and cold, a reminder of the strength coiled beneath her silk blouse. His clavicle ached under her grip. "Do not let your misplaced affection for those girls cloud your judgment at this critical juncture. They were your assignment, not your family. If you betray us now, if you waver even for a second, there is nowhere on God's green Earth you can hide from me. You won't just die; you will unravel."

Jon forced himself not to flinch, to hold her gaze. The threat wasn't hyperbolic; he had seen what happened to failures in this family.

"I'm not going anywhere, Mother. I'm in too deep." He paused, licking his dry lips. The next words felt dangerous to speak, but keeping them inside felt worse. "But... I think Unity knows."

Mother's eyes narrowed slightly. The pressure on his shoulder increased. "Knows what? Be specific."

"Everything. She remembers me. Not just as the caretaker, but from *during* the coma. I see it when she looks at me." He fumbled for words to describe the unsettling shifts he'd witnessed. "It's not just physical recovery. She's fluent in Italian, Mother. I heard her muttering to herself yesterday. And she watches us. When she thinks I'm not looking, her eyes... they aren't vacant anymore. They're calculating. She's not just recovering; her mind is... expanding."

Mother removed her hand slowly, the absence of weight almost as jarring as its presence. She walked to the grime-streaked window, looking out at the overgrown backyard of the rental property.

"I was wondering when you'd notice," she murmured, almost to herself.

Jon frowned at her back. "You knew?"

"Mia's serum was a crude instrument. It didn't just jumpstart Unity's brain; it unlocked something that had been dormant." She turned back, her face serious, stripped of the theatrical menace, replaced by cold pragmatism. "Listen to me closely, Jon. Jeffrey Peers was an arrogant fool, but he was brilliant. He designed Mia to be a genius, yes. A tool to fix his mistakes. And now... Unity is something new. She *and Mia,* combined, are... a force."

The implication hung in the sterile air.

"Listen to me," Mother repeated, her voice low. "Unity may be more dangerous than Mia, the US government, and all my disappointing daughters combined."

Jon frowned, grappling with the concept. "She's a ninety-pound cripple in a wheelchair. She can barely lift a spoon."

"For now. The body will catch up to the mind. Do not underestimate her. If you think she is harmless because she is physically weak, you are a fool, and fools do not survive in this family." Mother walked back to the desk and picked up the axe again, weighing it in her palm. "Watch her. Closely. Report everything—every muttered word, every drawing, every flash of anger. If she so much as twitches a finger in a way you don't understand, you tell me immediately."

"Understood," Jon whispered.

"Go."

Jon stood up, his knees popping. He bolted from the room, feeling her eyes on his back like bores. He kept his pace steady, controlled, until he was out of sight of the door and around the corner. Then, he leaned against the wall, his breath coming in short, shallow gasps.

For years, he had viewed Unity as the ultimate victim. The leverage. The sleeping damsel in distress, waiting for a savior or a quiet death. He had pitied her.

He pushed off the wall and headed toward the stairs. As he passed the closed door of the second bedroom—Unity's holding cell—he saw a sliver of yellow light under the frame. She was awake.

He paused, his hand hovering over the knob, remembering the moment Mother had taken that note from Unity. The clarity in Unity's eyes, that split second. The rage.

He pulled his hand back. Mother was right. That wasn't the look of a victim. That was the look of a player who had just sat down at the board, already knowing the rules better than the people who invented the game. And Jon was terrified he was standing on the wrong side of the table.

Machines

Brian

Brian Carter and Roger, the hacker whose last name Brian still hadn't learned, sat cross-legged on the cool, anti-static tiled floor of Lab 4. The air in the secure room was crisp, recycled, and smelled faintly of hot solder. They were surrounded by the disemboweled guts of Romano technology, a mechanical graveyard spread out like a sacrificial offering.

They worked in a comfortable, almost sacred silence, the kind shared by people who speak the same native language of circuit boards, binary code, and schematics. Brian, wearing his faded denim bell-bottoms and a t-shirt advertising a long-defunct computer parts store, had disassembled both stasis pods down to their chassis. He was a meticulous dissector, organizing screws, washers, and mysterious proprietary microchips into neat, obsessive piles on a labeled anti-static mat.

Roger, looking like a college sophomore living on energy drinks and anxiety in his oversized hoodie, had the brain implant—a small, dark, terrifyingly advanced bio-chip recovered from the skull of a liquefied clone—hooked up to his ruggedized laptop via a jury-rigged interface Brian had soldered together in an hour.

"What's the endgame with the hardware?" Roger asked, breaking the silence. He didn't look up from his terminal, his eyes reflecting the rapid cascade of green code scrolling across the black screen. His fingers moved in a blur, a pianist playing a concerto only he could hear. "I can't imagine Mia has much use for cryo-tubes, unless she plans on putting Chris on ice when he gets annoying."

"Everything is useful," Brian murmured, distractedly. He was testing a capacitor from the pod's power regulation unit with a high-end multimeter. The readout fluctuated wildly, showing efficiency ratings that shouldn't be possible with current technology. "We don't just need to know what it does; we need to know *how* it does it. The philosophy behind the engineering." He gestured with the probes toward the far corner of the lab. "The small units in the back... they aren't just storage for biological material. They're incubators."

Roger paused, his hands hovering over the keyboard. "Incubators? Like, baby makers?"

"Growth chambers. Accelerated gestation and maturation. That's how they make an army without waiting eighteen years. They grow them. Like corn." Brian set the meter down carefully. His lower back ached, a dull, persistent throb at the base of his spine from hours of hunching over, but he ignored it. It was background noise. He was close to understanding the unique power supply architecture, and if he understood the power, he could understand the neural interface.

"They didn't find any... product inside when they raided the farm?" Roger asked, his voice quieter now.

"Empty. We got the leftovers. The obsolete models."

Brian picked up a backup power coupling made of a ceramic-metal alloy that felt warm to the touch. It was elegant engineering, brutal in its efficiency, far superior to standard military spec. There were no wasted wires, no redundant systems. He admired it even as he feared what it represented. If he could reverse-engineer this power flow, he might be able to build something new. Something impossible. Something that could bridge the gap between two sisters sharing one soul without burning them both out.

It was a crazy idea. A dangerous, ethically gray idea that Mia would probably hate. But Brian didn't know how to operate any other way.

A sharp, digital *ping* from Roger's laptop cut through the low hum of the lab's equipment.

"We're in," Roger whispered, the words heavy with disbelief.

Brian slid across the floor on his knees, abandoning his tidy piles of screws, ignoring the protest of his joints. He leaned over Roger's shoulder. "Show me."

"The encryption was layered like an onion, nasty biometric keys, but the root access key... it was static. Careless." Roger's fingers flew across the keyboard, executing final commands. "Okay, bypassing the final firewall. Initializing the data dump. Let's see what these dead guys saw."

The screen flickered, went black for a heart-stopping second, then flashed white.

Then, a window popped up. Then another. And another. Within seconds, a dozen separate video feeds were tiled across the high-resolution monitor, each one a grainy, fish-eye view of the world.

"Is that..." Roger pointed at the top left tile.

The feed was pitch black. Then, slowly, a horizontal line of light appeared in the center. It widened, blinking rapidly.

Brian realized with a jolt what he was looking at. Lashes. Light. A blurry, close-up view of a curved glass surface covered in condensation.

"We're seeing through their eyes," Brian said, his voice hushed with awe and horror. "This isn't just data; it's the visual recording from the implants' optical nerve interface."

On the screen, a pale hand reached out and pressed a

sequence of buttons on a panel inside the glass. The pod door slid open with a hiss of hydraulics. The viewpoint shifted wildly as the clone stumbled out, looking left at the concrete wall, then right at the row of identical pods.

In the other windows, identical scenes played out simultaneously. A dozen men waking up from the void. A dozen men stepping into the cold air of the bunker.

They were naked. They were shivering. They looked confused, vulnerable, their eyes darting around the unfamiliar space.

Then, simultaneously, every clone in every video feed stopped moving. It was eerie, like a film reel jamming. They went rigid. Then, they raised their hands to their temples in perfect, terrifying unison, pressing against the skin right above the ear.

A stream of dense, complex code cascaded across the top of the video overlay in red text.

"What is that?" Roger whispered, shrinking back slightly from the screen. "Are they talking to each other? Is it telepathy?"

"It's a broadcast," Brian said, leaning closer, his nose almost touching the monitor, trying to read the impossible language of the code. "A command signal override. They're being activated."

The clones lowered their hands. The confusion was gone from their eyes, replaced by a dead, flat purpose. As one organism, they turned toward the metal armory lockers against the far wall. As one, they opened them and grabbed weapons—rifles, pistols, combat knives. As one, they turned and marched in lockstep toward the stairs leading to the surface.

It wasn't a squad. It was a hive mind.

"Turn it off," Brian said, revulsion churning in his stomach.

Roger killed the feed. The screen went mercifully black, leaving only their own reflections staring back at them.

Brian sat back on his heels, his mind racing, connecting dots he hadn't known were there. The implants weren't just passive recording devices; they were sophisticated two-way receivers. The clones weren't just trained soldiers; they were remote-controlled drones receiving real-time tactical data and override commands synchronized down to the millisecond.

If the Romanos could control an army like that... if they could override free will with a broadcast signal...

"Where did the signal come from?" Brian asked, the implications terrifying him.

"I don't know. That part of the log is encrypted differently. It's not internal to the chip. It looks like... like an external handshake from a massive network." Roger rubbed his face, smearing grease across his cheek. "We need an AI to parse this, Brian. I can crack the door, but I can't read the language once I'm inside. It's too dense, too—"

"Mia has someone for that," Brian said, standing up suddenly, his knees popping loudly. He brushed dust and solder filings from his bell-bottoms. "The woman from the playland meeting. Cynthia."

"The Intel analyst? I didn't know she was—"

"She used to run threat assessment AIs for the CIA. If she's good with pattern recognition, we need her yesterday." Brian glanced back at the pile of incubator parts, the idea in his head crystallizing into a plan. He had a theory about how to save Mia and Unity, but it required a neural interface that could handle two consciousnesses at once without overloading. And if these chips could network dozens of brains together flawlessly...

"Get Cynthia down here," Brian said, his voice flat, professional, but his mind was on fire with possibilities. "Tell Mia to give her full clearance. I... have an idea."

Date

Mia

The helicopter cut through the Virginia twilight, a black insect against a bruising sky that was rapidly bleeding from deep purple into charcoal gray. Below, the Shenandoah River was a ribbon of spilled ink, reflecting the last gasps of daylight.

Mia gripped the worn leather armrest, her knuckles aching. Even with the custom noise-canceling headset clamped tight over her ears, muffling the world to a dull roar, the rhythmic *thwack-thwack-thwack* of the rotors acted as a sensory trigger. It was a physical echo of one of the worst moments of her life. Perhaps she needed to rethink the merits of flying.

She breathed through her nose, forcing the air deep into her diaphragm. *In. Hold. Out.* She repeated the mantra of the therapy she hadn't had time for.

Opposite her in the cramped cabin, Major Washington and Tony scanned the horizon through their respective windows with professional, practiced paranoia. Their bodies were relaxed, loose, but their eyes were restless. Tony was muttering into his comms microphone, his British accent from earlier replaced by a clipped cadence that sounded vaguely like a Navajo code-talker.

Beside her, Chris stared down at his hands, which were clasped tightly in his lap. His tailored suit looked out of place here, a costume from a simpler life as a lawyer.

Mia reached over and covered his fingers with hers. His skin was cool. He looked up, startled, then offered a sad, lopsided smile that didn't reach his eyes. They hadn't spoken since takeoff from the lab's roof. The silence between them was heavy, pressurized like the cabin, weighted with the secrets Mia was keeping and the fear she couldn't share.

The chopper banked sharply, descending into a private clearing near Front Royal, the skids settling onto the dewy grass with a gentle bump that still jarred Mia's spine. The engine began its high-pitched whine-down.

"Green Tail Ops, Alpha Leader and M.1.A. are on the ground," Lethabo announced over the shared channel, his voice flat.

Tony escorted them to the restaurant—a rustic, timber-framed lodge tucked discreetly into the edge of the Appalachian Trail, usually bustling with hikers and tourists. The owner, a nervous man with a forced smile, met them at the heavy oak door. His eyes went wide as he took in the armed escort flanking Mia and Chris, their weapons held at the low ready. He had closed the entire place for the night at Mia's request, a transaction that had cost more than her wedding ring.

"Thanks for the ride," Mia told Lethabo, shouting over the fading rotor noise. "You boys go play in the woods. Set up a perimeter. I can handle dinner."

Lethabo nodded once, a silent acknowledgment of the order, and retreated into the shadows of the tree line with Tony, dissolving into the landscape like smoke.

Inside, the restaurant was warm and cavernous, smelling rich with woodsmoke from the massive stone hearth and the savory scent of roasting meat and herbs. They were shown to a prime table near the fire, which crackled cheerfully, casting dancing orange shadows on the sea of empty chairs and white tablecloths surrounding them.

"This is nice," Chris said, loosening his tie and unbuttoning his collar as they sat. He glanced around at the emptiness. "Quiet. I wish it didn't require buying out the entire venue just to get a meal together."

"Security protocol," Mia murmured, picking up the heavy linen napkin. "Normal is a luxury we can't afford right now. Not with what's out there."

"I miss normal, Mia. I miss you. The real you, not this... general."

Mia stared at him across the flickering candlelight. He was her rock, the man who had stood by her through explosions, arraignments, and the revelation that her entire life was a lie. He loved her without condition. And she was repaying that love by lying to him by omission every single day. The weight of it was crushing.

"I've missed you too," she said, her voice softer, genuine.

Chris reached across the table, covering her hand with his. "Okay. Lay it on me. Why the sudden date night? Why the helicopter evacuation from your own lab? You don't do spontaneous dates, Mia. Not anymore."

Mia pulled her iPad from her large purse. She navigated through the encrypted folders until she found the file: *Operation Farmhouse_Redacted.*

"This has a TV-MA rating," she warned, her voice tight, sliding the tablet across the white tablecloth. "Just watch the end. The time stamp I marked."

Chris tapped the screen. The video began to play—the shaky body-cam footage from the raid on the clone bunker. He watched in silence, his brow furrowing. Mia watched his face. She saw the confusion as the naked men swarmed out of the ground, then the horror as the grenades went off, then the stark, unblinking shock as the clones on the screen stopped moving and began to steam in the cool air.

He watched as their flesh bubbled, as their faces collapsed inward, as they dissolved into puddles in a matter of seconds.

He watched until the end, then pushed the tablet away as if it were contaminated. He rubbed his face with both hands, dragging the skin down, leaving red marks.

"What... what was that?" he whispered.

"The government analyzed the residue," Mia said softly, forcing herself to look at him. "Their functional DNA age was forty. It's a cellular meltdown. They don't die, Chris. They expire."

Chris glanced at her, his eyes sharp, his lawyer's brain connecting the dots instantly, brutally.

"And you're thirty-eight," he whispered, the realization hitting him like a physical blow.

Mia nodded slowly. "Eighteen months, Chris. Maybe less. That's what the Matriarch's letter meant when she said 'tick tock.' The Syndrome isn't just tremors and headaches. It's this." She gestured to the dark screen of the tablet. "Liquefaction. Total cellular dissolution."

Chris sat back, his face draining of color until he looked like one of the ghosts on the screen. "But... you're the scientist. You're the best there is. You have the serum. It heals bullet holes in seconds. It brought you back from the dead. It has to be able to heal this."

"It's not healing me fast enough. It's fighting a losing battle against my own programming. My hands still shake every morning. My toes are starting to tremor now. It's spreading." Mia looked away, staring into the heart of the fire, watching the wood turn to ash. "The Romanos want a cure. They think I can make one. They think I have the missing piece."

"So make it! Save yourself!"

"If I do... I hand an army of immortal super-soldiers the keys to the kingdom. I give them the power to rule forever."

"So you're saying you won't do it?" Chris's voice rose, echoing in the empty dining room. "You're saying you'll just... sacrifice yourself? Let it happen?"

"If the choice is between saving myself and saving the rest of the world from a super-powered mafia that views humanity as cattle? Yes. I have to."

"You don't get to make that choice alone, Mia!" Chris slammed his hand on the table. The silverware rattled violently on the china.

The waiter, approaching with a bottle of expensive red wine, froze in his tracks a few feet away, eyes wide. Mia waved him off sharply.

"I'm your husband," Chris hissed, leaning over the table, his eyes burning with fear and anger. "I get a vote in whether you live or die."

"You don't," Mia snapped back, the anger flaring hot and sudden in her chest, burning away the guilt. "You saw them, Chris. You saw the way Sophia and Livia moved. You saw the coldness in their eyes. If I cure the Romanos, if I make them stable, they will burn everything down. They will take everything. Including you."

"I don't care about them! I care about you!"

"And I care about you enough to not leave you alone in a world run by monsters I helped create!"

Silence fell over the table, heavy and suffocating, broken only by the crackle of the fire.

Mia picked up her wine glass, her hand shaking so hard the liquid sloshed over the rim, and downed half of it in one swallow. The expensive vintage tasted like vinegar. The shaking wasn't fear or the Syndrome this time. It was rage. At the Romanos. At her father. At the unfairness of it all. And beneath the rage, a terrifying desperation.

She stood up abruptly, her chair scraping loudly on the wood floor. "I'll be right back."

She grabbed her purse and marched to the bathroom, ignoring Chris's stricken look. The door clicked shut behind her, cutting off the rustic warmth of the dining room.

The bathroom was brightly lit, decorated in white subway tiles that felt sterile and cold. Mia stared at herself in the large mirror. Bloodshot eyes ringed with fatigue. Pale, tight skin. A woman running out of time, her biology turning against her.

She opened her purse, her fingers fumbling with the zipper. Hidden in a secret lining was a small, crush-proof silver case. Inside, nesting in velvet foam, lay a single glass syringe filled with a white liquid.

The Twin Variant. A final dose she had created. The volatile version meant for Unity's body if her sister's recovery after twenty years as a vegetable proved less than optimal.

Mia hadn't planned to take it. It was a desperate Hail Mary. But the argument with Chris, the visceral image of the melting clones on the tablet, the crushing weight of the deadline ticking away in her cells... she needed something. Clarity. Strength. A connection to Unity, however tenuous. A chance.

She rolled up the sleeve of her silk blouse. Her arm was pale, the veins standing out blue against the skin.

If I'm going to die anyway, let's see what this does.

She jammed the needle into the crook of her arm with a gasp and depressed the plunger, emptying the thick liquid into her bloodstream.

She gripped the sink, bracing herself for the rush—the sensory explosion, the burning fire in her veins, the sharpening of light and sound she'd felt back at Cabela's when she had taken the second dose.

But there was nothing. No fire. No electric jolt. Just the cold, dull sting of the injection site and the rapid thudding of her own terrified heart.

Mia waited. One minute passed, marked by the rhythmic dripping of a faucet. Two minutes.

Nothing changed.

She let out a shaky breath that was half a sob. Maybe she was immune now. Maybe her body was too broken, too degraded by the Syndrome to accept the upgrade. Or maybe it was working silently, deep in the marrow, knitting the fraying edges of her DNA back together in ways she couldn't feel.

She tossed the empty syringe into the trash can and walked back to the table, feeling hollowed out.

Chris hadn't touched his food, which the waiter had silently deposited. He looked up as she approached, his expression softening from anger to misery.

"Mia, I'm sorry," he said, his voice rough. "I love you. We'll figure this out. We always do. But don't ask me to accept losing you. I can't do it again."

Mia sat down. The linen napkin felt cool under her fingers. She realized with a start that her hand was perfectly still on the table. The tremor was gone.

"We'll try," she lied, meeting his eyes, hating herself for the false hope she was offering.

The heavy front door to the restaurant burst open, banging against the wall. Tony strode in, not bothering to be stealthy, his hand pressed to his earpiece, his face grim.

"Package is secure, ma'am," he said, his voice clipped and professional, the fake accent gone. "But we have to move. Command has a priority update. Secure line only. It's a Situation Red."

Mia groaned, looking at the perfectly seared steak in front of her. "We haven't even eaten. Chris paid a fortune for this."

"This isn't optional, Dr. Peers. We need to be in the air five minutes ago. The threat profile has changed."

Mia stared at her untouched dinner, then at Chris's devastated face.

"Welcome to the new normal," she muttered, grabbing her purse.

As she walked toward the door, she flexed her fingers. The steadiness remained. It felt alien, unnatural. And somewhere in the back of her mind, past the fear and the anger, faint as a whisper across a canyon, she felt a pull. A tug in the direction of magnetic north.

Unity.

Perhaps the serum hadn't failed. Maybe it had just tuned the receiver. Like it had changed the frequency of her soul.

Mia smiled grimly into the darkness and followed the soldier out into the cold night air.

Something Odd

Unity

Something was wrong. Not just wrong, but fundamentally, disorientingly altered in the fabric of Unity's reality.

She sat in a high-end wheelchair at a table draped in thick white linen, sporting a dress made of indigo silk that felt impossibly smooth against her skin. The air was thick with the aroma of roasting garlic, rosemary, and expensive Italian perfume.

Unity was wearing wing-tipped eyeliner that made her blue eyes look enormous in the reflection of her water glass. She was sipping sparkling water from crystal stemware, the carbonation sizzling pleasantly on her tongue. She was in a five-star restaurant, and the sensory overload was threatening to drown her.

Across from her, Jon Turner adjusted his tie, his fingers fumbling slightly with the knot. He looked dapper, almost unrecognizable, in a tailored brown suit and a crisp silver shirt that caught the low light of the chandeliers. He was playing the role of the dutiful, slightly older date perfectly, even managing a relaxed smile for the passing waiter.

But his eyes told a different story. They were darting around the room like a trapped animal searching for an unlocked cage, scanning the exits, the kitchen doors, the faces of the large Romano family gathering.

"Don't stare," Jon murmured, leaning in as he cut into his prime rib, the knife slicing through the meat like butter. His voice was barely a whisper, lost under the clinking of silverware and the low hum of conversation. "Eat. Enjoy it. It's part of the show. If you look terrified, they'll notice."

Unity picked up her heavy silver fork. The aroma rising from her own plate of filet mignon made her mouth water so hard it was almost painful—a primal, visceral reaction she hadn't experienced since childhood. She took a small bite of the steak. The explosion of flavor—salt, fat, umami, the char of the grill—was overwhelming. It was, without a doubt, the best thing she had ever tasted. It tasted like life.

But even the ecstasy of the food couldn't make her ignore the room.

The restaurant was full, bustling with what appeared to be a typical Saturday night crowd. Young couples chatted across tables, families laughed over shared appetizers, groups of well-dressed friends toasted with wine. But as Unity scanned the crowd, the uncanny valley hit her with the force of a physical blow.

They were all the same.

It was subtle at first, masked by variations in styling. The men had different haircuts—some short and military, some trendy shags, some dyed with streaks of gray—but under the hair, they shared the same bone structure. The same strong, angular jaw, the same Romano nose, the same deep-set, dark eyes. The women were variations on a theme she knew too well: the Sophia model, the Livia model, the Caterina model. Different makeup, different dresses, but the underlying architecture was identical.

It wasn't a restaurant. It was a showroom. A diorama filled with living dolls.

"Cesaro's clones," Jon whispered, tracking her gaze without moving his head. "Mother reclaimed them from buyers in the States. They were in stasis too long; their social skills degraded. They need socialization protocols before they can be deployed."

Unity shivered, the silk dress suddenly feeling thin. A room full of manufactured humans, pretending to be real. Pretending to laugh at jokes they didn't understand, pretending to enjoy relationships that were fake, pretending to live. It was a grotesque pantomime of humanity.

"It's a lot of them," Unity said, keeping her voice low, fighting the urge to bolt for the door she couldn't reach. "How did they hide this many people?"

"Money," Jon said simply, taking a sip of his iced tea. "And influence. They own the building. The staff are all on the payroll. It's a closed ecosystem."

Their escort, a clone named Chiara with a predatory smile and a dress that cost more than an a private jet, had left their table minutes ago to mingle with her "friends" at the bar. Unity seized the moment of relative privacy.

"Why are you really doing this, Jon?" she hissed, leaning across the table as far as her limited mobility allowed. "You're not one of them. You're human. You're not a clone. What could they possibly have on you that's worth twenty years of your life?"

Jon took a long, slow drink of his tea. He set the glass down with a quiet clink. He didn't look at her; he glanced at his reflection in the dark liquid.

"My sister," he whispered, the words barely audible.

Unity froze. The piece of steak in her mouth turned to ash. "Your sister?"

"They killed my parents," Jon said, his voice flat, detached, as if recounting a story he had read in a newspaper. "Decades ago. My folks were engineers. Brilliant. They built some of the early stabilization tech for the cloning process. When they wanted out… when they developed a conscience… the Romanos made an example." He sliced his meat again, with unnecessary, savage force. "They let me live. As long as I serve, my sister is free. But I'm reaching my limit, Unity. I'm tired."

Unity watched him, seeing the man behind the mask for the first time. The kindly caretaker act was gone. Underneath was a man burning with years of suppressed rage and grief, a man held hostage by love.

"We can use that," Unity whispered, her mind racing. "You have access. You drive the van. You know the protocols."

"This isn't the place, Unity. The walls have ears."

"This is the only place. Look at them." She gestured with her eyes to the crowded room. "They're distracted by their little play. They're drunk on freedom."

As she spoke, a strange sensation washed over her. It wasn't just the adrenaline of plotting an escape, the frantic energy of fear and hope. It was something physical, something deeply internal. A sudden lightness bloomed in her chest, expanding outward. A low-frequency hum started in her ears, drowning out the restaurant noise.

The world seemed to sharpen. The edges of objects became razor-distinct. The clatter of silverware on china, the murmur of a hundred conversations, the clinking of ice in glasses—it all became hyper-focused, a symphony of sound that she could parse individually.

Then, a flash.

A vision, crystal clear and blindingly bright, overlaid on the restaurant scene. A bathroom mirror. A woman with blonde hair, gripping a white porcelain sink. Eyes that were bloodshot, wild with panic and resolve. A used syringe.

Mia.

The connection was instant and overwhelming, a psychic blow that knocked the breath from Unity's lungs. She gasped aloud, her hands gripping the edge of the table so hard her fingernails turned white. She could feel Mia's desperation, her towering anger, her sheer, terrifying force of will. It was a tidal wave of emotion crashing into her mind.

Mia? Can you hear me? I'm here.

Unity pushed the thought out into the void, straining against the barrier in her mind, trying to grab hold of the thread.

Nothing. The vision faded as quickly as it had come, leaving behind only the scent of the restaurant and the hum in her ears.

But the energy remained. It coiled in Unity's chest, hot and volatile, a sleeping dragon waking up. She looked around the room at the clones—these abominations wearing human skin, these pale imitations of life laughing and eating while her sister was suffering—and a wave of pure, unadulterated fury crashed over her. They had stolen her life. They had imprisoned her. They were hunting her sister.

She wanted to crush them.

Unity squeezed her left hand into a fist on her lap. The pressure built inside her, a physical force demanding release, a scream trapped in her bones.

She exhaled sharply and flicked her fingers open, pushing her palm outward toward Jon.

BOOM.

It wasn't a sound. It was a concussion. A force.

Across the table, Jon flew backward as if hit by an invisible truck. His chair tipped with a violent screech, his feet left the floor, and he crashed into the waiter passing behind him with a tray of drinks. The tablecloth ripped from the table, sending plates, heavy crystal glasses, and silverware clattering to the hardwood floor in a cacophony of shattering china and splashing liquids.

The restaurant went dead silent. The music stopped.

Every head turned. One hundred and fifty pairs of identical, dark eyes stared at them.

Unity sat frozen in her wheelchair, her hand still extended in the follow-through of the push. Her heart hammered against her ribs like a trapped bird.

Jon scrambled to his feet, dripping with red wine, iced tea, and bits of food. He gawked at Unity, his eyes wide with genuine shock and terror. Then, his survival instinct kicked in.

"Sorry!" Jon shouted into the silence, waving his hands in a placating gesture. "Leaned back too far! Grabbed the tablecloth! Clumsy! My bad, everyone!"

He forced a loud, braying laugh that sounded frantic, bending down to pick up a fork with shaking hands. "Can we get a mop over here? Sorry about the mess!"

The tension in the room broke, the spell shattered by his performance. Waiters rushed over with towels. Most of the clones, accepting the simple explanation of human clumsiness, turned back to their meals and conversations.

Jon leaned over the table as he helped clear the larger debris, his face inches from hers.

"What the hell was that?" he hissed, his voice trembling.

Unity stared at her own hand. It was trembling. Not with weakness or fear. With power.

"I don't know," she whispered, looking up at him. "I just... pushed. With my mind."

"You pushed me ten feet across the room without touching me? You threw a grown man with your mind?"

"I think so."

Jon stared at her. For the first time in years, he didn't look at her with pity or paternal affection. He looked at her with unmasked fear.

"Mother was right," he muttered, wiping wine from his cheek. "You're dangerous."

"Did I miss the party?"

Chiara slid back into her seat, grinning like a cat that just ate the canary. She glanced from the mess being cleaned up on the floor to Jon's stained suit.

"Just a little accident," Jon said quickly, his voice tight. "Everything is under control."

Chiara peered at Unity, her dark eyes narrowing slightly, calculating. She seemed to sense the shift in the air.

"Be careful, Jon," she purred, sipping her wine. "Accidents can be fatal in this family."

Unity put her hand back in her lap and clenched her fist again, testing the feeling. The power was still there, coiling and uncoiling, humming under her skin. Waiting for a command.

She smiled at Chiara, a smile that didn't reach her eyes.

"Don't worry," Unity said, her voice steady and cold. "Jon's a fast learner. He won't make the same mistake twice."

Muse

Mia

The Muse Paintbar in Gainesville was a sensory assault dedicated to the forced democratization of art. It smelled aggressively of cheap, oaky chardonnay, and the sharp odor of student-grade acrylic polymers. It was a factory line for mediocre landscapes, churning out half-decent paintings that would eventually collect dust in guest bathrooms or be passive-aggressively gifted to in-laws.

Mia sat perched on a metal high-top stool that dug into her thighs, feeling ridiculously conspicuous in her attempt at anonymity. She wore a floppy straw sun hat with a brim the size of a satellite dish and oversized tortoiseshell sunglasses that slid down the bridge of her nose every thirty seconds. She felt less like an incognito geneticist running for her life and more like a hungover D-list celebrity trying to avoid paparazzi at brunch.

Beside her, Ginger Matthews nursed a pint of lager, looking equally absurd but entirely unbothered in a rhinestone-studded denim jacket that caught the overhead track lighting like a disco ball.

"This is torture," Mia muttered, staring morosely at her canvas. It was supposed to be a sun-drenched Tuscan hillside, all rolling greens and warm ochres. Hers looked like a mudslide taking out a sewage treatment plant. She stabbed the canvas with a brush overloaded with burned umber, making a bad situation worse.

"It's therapy," Ginger corrected, taking a long sip of her beer. Her own canvas was irritatingly competent—a decent rendering of cypress trees standing sentry over a vineyard. "Look at Robert. He's soothing."

Mia glanced at the front of the room, where Robert, an instructor with too much energy and a headset microphone, was practically levitating with forced enthusiasm as he demonstrated how to paint a "happy little cloud."

"Robert is a liar and a tyrant," Mia said, reaching for her own drink. It was her fifth beer in ninety minutes.

She took a long pull, the carbonation biting her tongue, tasting thin. She waited for the familiar fuzzy warmth of intoxication, the softening of the edges. Nothing. Her enhanced metabolism, a gift from the serum, was burning through the ethanol like a blast furnace before it could even think about buzzing her frontal lobe. She was stone cold sober, filled with nervous energy, and utterly miserable.

She couldn't get drunk. She couldn't paint straight. And she couldn't stop looking over her shoulder.

Near the front door, Major Washington sat at a small table, nursing an iced tea he hadn't touched. He was in a tactical crouch disguised as a casual slouch, his shoulders tight under his civilian jacket. His eyes never rested, scanning every patron who walked in, probably assessing threats in soccer moms and date-night couples. At the rear emergency exit, Peyton leaned against the wall, chewing gum and looking like a bored teenager waiting for a ride, but Mia knew she was watching the parking lot like a hawk, calculating angles of fire.

Their presence was comforting, but also a suffocating reminder that Mia was bait hanging on a hook.

"You're thinking too hard. I can hear your gears grinding from here," Ginger said, nudging Mia's elbow gently. "Relax the wrist. Stop gripping the brush like it's a scalpel. Let it flow."

"My wrist doesn't do 'relax' anymore, Ginger," Mia snapped, immediately regretting the sharp tone. She dropped the brush into the water jar, where it clattered loudly. She held up her right hand.

Under the unforgiving gallery lights, the tremor was undeniable. It was a fine, high-frequency vibration, a constant thrumming beneath the skin that turned every attempt at a straight line into a seismograph reading of her own decay.

"See? It's getting worse. The meds Brian give me aren't touching it. I'm accelerating."

Ginger set her own brush down, the playfulness vanishing from her eyes, replaced by the steel core that had saved the press conference. "Okay. We don't talk about the painting. Let's talk about real life. Has Chris brought up next steps? Maybe... expanding the family?"

Mia felt like she'd been punched in the gut. She picked up the brush again just to have something to hold, jerking her hand so hard she painted a jagged brown scar across her sky. "Ugh. Seriously?"

"Sorry. Too soon? You guys have been married a year."

"No," Mia sighed, the fight draining out of her. "It's just... ridiculous. Look at me, Ginger. Really look at me. I'm melting. My cells are reaching their expiration date. I have eighteen months to live, best case scenario, before I turn into soup. I'm being hunted by an Italian matriarch who thinks I'm her property. And you think I should bring a baby into this?"

"People have babies in war zones every day," Ginger said softly, her voice unwavering amid the chatter of the room. "Sometimes, it gives them the only thing worth fighting for."

"I'm fighting for my life. And my sister's. Those should be enough." Mia lowered her voice, leaning in so the cheerful instructor wouldn't overhear. "Besides, you're forgetting that Chris and I aren't exactly the average couple. He's human. I'm... a science experiment. A clone with tweaked DNA. I don't even know if I *can* have children. And if I did... what if I passed this on? Would they have the Syndrome? Would I be giving birth to a ticking time bomb?" The horror of the thought nearly choked her.

Ginger reached out and covered Mia's trembling, paint-stained hand with her own warm, steady one. "Or maybe, Mia, that's exactly why you should. A legacy. Something beautiful that lasts longer than eighteen months. Something they can't take away."

Mia pulled her hand away sharply. The contact was too much. The emotions were too big for this stupid, brightly lit room.

"I can't talk about this," Mia whispered.

Suddenly, the pressure in her head spiked. It wasn't a normal headache. It didn't throb. It felt like static pressure, like deep underwater submersion, a tuning fork struck hard inside the base of her skull. A high-pitched whine, just on the edge of hearing, drowned out Robert's instructions on cloud shading.

The room tilted violently to the left.

Mia grabbed the edge of the high-top table to keep from falling off her stool.

For a split second, the paintbar—the easels, the beer, Ginger's worried face—vanished entirely.

The smell of acrylics was instantly replaced by a rich, overwhelming sensory wave: roasted garlic, sizzling rosemary, and expensive, heavy perfume. The hard wooden stool beneath her dissolved. She wasn't sitting up high; she was low, contained. The sensation of being in a wheelchair, the specific pressure on her hips and spine, was absolute.

She wasn't looking at a canvas. She was looking across a table covered in thick white linen, littered with broken glass and spilled liquid.

A man was there, scrambling backward, his chair tipped over. He was wiping red wine off a shimmering silver shirt, his face a mask of shock and fear.

Jon.

The recognition hit her with the force of a physical blow. He looked older, terrified, and completely real.

"Holy shit," Mia whispered, the words barely forming on her lips in the paintbar.

"Mia?" Ginger's voice sounded miles away, distorted, as if coming through dense water. "Mia, what is it? Are you having a stroke?"

The vision snapped off as abruptly as it had begun. The paintbar slammed back into focus—the bright lights searing her eyes, the smell of paint thinner returning with a vengeance.

Mia gasped, air rushing into her lungs as if she'd been drowning. Her heart hammered against her ribs.

The headache was gone instantly. But something else had taken its place.

A hum. A physical quivering that started in her shoulder and threaded down through her biceps, into her forearm, lighting up her nerves like a second circulatory system. It wasn't pain. It was presence. A connection.

Mia stared at the canvas. The ugly brown mudslide stared back at her.

Then, her hand moved.

She didn't tell it to move. She watched, detached, a passenger in her own body, as her fingers gripped the brush with a sudden, fluid confidence she hadn't felt in months. The tremor was gone. Completely gone. Her hand was as steady as carved stone.

Her hand dipped the brush into the viridian green acrylic. Then a touch of cadmium yellow. It moved to the canvas, slashing across the surface with speed and precision that Mia the scientist had never possessed.

"Mia?" Ginger whispered, pulling back slightly, alarmed by the sudden shift in energy. "What are you doing?"

Mia couldn't answer. Her throat felt tight, locked tight. She couldn't have stopped her hand if she wanted to.

The brush danced. It was aggressive, masterful. The brown mudslide disappeared under layers of complex green. A tree took shape—not a blob, but a living, breathing oak with intricate, gnarled branches reaching desperately for the sky. A bird appeared in the distance, a single, perfect stroke of black that conveyed flight and freedom.

It wasn't Robert's painting. It wasn't Mia's painting. It was something else entirely.

Mia watched, mesmerized and terrified, as the brush moved down to the bottom right corner of the canvas, right over the mudslide. It switched, her fingers deftly rolling the handle to use the fine-point detail tip. It dipped into the black paint.

Her hand wrote a single word in elegant, looping, undeniably familiar cursive.

Pact.

And directly below it:

Love, Unity.

The presence vanished as quickly as it had arrived. The hum in her arm ceased, leaving behind a cold emptiness. Mia's hand went completely limp, the brush clattering loudly onto the wooden table, splattering black paint.

She slumped forward, elbows on the table, gasping for air, sweat drenching the back of her shirt under the stupid floppy hat. She felt hollowed out, exhausted, as if she'd just run a marathon.

Ginger stared at the canvas, ignoring the surrounding chatter of the class. Slowly, she reached up and took off her rhinestone glasses, her eyes wide and stunned.

"What does that say?" she whispered, pointing at the script.

Mia stared at the signature. The handwriting was identical to the mysterious note found in her childhood journals. The same handwriting on the note delivered at the ceremony that had started this whole nightmare.

The Angels won 37-36. The Pact. Their childhood code.

Hot tears welled in Mia's eyes, spilling over before she could stop them. She grabbed the edge of the table, her own hands shaking again, but this time from pure, adrenaline-fueled shock.

"It says she's alive," Mia choked out, the relief so profound it was painful. "The serum worked. She's awake. And she's close enough to reach me."

Ginger didn't ask questions. She didn't hesitate. She grabbed the wet canvas, shielding it with her body like it was a newborn baby. She stood up, waving sharply at Lethabo near the door. The Major was on his feet instantly, hand moving to his waistband.

"We're leaving," Ginger announced, her voice fierce, pulling Mia up from the stool. "Right now. Move."

Livia

Lethabo

Guarding Dr. Mia Peers was a unique kind of assignment, composed of ninety percent mind-numbing boredom and ten percent sheer, existential terror.

Lethabo stood at ease near the desk outside Lab 1, his posture deceptive. To a civilian, he looked relaxed, a statue in black tactical gear. In reality, every muscle was coiled, every sense rocking at maximum output. The air in the subterranean facility always felt thin, recycled too many times. The fluorescent lights hummed a high-pitch frequency that grated against his enhanced hearing, a constant, nagging toothache behind his eyes.

He shifted his weight, the ceramic plates in his vest pressing familiarly against his chest. Four hours into this shift. Four hours of watching scientists pipette liquids and stare at monitors.

Tony leaned against the brushed steel doorframe of the lab's elevator, spinning his sidearm on his finger before holstering it with a practiced click. He checked the chamber indicator for the third time in as many minutes.

"The Romanos will be back," Tony intoned, dropping his voice into a passable, if cliché, Schwarzenegger growl. He scanned the empty hallway with theatrical intensity. "Come with me if you want to live."

"Stop," Lethabo groaned, not moving his eyes from the corridor axis. "You're degrading operational discipline."

Beside him, Kristin and Peyton, currently acting as the close-protection radius, rolled their eyes in perfect, synchronized exasperation.

"You guys have no appreciation for the classics," Tony said, switching seamlessly back to his normal, clipped voice. "Levity, Major. It keeps the reflexes sharp. Otherwise, the sheer excitement of watching agar jelly set might kill us before the super-clones do."

"Quiet," Lethabo snapped softly. The elevator hydraulics were engaging.

The heavy steel doors slid open with a pneumatic hiss. Mia stepped out.

The transformation was subtle but striking. Gone was the harried scientist in the oversized lab coat. The woman standing before them wore fitted tactical pants, sturdy boots, and a black t-shirt that emphasized the lean, unnatural musculature of her arms. Her hair was pulled back tight. She looked less like a researcher and more like an asset ready for a wet-work operation. She carried a heavy, antiquated iron key ring that jangled sharply in the silence.

Lethabo scanned her face. Her eyes were rimmed with red, the pupils slightly dilated. She was running on fumes, adrenaline, and whatever cocktail of drugs she was using to try and slow her cellular decay.

"We're going downstairs," Mia said, her voice devoid of inflection. "Weapons hot if I were you."

Lethabo straightened, the boredom instantly evaporating, replaced by the cold prickle of adrenaline. "Downstairs? The sub-basement is storage. Threat level?"

"Internal," Mia said. She didn't elaborate. She walked past

them, the scent of rubbing alcohol and cold sweat trailing in her wake, heading not for the main elevator banks, but for a nondescript fire door labeled 'MAINTENANCE ONLY'. "I need an escort for an extraction. It might get messy."

Lethabo signaled the squad with a sharp hand gesture. They fell into a diamond formation around her—Lethabo on point, Kristin and Peyton flanking, Tony bringing up the rear, walking backward to cover their six.

Mia keyed open the maintenance door, revealing a concrete stairwell that plunged into darkness. The air rushing up to meet them was significantly cooler, smelling of undisturbed dust and high-voltage machinery.

They descended. One flight. Two. Three. The sounds of the active lab above faded, replaced by the echo of their own boots on the metal-edged steps.

"This area isn't on the blueprints we were provided," Kristin murmured over the squad comms, her voice tight. Her helmet-mounted lights swept the bare concrete walls, searching for hidden sensors or cameras.

"That's because it doesn't exist," Mia said over her shoulder. "It's lead-lined and sits on independent bedrock stabilizers. A bunker for biological mistakes."

Lethabo's grip tightened on his rifle. He didn't like being off the grid, even inside a friendly facility.

They reached the bottom landing. It terminated in a hallway of imposing, steel doors, riveted and reinforced. Complex electronic keypads sat next to old-fashioned tumbler locks. Mia approached a door, ignored the keypad and inserted one of the large iron keys into the manual lock.

She paused, her hand on the key, her back to Lethabo.

"Wait," Lethabo said, his instincts screaming. This felt like a trap. "Before we breach, I need to know what's on the other side. And you know this deviation from protocol is being recorded. My audio feeds go directly to Sentry Blade command in real-time."

Mia turned her head slightly. In the harsh glare of his tactical light, her profile looked sharp, predatory.

"I know," Mia said softly. "I can hear your transmissions, Major. The bone-conduction tech in your helmet is good, but my hearing is better. 'Sending packet now.' Every night at 8:00 PM. You report on my tremors, my mood swings, my caloric intake."

Lethabo stiffened, a cold spike of violation piercing his professional veneer. He shouldn't have been surprised—the woman had survived falling from a jet without a parachute—but the casual reminder that she was constantly listening to his private channel, to the secrets he reported to his superiors about *her*, unnerved him deeply. It shifted the power dynamic in the dark stairwell instantly.

"We'll talk about the video you send them later," Mia continued, turning back to the door. "Right now, I need you to do the job I'm paying the government for. Watch my back. And try not to flinch."

She turned the key. The heavy internal bolts retracted with a deep, resonant *thud* that vibrated through the floorplates.

Lethabo swallowed hard, recalibrating. "Kristin, you're with me on entry. Peyton, Tony, hold the stairwell perimeter. Nothing comes down."

He pushed the heavy door open, leading with the muzzle of his rifle.

The sensory assault was instantaneous. The room wasn't dark; it was blindingly white. Padded walls, floor, and ceiling reflected high-intensity halogen lights that seared the retina. The smell hit him next—the unmistakable, primal stench of unwashed human body and ammonia, barely masked by disinfectant.

In the center of the stark room, suspended by heavy industrial chains from the ceiling and anchored to bolts in the floor, hung a woman.

She was filthy, her body smeared with grime and dried bodily fluids. But that wasn't what stopped Lethabo in his tracks, causing Kristin to gasp audibly behind him.

It was the missing arm.

The woman was strung up like a piece of meat in a butcher shop—her remaining wrist shackled high to the ceiling, ankles chained wide to the floor, spread-eagled to prevent any leverage or movement. Where her left arm should have been, there was only a smooth, rounded stump at the shoulder. The skin was perfectly healed, pink and seamless, a grotesque testament to the regenerative power of the serum Mia had created.

"Jesus, Mia," Kristin whispered, her weapon lowering slightly in shock. This was a black site detention. This was a war crime.

"It's not torture," Mia said flatly, walking past the stunned soldiers into the room. Her voice echoed strangely off the padding. "It's containment. Necessary containment. This is Livia. She's the clone who attacked the ceremony. The one who snapped my head of security's neck."

Livia lifted her head slowly. Her dark hair was completely matted, obscuring half her face. But the single eye visible through the tangle was bright, burning with a manic, terrifying intelligence that belied her wretched state. She peered at Lethabo, then Kristin, likely cataloging their gear, their stances, their weaknesses in a split second.

"I memorize your faces," Livia hissed. Her voice was unused, rough like gravel, her Italian accent thick and guttural. "My family see what I see. They see you now. You are marked."

"No, they don't," Mia said, circling the prisoner like a shark. "Your implants are dead. I fried the transmission capability weeks ago. You're broadcasting to no one."

"Why show us this?" Lethabo asked, forcing himself to keep

his rifle trained on the hanging woman, though every instinct rebelled against targeting a restrained prisoner. The moral gray area he was operating in had just turned pitch black. "If Command sees this feed... if they know you're holding a Romano subject..."

"They'll want her," Mia finished for him. "They'll want to take her to some black site in Nevada and vivisect her to get the serum. That's why I kept her hidden down here. You are the only people on earth besides me and Brian who know she exists."

Mia reached into a pouch on her tactical vest and pulled out a large syringe and a tourniquet.

"But today... things have changed. I need a fresh sample. Brian needs her blood," Mia explained, her tone clinical, detached, as if discussing a lab rat. "For the interface he's building. We need live, active serum markers. But she... reacts poorly to needles."

Mia stepped onto a metal folding chair she had dragged behind Livia. She grabbed a fistful of the clone's matted hair and yanked her head back violently, exposing the taut line of her jugular vein.

"Don't move," Mia whispered into Livia's ear, the threat intimate and chilling. "Or I'll pop your skull off your spine like a grape. You know I can."

Livia went rigid. Her remaining hand clenched into a fist so tight the knuckles cracked.

Mia didn't hesitate. She didn't search for a vein. She drove the thick needle straight into the side of Livia's neck.

Livia screamed.

It wasn't a human sound. It was a feral, animal shriek of fury and violation that tore through the padded room. The heavy chains rattled violently as she thrashed against the bolts, testing the limits of her restraints, her body contorting in impossible ways. Blood, dark and thick, filled the syringe barrel.

Lethabo felt sick. He'd seen interrogation, he'd seen combat, but this cold, scientific brutality was something else. Mia's face was a mask of stone as she drew the blood.

Mia capped the needle and pocketed it. She stepped down from the chair, breathing heavily.

"See?" Mia said, turning to Lethabo, wiping a single drop of bright crimson blood from her hand onto her tactical pants. Her voice was brittle. "Easy."

SCREECH.

The sound tore through the room, high-pitched and agonizing—metal grinding against concrete with immense pressure.

Lethabo spun around, weapon raised, searching for the threat.

The metal folding chair Mia had just vacated was moving.

No one was touching it. It was sliding across the concrete floor, grinding against the surface, moving away from Livia. It wasn't sliding downhill; the floor was level. It was being *pushed* by an invisible hand.

"Contact!" Lethabo yelled, his heart slamming against his ribs. He swept the room with his rifle, desperate for a target. "Front! What is it?"

But there was no one there.

The chair accelerated. It slammed into the padded wall with enough force to dent the plaster beneath the foam. Then, impossibly, it dragged itself sideways, scraping along the baseboard for three feet before coming to a halt.

"What the hell?" Kristin whispered, backing toward the door, her discipline fracturing.

Peyton and Tony burst into the room from the stairwell, weapons raised, drawn by the commotion.

"Clear! Clear! What's the target?"

Everyone stared at the chair. It sat against the wall,

inanimate once more. The silence that followed was heavier than the scream had been.

Lethabo slowly lowered his weapon, turning to look at Mia.

She was standing rigid in the center of the room. She was rubbing her temples with the heels of her hands, her eyes squeezed shut tight. Her face had gone deathly pale, drained of all blood. She looked like she'd just taken a physical blow to the head.

"Did you do that?" Lethabo asked, his voice low, dangerous. If she was telekinetic now, the threat profile had just changed catastrophically.

Livia began to laugh.

It started as a low chuckle, then built into a high, broken cackle that echoed off the padded walls. She threw her head back, staring at the ceiling, laughing at the terrified soldiers, laughing at the impossible chair, laughing at the look on Mia's face.

"The twin is learning!" Livia shouted between peels of laughter. "She is devious and she is angry! Oh, Mother will be so pleased!"

Mia opened her eyes. The pain in them was raw, terrifying.

"No," she whispered, her voice trembling. "I didn't."

She didn't look at the chair. She looked past it, as if seeing something through the wall. She walked past Lethabo, heading for the door, her steps unsteady.

"Send the video feed of this to your bosses, Major," Mia said over her shoulder, not looking back. "Tell them they can't have Livia yet. And tell them... if they want to know what just happened in this room, they need to find my sister. Now."

Mia vanished into the dark stairwell.

Lethabo watched her go. He stared at the dented wall, the silent chair, and finally at the one-armed woman hanging from the ceiling, who was still laughing softly to herself.

The parameters of the mission had just shifted into

nightmare territory.

He tapped the side of his helmet, activating the secure line.

"Green Tail Ops, this is Alpha Leader. Priority upload incoming. Encrypt to the highest level. You're going to want to see this. We have a new variable."

Hike

Caterina

The long black limousine climbed the winding, treacherous roads of the Blue Ridge Mountains, its tires crunching rhythmically on the frozen gravel and patches of black ice. Inside the plush leather cabin, the silence was colder and more biting than the Virginia winter raging outside the tinted windows.

Caterina sat rigid beside Mother Sophia, staring out at the skeletal, snow-dusted trees that blurred past like ghosts. The heated seat beneath her felt like a mockery; her blood was ice. She was carefully, rationally considering the merits of matricide.

The Matriarch was losing her mind. It was the only logical conclusion. She was pulling brothers out of deep stasis too early, leaving them disoriented and volatile. She was flooding the States with batches of clones, a terrible waste of resources. And worst of all, she was actively stirring up a war on American soil with the most powerful military complex on Earth.

It was reckless. It was arrogant. It was suicide on a grand scale.

And Caterina, the Daughter-in-Waiting, the designated successor programmed for pragmatism and survival, seemed to be the only one who saw the cliff edge they were hurtling toward. The rest of the family were lemmings following a mad queen.

The car slowed, lurching slightly as it pulled into a deserted trailhead parking lot that was little more than a widened patch of gravel. A few other vehicles were scattered around—Subarus with roof racks belonging to hikers crazy enough to brave the sub-freezing temperatures—but they were currently empty, buried under a fresh dusting of snow.

"We walk," Mother said abruptly, her voice cracking the silence like a whip. She began pulling on heavy, fur-lined leather gloves.

"Here?" Caterina asked, bewildered, glancing down at her canvas Converse sneakers, already damp from the walk to the car. She hadn't been allowed to change out of her "tactical" American disguise. "Mother, it's ten degrees out. There's a wind chill warning."

"The cold sharpens the mind. It burns away distractions." Mother opened her door, letting in a blast of frigid air that instantly frosted the leather interior.

They exited the vehicle. The air hit Caterina like a physical slap, freezing the moisture in her nose and making her lungs burn. Four large security guards piled out of the trailing SUV, fanning out in a practiced defensive perimeter, their breath puffing in thick white clouds that were snatched away by the wind. They kept their distance, hands hovering near concealed weapons beneath heavy wool coats.

Mother started up the narrow trail without waiting, not even looking back. For a woman of seventy—though her biological age was a carefully guarded secret—she moved with unnatural vigor, a mountain goat in a parka. Caterina scrambled to keep up, her thin soles slipping on icy rocks hidden beneath the snow. She nearly fell twice, cursing under her breath, her anger burning hot enough in her chest to keep her core warm even as her extremities went numb.

They climbed in silence for ten minutes, the only sounds their labored breathing and the crunch of shoes on snow. They reached a high ridge line that overlooked the Shenandoah Valley, a vast expanse of white and gray under a leaden sky. The wind up here was ferocious, whipping through the bare branches of the oak trees, howling like a dying animal.

Caterina stopped, leaning against a rock face, gasping for air that felt too thin. Her throat was raw. "Mother, enough. I'm freezing. What are we doing here? This is madness."

Mother stopped near the edge of the precipice, where a single misstep would mean a thousand-foot fall. She turned slowly, her face impassive, snowflakes catching in her dark hair.

"Livia is alive," she said, the words snatched by the wind but landing with the weight of a bomb.

Caterina froze, forgetting the cold. "Alive? But the feed cut... the damage..."

"Our intel from Sentry Blade confirms it. Likely at Mia's lab in a containment cell." Mother brushed a snowflake from the lapel of her expensive coat. "Which means we have an opportunity."

"Another assault?" Caterina stepped forward from the rock face, her fatigue forgotten in a rush of disbelief. "Are you insane? We lost Sophia. Livia failed and got captured. And now you want to send more family into the meat grinder against a hardened target? We are bleeding assets, Mother!"

"We need the cure, Caterina. We need Mia's brain. And we need Livia back before she breaks."

"We need to survive!" Caterina shouted, her voice echoing strangely off the snow-covered rocks. "We have time. The stasis machines work. We can retreat to the compound in Rome, regroup, let the heat die down. Why are you risking everything on this war right now? What is the rush?"

Mother watched her, unblinking, her dark eyes reflecting

the gray sky. "Because I am the Queen. And you... you are disappointing me."

"I am the future!" Caterina snapped, stepping closer to the edge, invigorated by her own rage. "I am the one who will have to clean up this mess when you're finally gone. I deserve to be heard. I deserve a say in my own inheritance!"

"You deserve nothing you have not earned."

In a blur of motion that defied her age, Mother lunged.

It happened too fast for Caterina to react. Mother's hand clamped around her throat, squeezing with a shocking, hydraulic strength that shouldn't have been possible for an old woman. Caterina stumbled backward, choking, her heels scraping on the frozen rock. She slammed hard into the rough bark of a massive tree growing near the edge.

Before she could raise her hands to fight back, the cold bite of steel pressed against her jugular. Mother held a switchblade, the four-inch knife gleaming dully in the winter light, the tip pricking the tender skin under Caterina's chin just enough to draw a single bead of warm blood.

"You are weak," Mother hissed, her face inches from Caterina's, her breath smelling of mint and old rage. "You hesitate. You question orders. You think small, like a frightened mouse."

Caterina clawed uselessly at Mother's iron grip, gasping for air, her vision spotting. The guards watched from ten yards away, statues in the snow. Antonio, the head of security, a man Caterina had known her whole life, had his hand on his pistol—but he wasn't aiming at Mother. He was just watching.

"I... I am loyal," Caterina choked out, the words strangling in her throat.

"Loyalty is easy. Any dog can be loyal," Mother sneered. "Vision is hard. At the restaurant last night... did you see it? Really see it? Did you see Jon fall?"

Caterina's vision blurred, tears of pain and cold freezing on her lashes. "He... he tripped. On the tablecloth."

"No," Mother spat, tightening her grip. "He was pushed. By Unity. Without touching him. She threw a grown man ten feet with her mind."

Caterina stopped struggling, her brain trying to process this new impossibility. *Telekinesis?*

"You missed it because you were too busy preening in that dress, too busy playing the role instead of observing the board," Mother said with utter contempt. "Unity is evolving. She is becoming a weapon right under our noses. And you want to retreat to Italy and hide in a hole while our enemies gain superpowers?"

Mother released her abruptly. Caterina slumped to the snowy ground at the base of the tree, coughing violently, massaging her bruised throat, gulping down the freezing air.

"You are no longer Daughter-in-Waiting," Mother said coldly, wiping the single drop of Caterina's blood from the blade onto her white coat. "I have replaced you."

Caterina glanced up from the snow, ice forming in her veins that had nothing to do with the weather. "What?"

"Chiara wears the title now. The family has already pledged allegiance to her as my successor."

"Chiara?" Caterina scrambled to her feet, slipping on the ice, her voice rising to a screech. "She's a child! She's vain, she's stupid, she knows nothing of strategy!"

"She knows how to obey without question. And she doesn't keep secrets from her Mother."

Mother signaled to Antonio with a sharp nod. He stepped forward instantly, grabbing Caterina's arms and pinning them behind her back in a painful professional hold.

"Check her pockets," Mother commanded.

"No!" Caterina screamed, struggling wildly. She twisted, trying to kick, but another guard grabbed her legs, immobilizing her. "Get off me! Antonio, don't!"

Antonio ignored her, reaching roughly into the front pocket of her tight jeans. He pulled out the small, protected glass vial. The white liquid inside glinted—the serum. Her insurance policy.

He tossed it to Mother. She caught it out of the air with ease.

"I suspected," Mother said, holding the vial up to the winter light, examining it like a jewel. "Sophia and Livia were fools to take it, but they were loyal fools. They shared everything with me. I knew one dose was missing. I knew you had it."

"I didn't use it!" Caterina sobbed, the fight draining out of her, replaced by a sickening dread. "I was saving it! For the family! In case we needed it!"

"You were saving it for yourself," Mother corrected, her voice dripping with disdain. She pocketed the vial. "Because you are afraid to die. You are afraid of the Syndrome. And a leader cannot fear death. A leader must be willing to burn to ash if it means the legacy survives."

"Mother, please," Caterina begged, reduced to a terrified child, tears freezing on her cheeks. "I'll serve. I'll do whatever you want. I'll go into stasis right now. Just don't kill me. Please."

Mother smiled, a cold, terrible expression that held no maternal warmth.

"I'm not going to kill you, Cat. Not yet. You still have uses as a soldier." She turned her back on her weeping daughter and began walking back down the snowy trail. "Bring her. We have a war to plan, and we are down a commander."

Antonio shoved Caterina forward roughly. She stumbled, nearly falling again, looking at the receding back of the woman who had created her in a petri dish, the woman who had just stripped her of her title, her future, and her only hope for survival.

Caterina didn't scream again. She wiped her wet, frozen face with the sleeve of her thin sweater. The tears stopped. Her eyes dried, hardening into something brittle and sharp.

Mother was right about one thing. Caterina had been afraid. Afraid of dying, afraid of failing, afraid of her.

But the fear was gone now, left behind on the frozen ridge.

All that was left in its place was a pure, crystalline hate.

Pool

Mia

The lab below was a fortress of glass and steel, a hardened bunker built for biological warfare. But four hundred feet in the air, the penthouse suite was meant to be a sanctuary. Today, however, the silence up here felt less like peace and more like the pressurized hush before a hull breach.

Mia stood in the shadows by the polished rosewood minibar, watching her husband pace the sprawling living room. The floor-to-ceiling windows framed a panoramic view of nature at its best, untouched by human hands.

Chris was on the phone, tethered to the ground by bureaucratic red tape. His silk tie was loosened, hanging askew, and his dress shirt sleeves were rolled up, revealing forearms tense with frustration. He ran a hand through his hair, leaving it standing up in chaotic tufts. He looked exhausted, a good man drowning in a sea of bad options. The FDA was stonewalling the approval for Neuro-Regen, kicking the can down the road with endless requests for addenda while real people suffered.

"Yes, Fred, I understand the regulatory timeline," Chris said, his voice tight, fighting to remain civil. He pinched the bridge of his nose, squeezing his eyes shut. "But we're not talking about a new allergy medication here. We're talking about lives actively ending. Okay. Fine. I'll get Brian to send the data packet. Again."

He hung up with force and tossed his phone onto the plush charcoal sofa. It bounced once and landed face down. He stood there, shoulders slumped, staring at the Persian rug without seeing it. He didn't notice Mia standing in the periphery, wrapped in a thick white terrycloth robe that felt too heavy against her sensitive skin.

She watched him for a moment longer. He was human. Fragile. He didn't have titanium-laced bones or hyper-dense muscle fibers. He just had a massive heart and a stubborn streak a mile wide. He was fighting her battles with paper and phone calls because it was the only way he knew how to help.

Mia flexed her right hand beneath the long sleeve of the robe. The tremor was there—a low-frequency buzz inside her radius bone. The Syndrome. Tick tock.

"Ahem."

Chris jumped, spinning around. His brow furrowed in confusion as his eyes adjusted to the shadows, then softened instantly into a tired, relieved smile when he saw her.

"Hey," he said, exhaling a long breath. "Sorry. I didn't hear you come up. It's been a day."

"It's always a day now, Chris," Mia said, walking slowly out of the shadows toward him. The carpet was soft beneath her bare feet. "Ginger has a theory. She says we're letting the end of the world ruin our Friday nights."

Chris chuckled, a dry sound that didn't reach his eyes. "Ginger says a lot of things. Usually involving tequila."

"She's not wrong this time," Mia murmured, stopping inches from him. She could feel the heat radiating off him. "She says we need to live. Not just survive. She says if we're going down, we should go down fighting. Or... something else."

Chris peered down at her, his eyes searching hers. "Something else?"

She reached out and touched his chin. His skin was warm,

rough with a day's growth of five o'clock shadow. He smelled of coffee and the faint, comforting scent of his deodorant. It was the smell of normal life, a scent she was terrified of losing.

"I'm going for a swim," Mia whispered, her voice dropping an octave. "Join me?"

Chris blinked, momentarily thrown by the shift in gears. He glanced toward the panoramic window; the sun was still high. "Now? Mia, it's 2:00 PM on a workday. I have three briefs to review and the journalists are—"

"I'm the boss. I own the building. I make the schedule." Mia leaned in closer, letting her breath ghost across his neck. "And my schedule says I need my husband."

Mia reached for the sash of her robe. She untied it slowly, deliberately holding his gaze. She shrugged her shoulders, and the heavy terrycloth slid down her arms, pooling on the hardwood floor around her ankles.

Underneath, she wore a sapphire blue string bikini that felt impossibly light against her skin. It was a relic from a honeymoon they never really got to finish.

Chris's breath hitched audibly. His eyes traveled over her, not with the clinical detachment of the scientists downstairs, but with raw hunger. He stared at the strong slope of her shoulders and the definition of her flat stomach.

Mia turned, feeling his eyes on her back, and sauntered toward the glass doors leading to the enclosed pool deck. She swayed her hips slightly, a conscious effort to override the tension held in her spine, knowing exactly what she was doing. At the glass door, she paused, her hand on the latch, and glanced back over her shoulder.

With a subtle twitch of her fingers, she unhooked the clasp of her bikini top. She let the blue fabric drop to the floor.

"I'll be right there," Chris choked out, already stumbling toward their bedroom, loosening his belt as he went.

"Where are you going?" she asked, arching an eyebrow.

"To... get my trunks?"

Mia laughed—a genuine, throaty sound that surprised even her. She hadn't heard that laugh in weeks. It felt good in her chest, loosening the knot of anxiety that lived there permanently. "Not needed, counselor. Come on."

She slid the glass door open and stepped out into the humid warmth of the enclosed pool deck. The air instantly felt thicker, smelling of chlorine and damp tile. The water in the long lap pool was heated to a tropical eighty-five degrees, steam rising faintly from the surface.

Mia didn't wait. She dove in, in a shallow arc, breaking the glassy surface with barely a splash. The silence of the underwater world wrapped around her instantly, cutting off the hum of the facility, the worries about the FDA, the terrifying secret of Livia hanging in the sub-basement. Here, she was weightless. The tremor in her arm vanished in the buoyancy.

She surfaced at the deep end, shaking the water from her hair, resting her arms on the cool coping stones.

Chris appeared in the doorway. He had stripped down to his boxer briefs. Before stepping out, he paused, looking around nervously at the high corners of the atrium, checking for reflections on the glass, for the red blink of security cameras, for anything that might intrude on their bubble. He was living in a thriller movie too, she realized sadly.

"Chris," Mia said softly, her voice echoing slightly over the water. "Eyes on me. It's just us. I disabled the feeds."

He sighed, the tension finally draining out of his shoulders. He pushed his underwear down and kicked it aside. He walked to the edge, his body pale and lean. He wasn't enhanced. He couldn't heal instantly or hear a whisper through a steel door. He was perfect in his fragility.

He slipped into the water, the surface rippling toward her. He swam with smooth, powerful strokes, closing the distance.

When he reached her, Mia didn't hesitate. She wrapped her

legs around his waist, pulling him against the wall. The water buoyed them up, making them both weightless.

"So," he said, his voice husky, reaching up to brush wet strands of hair from her face. His thumbs traced her cheekbones.

"So," Mia replied, leaning into his touch.

"That journalist from the Post, he said—"

"Shh." Mia pressed a wet finger to his lips, silencing the world outside this pool. "No work. No FDA. No dying. Just us. Right here, right now."

She kissed him. It started slow, a tender testing of waters, an apology for the weeks of emotional distance. But it quickly deepened, fueled by the adrenaline coursing through both of them. It became desperate. She tasted the chlorine of the pool water on his skin, the lingering coffee on his breath. She pulled him closer, her nails digging into his shoulders, needing to feel the solidity of him, the undeniable proof that she was still here, still a woman, still human enough to want this.

Chris groaned low in his throat, his hands gripping her hips, pulling her firmly against him. His hands fumbled underwater, untying the side strings of her bikini bottom. The blue fabric floated away like debris.

He entered her, and the sensation was electric, grounding. The water sloshed rhythmically against the tiled sides of the pool, a tide of their own making. Mia closed her eyes tight, losing herself in the friction, the heat, the breath.

For a few glorious minutes, the countdown clock ticking away in her cells stopped. The Romanos didn't exist. Livia wasn't waiting in the dark downstairs.

There was only this. Connection. Defiance against the void.

The pleasure built, a tightening coil in her abdomen. As the waves crested, snapping her head back against the coping, Mia's mind drifted. The ironclad barrier she kept around her thoughts—the mental firewall she used to block out the trauma and focus on the mission—slipped.

She opened herself up completely to the moment.

And in that fraction of a second of raw, unfiltered openness, she felt it.

It wasn't a sound. It wasn't a physical touch. It was an intrusion.

A phantom echo resonated in her own nervous system. A sudden, sharp intake of breath that wasn't hers. A shiver of cold that had nothing to do with the heated pool. A profound, terrifying sense of *awareness* blooming in the back of her skull.

Somewhere, miles away, a ghost had just walked over her grave.

Mia gasped violently, her eyes snapping open, wide and terrified, staring at the ceiling girders.

Chris, mistaking her reaction for the peak of her climax, pulled her tighter, burying his face in her wet neck. "I've got you," he whispered fiercely. "I've got you, Mia."

Mia clung to him, her body trembling, but the pleasure had instantly transmuted into ice. Her heart was hammering a frantic, terrified rhythm against his chest.

It hadn't been a ghost. It had been Unity.

Her twin was connected. And her twin had just felt everything Mia had just felt.

Mia squeezed her eyes shut again, a wave of profound, sickening guilt washing over her, colder than any water. The connection went both ways. She wasn't just sharing a soul with her sister; she was sharing a life. And Chris was Unity's former boyfriend. Every sensation, every intimacy, every private moment was being broadcast.

And Mia had absolutely no idea how to turn the transmitter off.

An Ally

Unity

The new safehouse was practically a carbon copy of the last three, a testament to the Romanos' efficient, soulless logistics. Another anonymous white room, smelling faintly of fresh paint and bleach. Another high-definition camera mounted in the corner, its red recording light an unblinking eye. Another grueling day of physical therapy exercises that left Unity's long-atrophied muscles screaming in protest, her limbs feeling like lead weights draped over bone.

But the rules of her captivity were subtly changing.

Unity sat in a high-end titanium wheelchair, not a hospital loaner. She was wearing designer jeans that fit perfectly and a soft cashmere blouse that felt impossibly luxurious against her skin, a stark contrast to the scratchy hospital gowns that had been her uniform for months on end since waking. The food Jon brought her was no longer the flavorless protein muck designed for patients; it was real roasted chicken, steamed asparagus with lemon, and garlic mashed potatoes.

The Romanos were treating her like a guest, or perhaps a prized pet they were fattening up for slaughter.

She watched Jon move around the sterile room, tidying up physical therapy bands and wiping down equipment. He seemed tenser than usual today, his movements jerky and hurried, lacking his usual calm efficiency. Since the incident at the restaurant—since Unity had accidentally blasted him ten feet across the room with a burst of telekinetic energy—he looked at her differently. The paternal affection was gone, replaced by a complex mix of wariness, fear, and a grudging respect. He didn't turn his back on her anymore.

Unity closed her eyes, ignoring the ache in her shoulders. She tried to summon her power again, to locate the wellspring within her. She remembered the flash of the paintbar, the sensation of her consciousness sliding into Mia's arm like a hand into a perfectly fitted glove. She remembered the feeling of the brush in her hand, the smell of acrylics, the act of painting the tree over the mudslide, signing the pact. *Love, Unity.*

Did you see it, Mia? she thought, projecting the words outward into the void. *Did you know it was me? Are you there?*

She pushed her mind outward, searching for the familiar resonance of her sister, the psychic thread that connected them.

It hit her instantly, not as a whisper, but like a physical blow to the chest, knocking the breath from her lungs.

The overwhelming smell of chlorine. Humid, tropical heat that instantly beaded sweat on her skin. The profound, blissful weightlessness of being submerged in warm water.

Unity gasped, her hands gripping the armrests of her wheelchair. The safehouse room spun and dissolved. Suddenly, she wasn't in a house. She was in a pool.

She saw a man's face, close to hers, filling her vision. Chris. Her boyfriend. Mia's husband.

He was kissing her. No—he was kissing *Mia.*

Unity felt the scratch of stubble on his chin against her cheek, the desperate heat of his skin against hers in the water. She felt his hands, strong and urgent, on her hips, sliding the wet fabric of a bikini bottom away.

Oh God.

The sensation was overwhelming—intimacy, intense physical pleasure, and a raw, frantic emotional need that wasn't hers. It flooded Unity's senses, a sensory overload that left her gasping, drowning in someone else's experience. She was a voyeur trapped in her sister's body, feeling every touch, every breath, every heartbeat as if it were her own. The barrier between them had dissolved completely.

"Mia!" Unity blurted out, the name tearing from her throat in a strangled cry.

She slammed her eyes open, breaking the connection with a violent psychic snap. The room rushed back into focus—the blinding white walls, the blinking camera, Jon staring at her from across the room, a roll of athletic tape in his hand.

Unity squeezed her eyes shut again, fighting the residual waves of pleasure and adrenaline that washed over her own body. Her face burned with humiliation. It was violating. It was impossible. She was a virgin, trapped in a broken body, yet her physical self was reacting as if she were the one in that pool, in the arms of a man she barely knew.

Jon rushed to her side, dropping to one knee, positioning his body between her and the camera in the corner.

"What's wrong?" he whispered urgently, his hand hovering over her shoulder. "Are you hurt? Is it a seizure?"

Unity let out a strangled, hysterical laugh that sounded more like a sob. How could she possibly explain that she had just telepathically crashed her twin sister's afternoon delight?

"I'm fine," she choked out, her face still burning hot. "Just... a dizzy spell. Standing up too fast earlier."

Jon studied her face, his eyes searching hers. He didn't buy it for a second. He reached for her wrist, his fingers cool and professional as he checked her pulse.

"Your heart rate is spiking," he murmured, loud enough for the microphones to pick up. He leaned in closer, pretending to check her pupils with a penlight, blocking the camera's view of her lap. "Listen to me. Don't react. Don't look at the camera."

Unity stiffened, sensing the shift in his demeanor. This wasn't medical.

Jon pulled a small digital tablet from the large cargo pocket of his scrubs. He angled the screen toward her, keeping it shielded from the lens in the corner with his body.

He typed quickly, his thumb flying across the glass.

Overheard Mother and Chiara discussing archives. Your crash at sixteen. The truck. It wasn't an accident.

Unity stared at the words, the blood draining from her face. The truck. The massive semi that had t-boned their Hummer. The crash that had forever changed her parents' careers, left her father with a limp, and put her in a coma for twenty years, stealing her life.

She looked up at Jon, her eyes wide. He nodded once, slowly, grimly.

He typed again.

They cut the brakes. Paid the driver. They tried to kill the whole family in one shot. They found out about your parents' unsanctioned cloning project.

The breath left Unity's lungs in a whoosh. It wasn't just a tragedy. It wasn't bad luck or wet roads. It was a hit. A professional assassination attempt. The Romanos hadn't just capitalized on her coma for leverage; they had caused it. They had tried to wipe the entire Peers family off the map to bury the secret of Mia's creation.

And they had failed. They had all survived, broken but alive.

Unless the crash had just been a message.

Rage, cold and sharp as a scalpel, replaced the embarrassment of the psychic connection. The heat in her face turned to ice. Unity stared up at the camera in the corner. She imagined Mother Sophia watching her right now on a monitor somewhere, calculating, plotting, sipping tea in her expensive clothes.

She glanced back down at Jon. He deleted the text with a swipe and slipped the tablet back into his pocket.

"We need to get your blood pressure down," he said loudly, standing up and moving behind her wheelchair to unlock the brakes. "I'm taking you to the medical room for monitoring."

As he gripped the handles, he leaned down, his lips brushing her ear so lightly it felt like a breeze.

"Be ready," he whispered, the words barely a breath. "We're getting out of here soon."

Five Percent

Brian

B rian Carter sat cross-legged on the freezing concrete floor. He was still surrounded by the disemboweled guts of the Romano technology. He was trying to resurrect the former technological graveyard. He wore his signature Crocs, now scuffed and faded, paired with thick gray wool socks—a fashion choice that made Roger the hacker wince visibly every time he looked down from his workstation.

"You know, for a certified genius, you dress like a toddler who put his clothes on in the dark," Roger commented, his voice dry. He was perched precariously on a rolling stool, typing furiously on a laptop that was hardwired directly into the second blackened brain implant they were given, fished from a dead clone.

"Comfort is efficient," Brian muttered, not looking up from the circuit board he was examining under a magnifying lamp. He tightened a microscopic screw on the modified chassis of a stasis pod with a jeweler's screwdriver. "Fashion is a variable I deleted years ago. It consumes processing power for zero functional gain."

He picked up a heavy ceramic capacitor, retesting its load with a multimeter. The readout spiked, numbers dancing in red LED light. This basement had become their bunker, their Alamo. Since bringing the Romano hardware back from the farmhouse raid, Brian, Roger, and Cynthia had been working in punishing shifts, fueled by vending machine coffee and adrenaline, dissecting the tech with the fervor of religious zealots trying to translate a new scripture.

They weren't just studying it. They were building something new from the parts. Something unique that existed in the grayest area of ethics Brian had ever navigated.

"Status on the AI interface?" Brian asked, setting the capacitor aside in a labeled bin. His voice was flat, clipped, betraying none of the anxiety that gnawed at his stomach lining.

Cynthia, also sitting cross-legged on a cushion near the humming server rack, pushed a strand of errant gray hair out of her face with a grease-stained wrist. She looked exhausted, the skin beneath her eyes bruised purple with fatigue.

"The neural mapping is tricky, Brian," she said, sighing. "The Romano code isn't binary. It's... organic. It evolves based on input. It learns. I'm having to build a digital sandbox with triple-redundant firewalls just to keep it from infecting our local network and rewriting our OS."

"Keep it contained," Brian said, his tone hardening. "We need it docile, Cynthia. We need a tool, not a pet. And definitely not a smart one."

He glanced over at the machine he was painstakingly rebuilding in the center of the room. It was no longer a stasis pod intended for long-term sleep. He had stripped away the life-support systems, drained the noxious cryo-fluids, and removed the heavy, insulated bulk of the casing. Now, it was a sleek, terrifying chair made of polished chrome and black composite material, with a dense halo of biometric sensors and neural interface probes clustered at the headrest like a crown of thorns.

It was a consciousness transfer device. Or at least, that's what the schematics Brian was inventing on the fly suggested it could be. A lifeboat for a drowning mind.

"Five percent," he murmured to himself, adjusting the calipers on a delicate fiber optic cable.

"What was that?" Roger asked, pausing his typing.

"The probability of success. Based on current data and simulation models."

Roger stopped completely, swiveling his chair around. "Five percent? Brian, that's not a plan. That's a suicide pact with extra steps."

"It's infinitely better than zero," Brian said, finally looking up, his pale eyes intense behind his smudged glasses. "Mia has eighteen months. Maybe less, given the acceleration of her symptoms. If the Syndrome takes her body, if her cells liquefy like those clones in the video, we need a lifeboat ready for her mind. A place for her consciousness to go."

He glanced involuntarily toward the shadowed corner of the room, where two smaller, coffin-sized "incubator" units sat collecting dust under plastic tarps. They were originally designed to grow clones rapidly, accelerators for biological matter. But Brian wasn't interested in growing empty bodies. He was interested in the theoretical possibility of merging souls, of creating a vessel strong enough to hold two distinct consciousnesses.

It was a radical, terrifying theory he hadn't shared with Mia yet. She wouldn't understand. Not now. She would see it as giving up on saving her physical form, as a betrayal of the fight. But Brian saw it as the ultimate redundancy protocol. In engineering, if the primary hardware failed catastrophically, you needed a backup system to save the critical data. Mia's mind—her brilliance, her memories, her essence—was the data.

"We're completely stalled until we get the blood sample,"

Cynthia said, frustration edging her voice, snapping Brian back to the present. "I can't calibrate the neural interface to her specific biometric signature without a fresh, active sample of the serum in her system. And she's stonewalling us."

"She doesn't trust us," Brian said simply, returning to his work. "She thinks we're going to try to reverse-engineer her serum behind her back, maybe try to cure ourselves or sell it."

"We're trying to save her damn life!" Roger snapped, his patience fraying.

"She's been betrayed by almost everyone she ever trusted," Brian said, his mind flashing briefly to Bianca, the woman he had loved who had turned out to be a Mafia operative. The memory stung, sharp and fresh as a paper cut, but he pushed it down relentlessly. Emotions were inefficient variables. "Give her time. Trust is a slow algorithm."

The heavy security door to the lab slid open with a hydraulic hiss that made them all jump. Mia poked her head in. She looked pale, dark circles shadowed her eyes, and there was a tightness around her jaw, but her expression was resolute.

"You guys got a minute?" she asked, her voice quiet.

"Always for the boss," Roger said quickly, closing his laptop lid.

Mia stepped inside, shivering slightly in the colder air of the basement. She held a small, capped plastic vial in her hand. It was filled with dark crimson fluid that seemed to catch the light.

"I thought about it," she said, walking toward Brian, her voice steady but her hand trembling slightly. "The blood thing. I'm trying to... I need to *trust* people more. If we're going to win this. And by the way, I could hear you once I reached the basement."

She handed the vial to Brian.

"Just promise me it stays in this room," she said, her eyes searching his. "And that you're not trying to... you know. Make more of me in those things." She gestured vaguely to the incubators in the corner.

Brian took the vial. It felt heavy, warm from her body heat. It was the key to unlocking the machine, the missing variable.

"We're not making more of you, Mia," Brian said seriously, meeting her gaze without blinking. "One of you is quite enough trouble for the universe."

Mia cracked a small, genuine smile. "Thanks. I think."

Cynthia scrambled up from her cushion, taking the vial from Brian with something close to reverence. She hurried over to the complex blood analyzer unit. "I'll get the sequencing started immediately. This is... this is huge, Mia. Thank you. Really."

"Don't thank me yet," Mia said, crossing her arms and looking around. "I still don't know what you're actually building down here."

She walked over to the modified chair, running a hand over the cold chrome and the halo of sensors. Her eyes narrowed as she processed the design.

"I hope you're not planning to put me in stasis," she joked weakly, though the tension in her shoulders was palpable. "Although, I could use a nap right about now."

"Actually," Roger quipped, "Brian thought it might be the only way to get you to stop pacing for five minutes."

Mia laughed, but it sounded forced, brittle. She glanced around the room again, her gaze lingering on the tarp-covered incubators in the corner before quickly moving away.

"Lethabo has been asking questions," she said, her voice dropping. "About what we're doing down here. Why the power draw is so high. I told him I didn't know the specifics. He didn't believe me. He thinks we're building a weapon."

"Let him ask," Brian said calmly. "He's security. We're science. Need to know basis, and he doesn't need to know."

"Speaking of science..." Mia hesitated. She turned back

to Brian, her expression shifting from guarded leader to something younger, vulnerable. "There's something else. Something happened... in the pool. Yesterday."

"With the Syndrome?" Brian asked, stepping closer, his analytic mind shifting gears. "A new symptom? Accelerated tremors?"

"No. Not with me. With Unity."

The lab went dead silent. Cynthia looked up sharply from the microscope. Roger stopped spinning in his chair.

"You found her?" Roger asked, his voice hushed.

"Not exactly," Mia said, rubbing her left arm unconsciously, right over the injection site of the third serum dose. "But... I think I talked to her. Or she talked to me. I felt her."

Brian tilted his head, his brain racing to categorize this new data point. "Telepathy? A neural tunnel?"

"Something like that. It was... intense. Real." Mia took a deep breath. "Come with me. Upstairs. I need to show you something."

She turned and walked out of the lab without waiting for an answer.

Brian looked at Roger, who shrugged, bewildered. Then he looked at the blood sample beginning to spin in the centrifuge, a crimson blur. The probability of success just jumped from five percent to eight.

He adjusted his wool socks in his Crocs and followed her out into the corridor.

Contact

Mia

The painting from Muse Paintbar sat on Mia's polished rosewood desk in the penthouse, an ugly, undeniable window into a world science said shouldn't exist. Except for Unity's additions, it was a mess of aggressive green brushstrokes covering a brown smudge. And the words in the corner were clear, written in a looping script that wasn't Mia's: *Pact. Love, Unity.*

Mia stared at it, the late afternoon sun cutting across the brown grass four hundred feet below. The air up here usually felt rarified, removed from the grime of humanity, but today it felt thin, insufficient to fill her lungs.

She rubbed her temples, feeling the familiar, low-grade thrum of the Syndrome growing louder in the bones of her skull. The incidents at the paintbar and in the pool, and that moving chair, hadn't just shaken her foundation; they had jackhammered through the concrete. She was a geneticist. Her church was the laboratory, her scripture written in adenine, guanine, cytosine, and thymine. She believed in electrical impulses firing across synapses, chemical cocktails dictating emotion. She didn't believe in ghosts taking the wheel of her Porsche.

Yet, the signature was there, dried in black acrylic. It was real matter, created by an impossible connection.

Brian stood by the floor-to-ceiling window, obsessively adjusting the angle of the aluminum blinds, slicing the sunlight into thin ribbons on the carpet. He had a goofy, manic grin plastered on his face that looked entirely unnatural on him. It was the look of a man who hadn't slept in forty-eight hours and was surviving on caffeine and a dangerous idea.

"Why are you smiling like that?" Mia asked, her voice rough. She sank deeper into the French leather couch, pulling a cashmere throw over her legs despite the warmth of the room. "You wanted my blood. You got it. Now you're giddy about what was essentially several demonic possession events. What are you building in the basement, Brian? The power draw is flickering the lights up here."

Brian shrugged, finally turning away from the window. His grin faltered, replaced by a terrifying intensity in his pale eyes. "It sounds crazy, Mia. Even to me. But the simulations... we have an eighteen percent chance of success."

"Eighteen percent chance of *what?*" Mia demanded, sitting up straighter. "And since when is eighteen percent something to smile about?"

Before he could answer, the heavy oak bedroom door opened. Chris walked in, holding a thick sheaf of legal papers that smelled of toner and billable hours. He looked exhausted, his tie loosened to the second button.

He crossed the room and sat on the edge of the couch beside Mia, dropping the papers on the coffee table. He kissed her cheek, his lips warm, smelling faintly of a breath mint.

"Hey," he murmured, his hand lingering on her neck, his thumb stroking the pulse point. "How's the headache today? Any better?"

"Better," Mia lied automatically. The lie tasted like shit. She nodded toward Brian, who was fidgeting with suppressed energy. "We were just discussing the basement project. Brian was being characteristically evasive."

Chris raised a skeptical eyebrow at Brian. "Oh? Is it something that won't invite a Homeland Security raid?"

"We're improving the neural interface," Brian said, waving a hand vaguely. "Optimizing the hardware for... compatibility issues."

Mia opened her mouth to demand a real answer, to cut through the obfuscation, but a sharp, authoritative knock at the front door cut her off.

"It's me," Major Washington's voice called out, muffled by the heavy wood. "Urgent update, ma'am."

"Come in," Mia called, her stomach tightening.

Lethabo entered, closing the door swiftly behind him and locking it—a habit of his now. He looked grim, his usual professional mask showing cracks of genuine worry.

"We have chatter from Intel," he said without preamble. "NSA pick-ups. There's significant movement on the dark web encrypted channels the Romanos use. They're mobilizing assets."

Mia sighed, rubbing her face. Of course they were. The timeline was accelerating.

And then, the room tilted.

It wasn't the physical dizziness of the serum or the tremor of the Syndrome. It was profound and instantaneous, a sudden, sharp clarity cutting through the noise of the world, like a high-powered radio suddenly tuning into a frequency she hadn't known existed. The air pressure in the room seemed to drop, popping her ears.

Mia.

The voice wasn't in her ears. It didn't travel on sound waves. It bloomed in the dead center of her skull, resonating in her teeth, warmer and clearer than any memory.

Mia bolted upright from the couch, knocking the cashmere

throw to the floor. Her eyes darted around the luxurious room—the marble fireplace, the abstract art, the tense faces of the three men.

"Unity?" she whispered, the name tearing from her throat.

Chris grabbed her hand, his grip painfully tight. "Mia? Honey, what's wrong? You look like you've seen a ghost."

Mia. Can you hear me? I'm pushing hard.

The sensation was physical—a pressure behind her eyes, a scent of something floral and antiseptic that didn't belong in the penthouse.

"Yes," Mia said aloud, her voice trembling, her heart hammering against her ribs like a trapped bird. "Yes, I can hear you. Oh my God."

Lethabo took a sharp step back, his hand hovering instinctively near his sidearm, scanning the room for a threat he couldn't see. Brian stopped breathing, his eyes wide, staring at Mia as if she were a new scientific phenomenon. Chris looked terrified, watching his wife talk to thin air.

"Who are you talking to?" Chris asked gently, terrified of the answer.

"Unity," Mia whispered, tears pooling in her eyes, blurring the room. "She's here. She's in my head."

"Is now a bad time for an intel briefing?" Lethabo asked awkwardly, glancing at the door as if expecting a SWAT team of psychics.

"Be quiet. Please," Mia snapped, closing her eyes to shut out the distractions of the physical world. She focused inward, chasing the warmth of that voice. *Unity? Is it really you? How is this possible?*

A giggle echoed in her mind—a sound from their fragmented childhood, bright and mischievous, something she hadn't heard in twenty years.

Yes, it's me, silly. You're the genius scientist, Mia. You figure out the how. I'm just working the pedals.

Mia felt the hot tears spill over onto her cheeks. The emotional weight of two decades crashed down on her. *I love you. I missed you so much. I'm so sorry. I'm so, so sorry.*

Sorry for what? The thought was crisp, curious.

I had the drug for ten years, Unity. It was sitting in a fridge. I could have woken you up sooner. But I was afraid. I was afraid if I woke you up—I left you in the dark because I was a coward.

There was a pause. A silence in her head that felt heavy and old. Mia held her breath, waiting for the judgment, the anger that she deserved.

Water under the bridge, Unity's thought came back, splashing into Mia's mind, warm and infinitely forgiving. *I love you too. Now stop apologizing. We don't have time for guilt.*

Mia let out a shuddering breath she felt like she'd been holding since she was twenty-six years old. The absolution was physically weakening. *Where are you? Can we come get you?*

I don't know exactly. Virginia, somewhere rural. We move every week, sometimes twice. It's always white rooms and pine trees. But I'm okay. Better than okay. Jon is helping me. He's... complicated. Broken. But he's getting me out.

Jon? Mia frowned, the image of the caretaker flashing in her mind. *Jon Turner? The man who read you Dickens? Unity, he's a fake.*

He's their mole, Unity confirmed, the mental voice hardening slightly. *But he hates them now. He's trapped too. We're planning a breakout. Soon. Tonight, maybe.*

Mia opened her eyes, the room rushing back in—Lethabo's impatience, Chris's fear. She relayed the information quickly. "She's with Jon Turner. He *is* the mole, just like we thought, but she says he's flipping. They're planning an imminent escape."

Chris stared at her, trying to process the impossible. "You're... you're having a real-time conversation right now? Like a phone call in your brain?"

"Yes. It's... it's real, Chris. She says the Romanos have

hundreds of clones out of stasis. They're ramping up for something big."

Mia, Unity's voice sharpened, cutting through the noise. The warmth vanished, replaced by a cold, hard edge. *There's something else. You need to know. The accident. Twenty years ago. The semi-truck on I-95.*

Mia stiffened, her blood running cold. The worst night of their lives. *The truck? What about it?*

It wasn't an accident. Jon showed me the files. They cut the brakes. They paid the truck driver. They tried to kill the whole family in one shot because Dad cloned me without permission. They tried to wipe us off the map.

Mia felt the blood drain completely from her face. The room seemed to fade at the edges. Her parents hadn't just been negligent victims of bad weather and worse luck; they had been targets. And she—her existence—was the reason.

I'm sorry, Unity thought, the connection wavering slightly under the emotional strain. *I can feel you putting up walls. Don't shut down on me, Mia. We need to be clear-headed.*

I'm okay, Mia lied mentally, though her hands were shaking violently in her lap. *Focus. Can you tell me anything else about the location? Sounds? Smells? Landmarks?*

Nothing. Just nature and rental homes. But Mia... be careful. Mother Sophia is obsessed. They want you alive. They want you to cure the Syndrome before the new batch melts. And they don't think you'll give it willingly. You know about the Syndrome, right?

Yes, I know. I've seen videos.

Good. Then you know the stakes. Don't let them take you.

Lethabo cleared his throat loudly, stepping forward, breaking the spell. Mia opened her eyes again. The three men were staring at her like she was a ticking bomb that had just started counting down.

"Ma'am," Lethabo said, his voice urgent. "I hate to interrupt, but we need to move. Now. The chatter isn't just mobilization.

It's an imminent attack protocol. They've identified a primary target."

"Where?" Mia asked, her voice hollow.

"The Pentagon. SecDef is calling an emergency briefing in the tank. They requested you specifically. The chopper is spinning up on the roof."

Mia nodded numbly. "Okay. We go."

She felt Unity's presence waver in her mind, fading like a radio signal driving into a tunnel, losing strength against the encroaching reality of the physical world.

Mia, Unity's voice came back, sudden, sharp, and incredibly urgent. *Wait. Don't go yet.*

Mia paused, one hand on the couch cushion. *What is it? Are they moving you?*

No. It's not me. It's you. I feel something.

What?

A pulse. A secondary rhythm. A... doubling. Unity's mental tone shifted instantly from tactical urgency to profound, earth-shattering shock. *Mia... please tell me you aren't cloning yourself in that lab.*

What? No! Of course not!

Then why do I feel multiple heartbeats inside you? The sense is faint... but it's there.

Mia froze. The penthouse went dead silent. The hum of the air conditioner, the breathing of the men around her—it all ceased.

The pool, Unity thought, the realization flooding across the connection, bringing with it a flash of the sensory memory—warm water, Chris's hands, the raw intimacy Mia had shared. *I was there. I felt it happen. I felt the spark.*

Mia's hand went slowly, instinctively to her flat stomach. The pieces slammed together in her mind. The low-grade nausea yesterday she had blamed on nerves. The profound, bone-deep fatigue she attributed to the Syndrome. The cycle she should have had already but blamed stress for its absence.

Oh my God, Unity whispered in her mind, her voice filled with awe and terror. *Mia, you fool. You wonderful fool.*

Mia glanced up at Chris. He was watching her with deep concern, completely oblivious to the thermonuclear bomb that had just detonated in her mind. He was worried about the FDA. He was worried about the Romanos.

I'm pregnant, Mia thought, the realization hitting her with the force of a physical blow, knocking the wind out of her. *I'm dying of a genetic disease, being hunted by super-soldiers, and I'm pregnant.*

Yes, Unity replied, her voice fading out rapidly now, distant but undeniable. *You are, sister.*

The connection broke with a finality that left a ringing silence in Mia's skull.

She sat on the couch, staring at her husband, the secret expanding between them like a sudden, new universe.

"Mia?" Chris asked, stepping closer, reaching for her hand. "Are you okay? Did she go? What did she say?"

"She's gone," Mia whispered, her voice unrecognizable to herself. She stood up, her legs feeling unsteady, like she was walking on the deck of a ship in rough seas. "We have to go. The Pentagon is waiting."

She walked toward the door, her left hand hovering protectively over her belly, the tremor in her fingers stilled by a terrifying new purpose. She was dying. She was hunting. And now... she was creating.

The stakes hadn't just raised. They had shattered the ceiling and reached for the stars.

Implant

Caterina

The holding cell didn't just smell; it had a physical atmosphere, thick and heavy. It was a miasma of stale, sour sweat—the kind generated by terror, not exertion.

Caterina, formerly the pristine Daughter-in-Waiting, sat curled in the farthest corner of the empty room. Her designer jeans were stiff with filth, and her soft blouse was torn at the shoulder, stained dark with crusted blood. She pulled her knees tightly to her chest, trying to conserve body heat in the drafty space.

She had been here for forty-eight hours. Time had become a blurry loop of darkness and gray light filtering under the door. No bed. No blanket. Just four walls, two of which bore the crescent-moon indentations of her own fists, and a beige carpet that was abrasive against her skin, mapped with the rust-colored continents of her own bleeding.

Her body was a landscape of aches. Her throat felt like it was filled with broken glass from dehydration. Her stomach gnawed at itself, a hollow, cramping pit. But the worst pain was centered behind her right ear, a throbbing, hot locus that pulsed in time with her racing heart.

Outside the door, the muffled sound of a phone notification

pinged, followed by a coarse laugh. Antonio. The head of security. The man who had taught her how to shoot a Sig Sauer when she was twelve, now guarding her like a rabid dog.

"Shut up!" Caterina screamed. The sound tore at her raw vocal cords, emerging as a ragged screech that surprised even her.

"Shut the hell up yourself, princess," Antonio yelled back, his voice muffled but dripping with amused contempt. He thumped the door with the heel of his hand, a dull boom in the small space. "Or I'll come in there and sedate you like the cripple next door. You want the needle, Cat? Keep screaming."

Caterina let out a guttural sob, rocking back and forth violently, letting her shoulders bang against the drywall. To Antonio, listening on the other side, it must have sounded like the final surrender of a broken woman, someone whose pampered reality had finally shattered against the hard concrete of her situation.

Good, she thought, the sob cutting off instantly in her throat, replaced by cold calculation. *Let him think I'm broken. Let him think I'm just a scared little girl throwing a tantrum.*

Because under the curtain of her matted, greasy black hair, shielded from the peephole in the door, Caterina was performing surgery.

She uncurled her right hand. Nestled in her sweaty palm, slick with blood, was a triangular shard of glass. It was perhaps two inches long, wicked and sharp. She'd palmed it hours ago when she'd smashed her head against the window casing in a performative fit of despair. Antonio had bought the suicide attempt act. He'd come in, cursed at her, slapped a gauze bandage loosely over the bleeding gash, and left her to rot. He hadn't bothered to sweep the floor. He was sloppy.

They were all sloppy. They underestimated her because Mother had discarded her.

Caterina took a shallow, shuddering breath. She reached up

behind her ear, her fingers trembling not from fear, but from exhaustion and the anticipation of agony. The skin was angry, swollen and hot to the touch.

She grit her teeth so hard her jaw ached, stifling a moan as she pressed the sharp point of the glass into the existing wound.

It wasn't a clean cut. The glass snagged and tore. Warm blood immediately welled up, thick and fast, trickling down the sensitive skin of her neck, soaking into the already stiff collar of her blouse. The pain was blinding—a white-hot spike driving itself into her skull, radiating down into her jaw and up behind her eye. It was nauseating in its intensity. Black spots danced at the edges of her vision, threatening to pull her under into unconsciousness.

Focus, Caterina. You are a Romano. You do not break. You break others.

She forced her hand to be steady, probing deeper into the bloody meat behind her ear. The tip of the glass scraped against something that wasn't bone. It was hard, unnatural, with a slight give.

The implant.

The tracking device. The audio recorder. The high-tech leash that Mother Sophia had embedded in all her "daughters" to keep her bitches in line. It had been humming faintly in her skull for years, a subtle vibration she only noticed when the room was dead silent. Now, it felt massive, an alien parasite fused to her mastoid bone.

Caterina probed the edges of the device with the glass tip, mapping its shape through waves of sickening pain. It was fused deep, woven into the fascia, wired directly into the auditory nerve bundle. Mother's scientists had ensured that removing it without a surgical team and general anesthesia would be torture. Pulling it out raw might leave her deaf in one ear. It might sever a facial nerve and leave her drooling. It might scramble her brain permanently.

But if she didn't get it out, she was dead anyway. As long as it was in, Mother knew where she was. As long as it was in, she was property.

She twisted the glass shard, using it like a crude saw to hack at the tough connective tissue anchoring the device. Her vision blurred into a watery, swirling tunnel. Sweat popped out on her forehead, mixing with the grime on her face.

Just a little more. Sever the anchor points.

A heavy *clack* echoed through the small room. The deadbolt.

Caterina froze, the glass shard buried half an inch deep in her own flesh. Adrenaline surged, icing over the pain. She dropped her hands instantly to her lap, bowing her head low so her hair fell sideways, a curtain hiding the fresh, copious flow of arterial blood. She curled tighter, making herself small, defeated, a lump of misery in the corner.

The door swung open with a groan. Light from the hallway sliced into the dim cell, blinding her momentarily.

Lorenzo stepped in. The family cook. A man who used to sneak her extra biscotti when she was a child. Now, he wrinkled his broad nose in disgust as the smell of the room hit him.

"Jesus, Cat. You smell like a sewer."

He didn't step fully into the room, as if afraid the failure might be contagious. He held a paper plate in one hand and tossed it onto the floor near her feet like he was feeding a stray dog.

The plate hit the carpet and flipped. A scoop of lukewarm mashed potatoes and three chicken tenders splattered onto the filthy fibers. A small paper cup of water followed, landing upright by a miracle, though half of it sloshed over the rim and soaked into the rug.

"Eat," Lorenzo muttered, wiping his hand on his apron. "Mother wants you alive for the flight to Rome. Don't die on my watch."

He backed out without another look. The door slammed shut, plunging her back into gloom. The lock engaged with a final, decisive click.

Caterina waited. She held her breath, listening to the light tread of his footsteps retreating down the hall, followed by Antonio's heavier gait. Only when silence returned did she move.

She scrambled on hands and knees to the food, ignoring the fresh wave of dizziness the movement caused. She was starving. Her body was cannibalizing itself for energy.

She didn't hesitate. She scooped the mashed potatoes off the carpet with her fingers, not caring about the lint, dust, and dried blood that came up with them. The texture was gritty and revolting, but she shoved it into her mouth, swallowing without tasting. She grabbed the chicken tenders, cold and congealed with grease, and chewed frantically, animalistically.

She needed the calories. She needed the salt. She needed the strength for what came next.

She washed the chicken down with the remaining half-cup of water, the cool liquid feeling like salvation on her parched throat. Then, panting, she crawled back to her corner, leaving a snail-trail of blood on the carpet behind her.

She reached up again. Her fingers were slick now with blood and chicken grease, making it hard to get a purchase. She found the wound by the pulse of agony that greeted her touch. The pain wasn't a spike anymore; it was a dull, roaring ocean, a constant companion that threatened to drown her.

She didn't use the glass this time. She jammed her thumb and forefinger into the open gash, digging until she got a tenuous grip on the slippery plastic edge of the implant with her fingernails.

She took a ragged breath, tasting blood in the back of her throat.

This is for Sophia, who died trying to be free. This is for me, who will not die a slave.

She braced herself against the wall. And she pulled.

A wet, tearing sound filled her head, louder than any scream. It sounded like fabric ripping inside her skull. A spike of agony so profound it stopped her heart, shot down her spine, paralyzing her lungs, locking her muscles rigid.

Caterina didn't scream. She couldn't. She bit her lip until it burst, tasting fresh salt, tears streaming silently down her grime-streaked face. She pulled harder, feeling the resistance of wires, the scrape of metal grating against bone. The world dissolved into white noise and red pain.

With a final, sickening, sucking *pop*, the device came free.

Caterina slumped sideways against the wall, gasping for air, her chest heaving. Her right hand was clutched tight to her chest, holding the bloody prize like a diamond.

Silence rushed into her right ear. It wasn't just quiet; it was a profound, heavy, absolute absence of sound. The faint electronic hum she had lived with most of her life was gone. The silence felt enormous. It felt pure.

She opened her hand. Lying in a pool of blood on her palm was a small, black, bean-shaped chip. It blinked a faint, dying red light. *Searching for signal.*

She looked at the paper cup, still containing a few drops of water. She dropped the chip into it. The red light flickered once, twice, and died as the water shorted the circuitry.

She was off the grid. For the first time since puberty, Mother Sophia did not know exactly where she was.

Caterina leaned her head back against the blood-smeared drywall, exhausted beyond measure. Blood was still pooling on the floor beneath her, soaking her jeans. She was filthy. She was injured. She was trapped in a locked room with armed guards outside.

But as she closed her eyes, listening to the beautiful, empty silence in her head, Caterina smiled. It was a grim, bloody baring of teeth in the dark.

She was free. Now, she just had to survive long enough to use that freedom.

The Pentagon

Mia

The Pentagon parking lot was a ghost town, a vast expanse of asphalt usually teeming with the hustle of national defense, now utterly deserted under the gray sky. The silence was unnatural, heavy, amplified by the distant hum of the D.C. beltway.

Mia Peers sat in the back of the armored government SUV, the leather seat cool beneath her. She wore a heavy tactical vest over her civilian clothes, the ceramic plates pressing against her chest like a second ribcage. Underneath the Kevlar, deep inside her, she felt a phantom flutter—a sensation that was probably just nerves, but her mind insisted was a second heartbeat.

Please be safe. Both of us.

She shouldn't be here. This was a combat zone, a pre-staged kill box. She was pregnant. She was dying of a cellular disease that made her hands tremor even now. She was the only hope for a cure, the only person who understood the biology of the enemy. But she had made a deal with the government: protection for her lab and her team in exchange for her presence on the field. They wanted her superhuman strength, her ability to read the clones, her insight into the Romano mind.

Beside her, Major Washington adjusted his noise-canceling

headset, his profile sharp against the tinted window. He was a statue of relaxed readiness, his rifle resting across his knees.

"Alpha Leader to Command. Perimeter is quiet. Too quiet. No movement on thermal," Lethabo murmured into his mic.

"Copy, Alpha Leader," the voice of Command crackled in Mia's earpiece, sounding tinny and distant. "Intel confirms a significant chatter spike on the dark channels. They're coming. ETA imminent."

Mia scanned the horizon through the thick, bulletproof glass. The Pentagon Force Protection Agency had cleared the area for a mile radius, turning the bustling hub into a silent stage. It felt wrong. Tactically unsound. Why would the Romanos attack the most fortified building on the planet with a handful of ground troops? They had money, influence, advanced tech. This felt medieval.

It was suicide. Or a distraction.

A sharp crack echoed in the distance, cutting through the silence.

"Contact!" Lethabo shouted, his voice tight. "Sector Four! Near the memorial."

Gunfire erupted—a dry, popping sound like firecrackers at first, then the heavier *thump-thump-thump* of high-caliber automatic weapons. The SUV rocked slightly as the driver shifted into gear.

"Let's move," Lethabo said, kicking the heavy door open before the vehicle even fully stopped.

Mia followed him out, her boots hitting the asphalt with a solid slap. The air instantly smelled different—acrid, metallic, the scent of cordite and burned ozone carried on the wind. She didn't have a weapon. She didn't need one. Her body was the weapon. She healed faster, moved faster, perceived faster than any human. But today, her job was observation.

"Alpha Three, report status," Lethabo barked into his comms as they jogged toward the sound of the fighting.

"Engaging," Tony's voice came back, clipped, professional, but with an undercurrent of confusion. "Hostiles down. Five confirmed kills. It's... pathetic, boss. They're just walking into the fire lanes. No cover, no tactics."

Mia frowned, her stride hitching slightly. Walking into fire? The Romanos trained their assets from birth. This wasn't an assault. That was a sacrifice. A purge.

They jogged past the rows of empty parking spaces toward the Air Force Memorial, the three stainless steel spires piercing the leaden sky like curved swords. The gunfire was sporadic now, dying down.

They rounded a concrete retaining wall and stopped. The scene was surreal.

Bodies littered the manicured grass near the concrete benches and the base of the spires. There were maybe twelve of them. Male and female clones, dressed not in tactical gear but in plain civilian clothes—jeans, jackets, sneakers. They lay in crumpled heaps, bleeding out onto the federal lawn. No heavy weapons, no armor. Just pistols and knives against a battalion of entrenched special forces.

It was a slaughter. A grotesque, pointless waste of life.

"Clear!" a soldier shouted from the tree line, lowering his rifle.

Mia walked forward, the grass slick under her boots. She stepped over a woman who looked exactly like Sophia, only younger, her eyes staring blankly at the sky, a single bullet hole in her forehead. Dead. A copy of a copy, discarded.

"Why?" Mia whispered, her voice lost in the wind. "Why throw them away like this? What does Mother gain?"

She heard a wet cough to her left.

A male clone, lying near a concrete bench, was trying to crawl. He was bleeding from four distinct wounds in his chest, his breath bubbling in his throat.

"Lethabo," Mia said, moving toward him. "Cover me. I'm

going to talk to him."

"Clear," Lethabo said to the perimeter team. "Hold fire. Dr. Peers is moving in."

Mia knelt beside the dying man on the damp grass. He was a Cesaro copy—dark hair, angular jaw, identical to the melting men from the farmhouse video.

"Wakey-wakey," Mia said roughly, pressing a QuickClot dressing onto his chest wound with one hand, feeling the heat of his blood.

The man groaned, his eyes fluttering open. They were unfocused, glazed with pain. He looked up at her, his vision clearing for a moment. A bloody, humorless grin spread across his face, staining his teeth.

"Mia," he rasped. His voice was clear, perfect unaccented English. "Fancy meeting you here. I was wondering if you'd show up for the show."

"Where is Unity?" Mia demanded, leaning close so only he could hear, her voice hard. "Tell me where the safehouse is. Give me a location."

"Unity?" The clone chuckled, a wet, rattling sound. Blood bubbled at the corner of his lips. "I don't know any Unity. I just know the mission parameters."

"The mission was suicide," Mia said, pressing harder on the wound, feeling his ribcage hitch. "You failed. You're all dead."

"Did we?"

Mia stiffened. The tone was wrong. Triumphant. She grabbed his throat with her free hand, squeezing just enough to cut off his air, to focus his fading mind. "Talk! What was the real target?"

The clone clawed weakly at her hand, his strength fading fast. "You don't get it, do you? You're so smart, Mia... but you're so slow. Always one step behind."

"Talk, damn you!"

"Mother sends her regards," the clone whispered, his eyes

rolling back, glazing over. "She says... thank you for taking such good care of Livia. She'll take it from here."

Mia froze. Her heart stopped.

Livia.

Livia was in the sub-basement of the lab, an hour's flight away. Guarded by Peyton and Kristin. The lab that was currently understaffed because half the team was here, chasing ghosts at the Pentagon.

If the Romanos knew Livia was there... and if this attack, this suicidal charge of clones, was just a distraction to pull Mia and Lethabo and the bulk of the Sentry Blade force away from the real target...

"Oh my God," Mia breathed, the realization hitting her like a physical blow.

She dropped the dying man, scrambling to her feet, her hands slick with his blood.

"Lethabo!" she screamed, turning and sprinting back toward the SUV, her breath tearing in her lungs. "It's a diversion! The Pentagon isn't the target! They're hitting the lab! They're going for Livia!"

Lethabo was already on the comms, his face pale under his helmet. "Alpha Two, report! Kristin, Peyton, come in! Status report now!"

Static hissed in their earpieces. Dead air.

"Get the chopper!" Mia yelled, tearing off her helmet and throwing it on the asphalt as she ran. "Get us back there now! Before they kill everyone!"

Visitors

Brian

Brian Carter sat on the plush French leather couch in Mia's penthouse, hunched over his tablet, his body a testament to ergonomic failure. The screen illuminated his pale, tired face in the dimly lit room, displaying a complex schematic of the modified stasis pod sitting four floors below in his lab. The probability of success for the consciousness transfer protocol had risen to twenty-two percent after he'd recalibrated the neural uptake rate based on the latest simulations.

Twenty-two percent. Not great. In fact, terrifyingly low if you were the one about to plug your brain into it. But it was infinitely better than the big, fat zero it had been several weeks ago.

A low, rhythmic thrum vibrating through the hardwood floorboards pulled him from the digital maze. *Thump-thump-thump-thump.*

The helicopter.

Brian frowned, pushing his smudged glasses up his nose. The Pentagon operation must have been canceled.

He stood up, his knees popping loudly. He adjusted his signature Crocs, which let out a cheerful, incongruous squeak on the expensive wood floor. He needed to go up there and politely but firmly ask the pilot about the status of the rooftop vibration dampeners anyway. They were due for a calibration.

He walked to the heavy, fire-rated door of the stairwell that led up to the roof access. He pushed the crash bar. The door swung open, and the noise of the rotors instantly grew from a thrum to a roar, accompanied by a blast of cool air smelling of aviation fuel.

Brian stepped out onto the metal grate landing, ready to complain. The words died in his throat.

Six women stood on the helipad, illuminated by the red and green landing lights. They weren't the pilots. They wore identical black tactical gear—heavy vests, utility belts bristling with equipment, drop-leg holsters. Their faces were covered by balaclavas, leaving only their eyes visible—cold, identical eyes that scanned the perimeter with professional detachment.

"Well, ladies," one of the women said, her voice filtered through a comms mask but still terrifyingly familiar. She spotted him instantly. "Looks like we don't have to blow the door after all. The mouse came to the trap."

Before Brian could react, before his brain could even process the threat, she lunged. A hand clad in a reinforced glove grabbed the front of his lab coat, yanking him violently off the landing and onto the abrasive non-slip surface of the roof.

He stumbled, his Crocs losing traction. A hard, cold object—a pistol barrel—pressed firmly into the small of his spine, right between his vertebrae.

"Emma, Anna, hold the perimeter here," the leader commanded over the roar of the engine. "The rest of you, with me. We're going down."

She spun Brian around with bruising force, shoving him toward the open stairwell door.

"You're Brian Carter, right? Head of Research and Development?"

Brian nodded numbly, his throat sandpaper dry. Up close,

even with the balaclava, he recognized the structure of the face, the specific tilt of the eyes. It was the same face he saw in the mirror of his nightmares, the face of the woman who had betrayed him and Mia, then kidnapped him, tying him to a chair in a hangar.

Sophia. Or a perfect copy of her. A ghost with a gun.

"Don't be shy, dear," she purred, the tone a terrifying, mocking echo of the dead woman. "We have a lot of catching up to do. You're going to take us to Livia."

They descended the stairs in a tight formation, a phalanx of clones moving with silent, deadly precision around their stumbling captive. Brian's mind raced faster than the helicopter rotors. Where was everyone? Peyton and Kristin were supposed to be on patrol on the second floor. The regular security guards were at the front gate, hundreds of feet away. The penthouse was empty; Chris was still at the FDA office, Mia was... at the Pentagon.

He was alone.

"Where is she?" the leader hissed in his ear, prodding him sharply with the gun barrel to speed him up.

"Basement," Brian squeaked, his voice an embarrassing octave higher than usual. "Secure wing. Sub-level two. No windows. Reinforced concrete."

"Lead the way, mouse. And don't get creative."

They moved fast, descending flight after flight of concrete stairs. On the second-floor landing, Brian heard a sudden shout from the corridor beyond the fire door. Kristin's voice, sharp and urgent.

"Contact! Roof access stairwell! Multiple bogeys! Seal the—"
CRACK-CRACK-CRACK.

Gunfire erupted above them, the sound deafening in the confined stairwell. The leader didn't even flinch. She shoved Brian down the next flight of stairs so hard he nearly tumbled headfirst.

"Ignore it," she ordered her sisters, her voice flat. "They're distractions. Eyes on the prize."

They reached the bottom level. The air here was significantly cooler, smelling faintly of damp concrete. Brian hesitated at the heavy steel door marked 'SECURE STORAGE - AUTHORIZED PERSONNEL ONLY'.

"It's locked," he lied, his voice shaking. "Biometric scanner and keypad. I don't have the clearance code for this door. Only Mia does."

"We brought our own key."

The leader pulled a silver pouch from her vest and slapped a thick strip of gray thermal putty over the lock mechanism. She shoved Brian back against the concrete wall.

"Cover your ears."

She pressed a detonator. *FZZZT-POP.*

A blinding flash of white light was followed by a sharp concussive crack. The smell of burning metal filled the air. The lock mechanism melted into slag, dripping onto the floor. The heavy door groaned and swung inward a few inches.

The leader kicked it open.

Brian was shoved through the doorway into the hallway. At the far end, light spilled from the open door of his main lab—Lab 4. He saw Roger's shaggy head poke out, a confused, sleepy smile on his face, holding a lukewarm cup of coffee.

"Hey, Bri, what was that noi—"

"Shut the door!" Brian screamed, putting every ounce of terror into his voice. "Roger! Shut the door and lock it! Now!"

The clone leader snarled and slammed the butt of her rifle into the back of Brian's head with sickening force.

He crumbled to the cold floor, stars exploding behind his eyes, the taste of blood filling his mouth. The world spun violently.

But through the haze of pain, he saw it. Roger's face went pale with realization. The lab door slammed shut with a heavy clang. The electronic deadbolt engaged with a loud *clack*.

Secure. For now.

"That wasn't smart, mouse," the leader growled, reaching down and hauling Brian to his feet by his collar. His head throbbed in agony.

"They're just tech support," Brian wheezed, swaying on his feet, blood trickling down his neck. "Civilian contractors. Harmless. You're here for Livia. She's down there." He pointed with a trembling hand to the reinforced door at the very end of the dead-end hallway.

The clones moved past the locked lab door, ignoring Roger and Cynthia inside. They stopped at Livia's cell.

Another strip of putty. Another blinding flash and pop.

The heavy door drifted open on silent hinges. The smell hit them first, rolling out into the sterile hallway like a physical presence—a thick, scent of human waste, sweat, and the underlying hint of madness.

The clones gasped in unison, recoiling slightly. Even Brian, who had seen it before, felt his stomach turn violently.

Livia hung in the center of the stark white padded room, a broken marionette suspended by heavy chains from the ceiling. Her remaining arm was shackled high, her body limp. The smooth, healed stump of her missing arm was stark against her filthy skin. Her hair was a matted, greasy curtain hiding her face.

"Get her down," the leader commanded, her voice thick with revulsion and fury at the sight of her sister's degradation.

Two sisters rushed forward with heavy bolt cutters. *Snap. Snap.* The chains fell away clattering.

Livia dropped like a stone. The leader caught her, grunting with the effort, and lowered her gently to a metal folding chair propped against the wall.

Livia sat there, hunched over. She didn't speak. She didn't look at her rescuers. She just stared at the padded wall, her eyes wide, unblinking, and utterly vacant.

"Livia?" the leader asked gently, crouching in front of her, pulling off her balaclava to reveal the face of Sophia. "Sister? Can you hear me? It's us. We're getting you out."

"Mother sent us," another clone said, placing a hand on Livia's shoulder. "She wants to see you. You're going home."

Livia's head snapped up at the word 'Mother.' A slow, terrible, beatific smile spread across her grime-streaked face, showing teeth that looked too large for her mouth.

"Mother," she whispered, the word a reverent prayer.

"Yes," the leader said, relieved, standing up. "Come on. We have to move fast. The security team is swarming. We need to get to the roof."

Livia stood up. She stretched her neck to the side, a sickening, loud *crack* sounding in the small room. She seemed to grow two inches, her posture shifting from broken victim to something else entirely.

"I can help," Livia said, her voice raspy but clear.

"Good. We need you to—"

Livia moved.

It was a blur of violence so fast Brian's eyes couldn't track it. Her remaining hand shot out like a striking cobra, grabbing the leader by the throat. The leader's eyes bulged in shock.

With a wet, sickening *crunch*, Livia crushed the woman's windpipe.

The leader dropped to the floor without a sound, gargling blood, drowning in her own fluids.

The other three sisters froze, shock paralyzing their highly trained reflexes for a fatal split second. As if they couldn't process what they were seeing. This was their sister.

It was enough time.

Livia spun, grabbing the pistol from the dead leader's holster in one fluid motion. She didn't hesitate. She didn't move. She just fired point-blank into the stunned face of the nearest clone.

Bang.

The woman fell back, a ruin of blood and bone where her face had been.

"Livia!" the third clone screamed, finally raising her rifle, her voice cracking with terror. "What are you doing? Stop!"

Livia laughed. It was a high, broken, ecstatic sound that scraped against Brian's soul. "Cleaning house."

She shot the third sister in the neck, two controlled rounds. Then she turned to the fourth, who was trying to raise her weapon. *Bang. Bang.*

Silence slammed back down onto the basement hallway, heavier and more suffocating than before. The air was thick with cordite and blood mist.

Four identical bodies in tactical gear lay in spreading pools of crimson on the concrete. Livia stood over them, the gun loose in her hand, grinning at the carnage she had created.

Brian didn't wait to see what she would do next. Adrenaline overrode his pain and terror. He scrambled backward on his hands and knees, crab-walking frantically toward the lab door, slipping in the blood of the clones.

He pounded on the metal door with both fists. "Roger! Cynthia! Let me in! Open the goddamn door!"

The lock clicked. The door cracked open an inch.

Brian threw his weight against it, diving inside just as Livia exited her prison. Her smile was gone. Her eyes were black holes, devoid of anything human.

Roger grabbed Brian by the collar of his lab coat and yanked him fully into the room. Cynthia slammed the heavy door shut and threw the electronic bolt with a shaking hand.

Brian collapsed onto the anti-static floor mat, gasping for air, his lungs burning, blood dripping from the back of his head onto the clean tile.

"What happened?" Cynthia asked, her voice high and terrified, clutching a soldering iron like a weapon. "Who was shooting? Where are the guards?"

"Livia," Brian whispered, staring at the sealed door, waiting for the inevitable pounding to start. "She... she killed them. She killed her own rescue team."

He looked up at his friends, his face paper-white, his eyes wide with the horror of what he had just witnessed.

"She's loose out there. She's armed with their weapons. And she's completely, homicidally insane."

Chiara

Unity

T he backyard of the safehouse was less a sanctuary and more a holding pen. It was a postage stamp of dormant, frost-bitten grass, hemmed in on all sides by an eight-foot privacy fence that blocked out the rest of Virginia.

Unity sat in a wrought-iron patio chair that sucked the heat right through her designer jeans. She was bundled in a thick wool pea coat Jon had sourced for her, but the chill found its way in at the collar and cuffs. Still, she refused to go inside. She tilted her face toward the weak, winter sun hanging low over the tree line, trying to absorb its meager warmth.

For twenty years, her skin had known only fluorescent hums and cotton sheets. The sensation of actual wind—even this biting, bitter breeze—moving across her cheeks felt like a violent awakening.

Jon sat beside her, huddled deep inside his puffy thermoball North Face jacket, his shoulders hunched nearly to his ears. He wasn't just shivering from the temperature; he was shaking with a nervous energy that had consumed him since the disastrous rescue attempt of Livia.

"It's freezing, Unity," Jon muttered, rubbing his gloved hands together, the nylon loud in the quiet yard. His breath plumed in thick white clouds. "My toes are numb. We should go in before you catch pneumonia. Their doctors will blame me."

"Five more minutes," Unity said, her voice raspy. "Please, Jon. I need the air."

She needed the distance. The house felt like a coffin waiting for a lid. Ever since the news broke among the Romanos about Livia—how she had snapped, slaughtering her own rescue team in Mia's basement—the mood inside the house had shifted from tense to toxic. The air indoors was thick with Mother Sophia's silent, terrifying rage.

Only Chiara seemed calm. The new Daughter-in-Waiting was thriving in the chaos, preening like a vulture that had just inherited a carcass.

As if summoned by the thought, the back door clicked open.

Chiara stepped out onto the small concrete patio. She was dressed not for the weather, but for an audience, bundled in a sculpted black wool coat, topped with a chic cashmere beanie. She spotted them and smiled, a slow, stretching expression that held all the sweetness of arsenic.

"Mind if I join you?" she asked, her voice light, already walking toward them before they could answer. Her boots crunched loudly on the frozen grass.

Jon practically jumped out of his skin, scrambling to grab a third, rusted metal chair. "Of course. Be our guest, Chiara."

Chiara sat opposite Unity, crossing her legs elegantly. She didn't look cold; she looked untouchable. Her dark eyes scanned Unity's face like she was reading a disappointing menu.

"You look good," Chiara said, cocking her head. "The fresh air suits you."

"Thanks," Unity said cautiously, keeping her hands tucked deep in her pockets to hide the sudden tremor. Every conversation with a Romano felt like navigating a minefield blindfolded. "It's nice to be out of the room. Jon has been very helpful with my rehabilitation."

"I'm sure he has. Enjoy the view while it lasts," Chiara murmured, looking past Unity toward the trees, her expression wistful. "I love winter. Real winter, not this damp American nonsense. My favorite holiday spot is the Alps. St. Moritz. Skiing all day, tea by the fire at night. You used to ski, didn't you, Unity? Before the accident?"

Unity stiffened. The reference was cruel and deliberate. "A long time ago. In another life."

"Shame you'll never do it again. Those legs... well." Chiara sighed theatrically, then turned her gaze back to Unity. The smile vanished instantly, replaced by a flat, dead stare. "Have you heard from Mia lately?"

Unity's heart skipped a beat, then slammed against her ribs. The sudden pivot stole her breath. "How would I hear from her? I'm completely cut off."

"You know what I mean." Chiara leaned forward, her expensive perfume—something heavy with musk and jasmine—overpowering the smell of the cold air. "I mean... the spooky way."

Jon shifted uncomfortably in his metal seat, the chair screeching slightly on the concrete pavers. Unity kept her face blank, a skill she was rapidly relearning.

"I don't know what you're talking about. If this is about the restaurant, Jon told you, the tablecloth—"

"Don't lie to me, dearie," Chiara purred, cutting her off. Her voice dropped to a conspiratorial whisper. "I hate liars. Almost as much as Mother does. Livia was a liar. Caterina was a liar. That's why Caterina is rotting in a cell right now and I'm sitting here wearing silk underwear."

Chiara reached out lightning fast and grabbed Unity's chin. Her grip was surprisingly strong, her fingers digging into Unity's jaw, forcing eye contact.

"I heard you," Chiara whispered, her eyes gleaming with

malice. "In your room. You thought you were alone. You were staring at the wall, muttering to yourself."

Unity's stomach bottomed out.

"'I'm surprised you don't have morning sickness yet.'" Chiara repeated the words slowly, savoring them. "That's what you said. Clear as a bell."

Unity froze. Ice flooded her veins, colder than the Virginia winter. She *had* said that. In the middle of an intense psychic conversation with Mia, overwhelmed by the shared sensory input of Mia's pregnancy, she had slipped and spoken the thought aloud.

"Mia is pregnant," Chiara said, triumph radiating from her. "And you know it. Which means you're talking to her. Right under Mother's nose."

"I was daydreaming," Unity lied, jerking her chin out of Chiara's grip. Her voice shook. "It was just... wishful thinking. A fantasy about a normal life I'll never have."

Chiara laughed. It was a cold, sharp sound like breaking glass. "A fantasy? Please. You don't have the imagination for that. And the restaurant? Was throwing Jon ten feet across the dining room with your brain a fantasy, too?"

Jon flinched violently beside her. Chiara turned her predatory gaze on him.

"You're a terrible liar too, Jon. 'Slipped on the tablecloth?' Did you really think Mother bought that pathetic story for a second?"

Chiara stood up abruptly. Before Jon could react, she slapped him across the face.

The crack of flesh on flesh echoed shockingly loud in the cold, quiet yard.

Jon rocked back in his chair, clutching his cheek, his eyes watering. A bright red scratch bloomed instantly on his dark skin.

"Mother knows everything," Chiara said, turning back to

Unity, looming over her chair. "She knows you're evolving. She knows you're dangerous. She knows you're connected to Mia. And she's done playing nice with her little science experiment."

"Then kill me," Unity spat, adrenaline surging through her, burning away the cold. "Do it right now. I'd rather die than help you monsters."

Chiara's sneer vanished. Her eyes went flat.

"You think death is the worst thing we can do to you? You poor, naive girl." Chiara leaned down until her nose was inches from Unity's. Her breath clouded in Unity's face. "We have stasis pods in storage. We can put you back to sleep. Not for twenty years. For a hundred. We can wake you up when Mia is long dead and buried, when her children's children are dust. You will be alone in a future you don't understand, owned by us forever. Of course, only if Mia finds a cure. If she can't... or won't, well, game over for you anyway."

The threat hit Unity harder than any physical blow. To go back into the dark... the thought was a suffocating terror that clawed at her throat.

"Consider the honeymoon over," Chiara whispered. "From now on, you stay in your room. No more fresh air. No more nice meals. If you speak, if you twitch a finger wrong, if you so much as *think* about Mia, I will hurt Jon. I will take him apart piece by piece while you watch. Do you understand me?"

Unity glared up at her, trembling with a mixture of terror and incandescent rage. "Go to hell."

"I'm already there, dearie. I'm just giving you the tour."

Chiara straightened up, adjusted her beanie, and marched back into the house, the door slamming shut behind her with finality of a prison gate.

Silence rushed back into the yard, heavier now, loaded with immediate threat.

Jon let out a long, shaky breath. He lowered his hand from his face. A trickle of blood leaked from the corner of his lip where

Chiara's fingernail had caught him.

"She knows," he whispered, his voice hollow. "They know it all. We're completely out of time."

Unity looked at the closed door. The sun had dipped below the tree line, and the yard was suddenly plunged into deep gray shadow. The cold was agonizing now, seeping into her bones.

The idea of a stasis pod, like the coma she had endured for twenty years stung, threatening to crush her. But for now, she wasn't asleep. She was awake, and she was furious.

"We need help," Unity said, her voice steely. "We can't do this alone. Not against all of them."

Jon nodded slowly, wiping the blood from his lip with a gloved hand. He stood up, wincing, and bent down to pick her up.

"So it's decided?" he asked quietly. "Caterina?"

"She's in a cell because of them. She hates Mother more than we do right now," Unity said. "She's the only option we have left."

Jon held Unity against his chest. His arms were trembling slightly, whether from the cold, the fear, or her weight, she couldn't tell.

He looked down at her, his eyes grim. "Let's go inside. We have a jailbreak to plan."

Chester Gap

Mia

The view from the cantilevered timber balcony of Chester Gap Winery was undeniably breathtaking—a sweeping, cinematic vista of the Blue Ridge Mountains rolling out in undulating waves of hazy blue and dying rust toward the Shenandoah Valley floor. The falling sun was setting the western horizon on fire, bleeding deep oranges and bruised purples across the sky.

Mia Peers hated every inch of it. The vast, echoing gap between the peaks reminded her too much of the chasm that had opened up between her and her husband sitting three feet away.

She took a sip of her sparkling water, the lime twist tasting sour and thin against her tongue. The carbonation bit at her throat, a poor substitute for the numbness she craved. Beside her, Chris nursed a bottle of expensive Pinot Noir like it was a life preserver. The bottle was sweating in the cold evening air. He was on his third large glass. Or maybe his fourth. Mia had stopped counting when he stopped making eye contact.

He was drunk. Not sloppy, shouting drunk, but a cold, simmering, resentful drunk that was infinitely harder to handle. And God help her, she was jealous. Her enhanced metabolism burned through alcohol faster than she could drink it; she was trapped in high-definition sobriety while he got to blur the edges.

A biting wind whipped up the valley, rustling the dry leaves on the vines below and cutting through Mia's jacket. She shivered, wrapping her arms around herself, feeling the ultraslim ceramic plates of the ballistic vest she now wore under everything.

"You know what they call me?" Chris slurred slightly, his gaze unfocused as he stared at the elegant script on the wine label. His voice was low, roughened by the alcohol and weeks of suppressed anger.

Mia kept her eyes on the sunset, watching the light die. "Who calls you what, Chris?"

"The staff. The private security goons you hired to turn our home into a FOB. The ones who pat me down when I come home from one of your errands." He chuckled bitterly, picked up his glass, and swirled the dark red liquid. "They call me Saint Christopher."

Mia winced. The nickname hit its mark like a physical blow. It was mean, petty, and entirely accurate.

"Because I put up with it," Chris continued, taking a heavy swallow of wine. "Because I'm the patient, long-suffering human husband married to the walking science experiment."

"Chris, please," Mia whispered, the fight draining out of her. "Don't do this here."

"Why not? It's a lovely view for a dissection." He turned to look at her then, his eyes glassy and hard, stripped of their usual warmth. "I'm tired of being a saint, Mia. I'm tired of living in a Tom Clancy novel I didn't write."

"I'm sorry," Mia said, the words feeling inadequate and small in the vast mountain air.

"Don't apologize," Chris snapped, slamming the glass down a little too hard on the teak table. A few drops of red splashed onto his cuff, staining it like blood. "Just... stop lying to me. Stop hiding things in the basement."

He wasn't talking about wine storage. He was talking about Livia. The disaster at the lab—the failed rescue attempt where the psychotic clone had butchered her own sisters before escaping—had cost lives. Good security guards were dead. Brian was traumatized. It was a catastrophe born of Mia's arrogance, her desperate attempt to play god and control a variable that refused to be controlled.

Chris hadn't forgiven her for bringing that kind of danger into their world. More importantly, Mia hadn't forgiven herself.

"I was trying to protect you," Mia said, her voice trembling. "I thought if I could contain her, study her—"

"You weren't trying to protect me. You were trying to control everything," Chris corrected, pouring more wine with a hand that shook noticeably. "You think because you have this... this *power*, that you know better than everyone else. You're just like your father."

The comparison stung worse than the alcohol he was consuming. Jeffrey Peers, the brilliant, amoral narcissist who had created Mia in a test tube. To be compared to him by the man she loved was a knife twist in her gut.

Mia glanced down at her hands resting on the table. They were steady today, rock solid. But underneath the skin, beneath the muscle and bone, she could feel the foreign workings of the Syndrome. It was waiting patiently for her to turn forty so it could finalize its work of turning her nervous system into puddy.

She was falling apart. She was being hunted by an Italian matriarch. And she was keeping secrets that could sink a battleship.

She needed to tell him. The weight of the secret was becoming physically painful, a pressure behind her ribs that rivaled the Syndrome. She needed to tell him about the pregnancy. About the impossible extra heartbeat she could feel fluttering inside her, a tiny, terrifying miracle amid the chaos. She wasn't just fighting for her own life anymore; she was fighting for their future.

But looking at him now—sullen, drunk, lashing out from a place of deep hurt—the words stuck in her throat.

"Chris," she started, forcing herself to meet his gaze. "There's something else. I need to tell you something."

He stared at her, his expression weary and cynical. "What now, Mia? Another secret prisoner? Did you hide a tactical nuke in the attic this time?"

"No. It's... it's personal. About us."

Chris leaned back in his chair, crossing his arms over his chest defensively. The wind ruffled his hair. "Go ahead. Lay it on me. I'm numb anyway."

Mia took a deep breath, tasting the overripe winter in the air. She opened her mouth to say the impossible words: *I'm pregnant.*

Mia.

The voice sliced directly into the center of her skull, severing her connection to the physical world.

Mia gasped, jerking upright in her chair, her water glass tipping over and spilling onto the deck. The sunset, the winery, Chris—it all receded behind a veil of sudden, sharp psychic pressure.

"Unity?" Mia whispered, her eyes darting around, seeing nothing but the encroaching twilight.

Chris groaned loudly, throwing his head back. "Oh, great. Perfect timing. Now we're doing the spooky voice thing again."

"Shut up, Chris," Mia hissed, holding up a hand to silence him. The intensity of the connection was stronger than ever before, almost painful. She closed her eyes to focus. *Unity? What is it? Are you okay?*

We're going, Unity's thought came crashing into Mia's mind, urgent and sharp as broken glass. *Tonight. It has to be tonight.*

Mia frowned, her physical body tensing. *Tonight? Why the rush? You said you needed more time to plan.*

Plan changed, Unity replied. Mia could feel her twin's terror, a cold knot in her own stomach. *Chiara knows. She knows I can talk to you. She overheard me. She knows about the telekinesis at the restaurant. She revoked our privileges. We're locked down. If we don't move now, while they think we're cowed, we never will.*

Mia's heart hammered against her ribs, a frantic counterpoint to the smaller rhythm lower in her abdomen. *Are you ready? Do you trust Jon to pull this off?*

A flash of emotion from Unity—a complex tangle of fear, pity, and desperation. *I have to. He's terrified, Mia. He's coming apart. But he hates Mother more than he fears her now. We're going to break Caterina out first.*

Caterina? Mia almost laughed out loud, a hysterical sound bubbling up in her throat. *The enemy?*

The enemy of my enemy is my ticket out of here, Unity corrected grimly. *Mother locked her in a cell. Caterina is furious and she knows the escape protocols. We need her help.*

Mia opened her eyes. The reality of the winery crashed back in—the murmur of other patrons, the clink of glass. She turned to Chris, speaking quickly, adrenaline burning away her hesitation.

"They're moving. Tonight. The timetable moved up."

Chris blinked slowly, the alcohol fog lifting slightly at her tone. "What? Who is?"

"Unity and Jon. They're breaking out. Tonight. And they're busting out one of the Romano sisters to help them escape."

Chris stared at her blankly. "Wait. They're recruiting one of the clones? That sounds like a disaster waiting to happen."

Where are they, Unity? Mia pushed the thought hard. *Give me something. A road sign. A smell. Anything.*

I don't know. I've never seen the outside of the fence. Mia felt

Unity's frustration. *It's cold. There are pine trees. The air smells thin. But we're close, Mia. I can feel your pull. I can feel... you.*

Be careful, U, Mia thought, projecting as much strength as she could muster. *Please. Don't take unnecessary risks.*

I won't. The hardest part is getting past the gate. There was a pause in the connection, a hesitation that felt heavy. *Mia... you need to tell him.*

Mia froze. The wind seemed to stop. *Tell him what?*

About the baby. Unity's mental voice was gentle now, but firm as bedrock. *He's hurting. You're both hurting. He deserves to know what you're fighting for.*

Mia glanced at Chris. He was watching her, waiting for translation, the drunken anger in his eyes replaced by a flicker of the old worry, the old love. He looked lost.

I will, Mia promised her sister. *As soon as you're safe. I can't lay this on him when I might have to leave in five minutes to come get you.*

Good luck, Mia. See you on the outside.

The connection broke with a snap that left Mia's ears ringing.

She opened her eyes again. The sun was completely gone now. The valley below was a bowl of deep shadows, the mountains reduced to jagged black silhouettes against a dying indigo sky.

"She's gone," Mia said, her voice hollow. She stood up abruptly, her chair scraping loudly on the wood decking. She grabbed her purse. "We have to go."

"Go where?" Chris asked, standing unsteadily, bracing himself against the table. "It's obvious they don't know where they are. We can't just fly around Virginia aimlessly."

"We're going back to the lab," Mia said, already moving toward the exit. "I need to be in the chopper when they make their move. If they get out, they'll need immediate extraction. And if the Romanos come for them before we get there... I need to be ready to meet them."

Chris grabbed her arm as she passed, his grip clumsy but firm. "Wait. Stop for a second. You said... before Unity interrupted, you said it was personal. You said you had something to tell me."

Mia looked at him. She saw the red wine stains on his teeth, the glazed look in his eyes, the defensive set of his shoulders. Then she thought of the baby, the impossible secret curled inside her, a secret that deserved a sober father and a safe world.

"Later," she said softly, pulling her arm free. "When we're sober. And when my sister is safe."

She leaned in and kissed his cheek quickly. His skin was cold and tasted of expensive, sour wine and regret.

"Let's go, Saint Christopher," she whispered. "We have a gift to find."

Breakout

Unity

T he hallway outside Caterina's holding cell hummed with boredom, complacency, and weariness.

Marco and Giovanni guarded the door. They looked like zombies, leaning against the beige drywall, pistols holstered, chewing gum in synchronized rhythm. They were disposable muscle, unaware they were standing on a fault line.

Jon pushed Unity's wheelchair around the corner, his breathing erratic and loud.

"Ready?" he murmured, the word barely audible over the light friction of the chair's wheels on the tile.

"No," Unity whispered. Her palms were slick with sweat against the vinyl armrests. Her heart hammered a frantic rhythm against her ribs. "But let's do it anyway."

Jon took a breath and rolled her toward the guards. "Gentlemen," he said, feigning a casual air that felt brittle enough to crack. "Chiara wants Cat prepped for immediate transport. Flight's moved up."

Marco frowned, stopping his chewing. He straightened up, dropping a hand to his belt. "We didn't get an order from Antonio."

"That's why I'm here. Comms are down at the main desk,"

Jon lied smoothly. He stopped the chair directly in front of the locked door. "Damn shoe." He bent down to tie a lace that wasn't loose, stalling.

It was the signal.

Unity closed her eyes, tuning out the whisper of reality, the smell of cleaner, the thud of her own pulse. She reached out with her mind, pushing past the physical world into the dense, cold certainty of matter. She felt the deadbolt inside the door. She sensed the tumblers, the tension springs, the sheer weight of the metallic complexity.

It felt like pushing through half-frozen molasses. She gritted her teeth, sweat popping on her forehead, and *shoved* with her mind.

Click.

The lock disengaged with a mechanical snap loud enough to echo in the sudden silence.

The guards reacted instantly, training kicking in. Polymers rasped as they drew their weapons.

"What the hell was that?" Marco barked, leveling his Sig Sauer at Jon's crouching form.

Jon lunged upward, tackling the door with his shoulder. He disappeared inside the dark room.

Marco raised his gun higher, aiming at Jon's back.

Unity pushed.

She didn't touch him physically. She threw her will at his center of mass like a battering ram. The impact shuddered back up her own spine. Marco flew backward, his feet leaving the floor. He slammed into the opposite wall with a bone-jarring thud, his head cracking against the drywall, leaving a dent. He slid to the floor, unconscious before he landed.

Giovanni spun toward her, eyes wide with dawning horror. "You—you freak—"

Unity squeezed her left fist. Across the small space, Giovanni choked. He clawed at his own throat, his face purpling as an invisible vise clamped down on his trachea. It felt sickeningly intimate, feeling the cartilage compress under her mental grip from ten feet away. He dropped to his knees, gasping silently for air that wouldn't come, then collapsed onto his side.

Unity slumped in her chair. A spike of agony drove itself behind her eyes, blinding her for a second. Her nose began to bleed, warm and dripping onto her lips.

Two down. So many to go.

Jon burst out of the room, dragging a disheveled creature that used to be Caterina. She was filthy, smelling of dried blood and vomit, her eyes wild.

"Let's go!" Jon hissed, grabbing the wheelchair handles.

They ran—Jon pushing the chair at a dangerous speed, Caterina stumbling alongside, coughing—toward the secure storage room near the kitchen where the confiscated serum was kept.

They turned the final corner and ran straight into a wall of muscle.

Antonio.

The head of security stood like a mountain blocking the narrow hallway. He took in the scene instantly—the running prisoners, the rolling invalid. He smiled, a cruel twisting of thick lips.

"Going somewhere, little birds?"

He reached for the radio on his shoulder.

"Unity! Now!" Jon yelled, shoving the chair forward.

Unity wiped blood from under her nose and focused on Antonio. He was bigger than the others. Denser. His mind was a fortress of simple, brutal aggression. She gathered the remaining scraps of her energy and *pushed.*

Antonio grunted. He braced his legs, leaning into the invisible force like a man walking into a hurricane. His boots squeaked on the tile, sliding backward an inch, but he didn't fall. He took a heavy step forward, fighting the pressure, his hand moving toward his holster.

Unity groaned aloud, the strain tearing at the fragile synapses of her mind. She couldn't hold him. He was too heavy, too grounded in reality.

"Get back!" Caterina screamed, her voice raw granite. She shoved past the wheelchair, nearly knocking Unity over, and kicked the storage room door open with manic strength.

She disappeared inside.

"She's going for the serum!" Antonio roared, realizing the bigger threat. He shoved past Unity and Jon, knocking the wheelchair into the wall.

Inside the small room, Caterina was tearing through cardboard boxes like a rabid animal. Equipment shattered on the floor.

She found it. The single glass vial of clear liquid. No syringe. No time.

"Damn it!"

She popped the cork stopper with her teeth and downed the raw, volatile liquid in one gulp.

Antonio burst into the doorway, gun raised.

Caterina convulsed. It wasn't a normal spasm. Her back arched violently, snapping backward so hard her vertebrae cracked. She dropped to her knees, clutching her stomach, a guttural, wet sound tearing from her throat. Foam bubbled between her teeth. Her eyes rolled back into her head, showing only whites. She collapsed onto the carpet, seizing violently.

"Idiot," Antonio sneered, stepping over her thrashing body. He aimed his gun at the back of her head to finish the job.

NO.

Unity didn't have the strength to push Antonio again. Her mind was empty. In desperation, she threw her focus at the floor beneath his boots.

The tile buckled. Wood subflooring snapped upward with the sound of a gunshot. Antonio lost his balance, flailing, firing a round wildly into the ceiling plaster as he fell backward.

Before he could recover, the thrashing in the storage room stopped dead.

Silence.

Then, Caterina stood up.

It wasn't a normal movement. She didn't scramble or climb. She *unfolded,* joints articulating at impossible angles, rising from the floor with the fluid, unnatural menace of hydraulic machinery. She turned to face the door. Her eyes snapped open.

The irises were gone. The whites were gone. Her eyes were enormous, abyssal black holes swallowing the light in the room.

She stared at Antonio, who was scrambling to his feet. The bloody ruin of her face stretched into a smile that showed too many teeth.

"Hello, Antonio."

She moved faster than thought. One second she was by the counter; the next she was a blur of motion crossing the room. She stood over him, grabbing his head with one hand.

Crunch.

Antonio went limp, his neck twisted at an impossible angle.

Caterina stepped over the body, pulsing with raw, terrifying power. The air around her seemed to crackle.

"Let's go," she said, her voice distorted, deeper, echoing in Unity's chest.

They moved into the main hallway just as the rest of the family arrived, drawn by the gunshot. Mother Sophia stood at the far end near the foyer, flanked by a dozen armed guards with rifles raised. Chiara was beside her, looking pale and small.

"Stop them!" Mother screamed, pointing a shaking finger. "Kill them all!"

The guards hesitated for a fraction of a second, terrified by the thing standing next to Jon.

Caterina charged.

It wasn't a fight. It was a slaughter. She was a wrecking ball in human form, a blur of motion that defied physics. She dodged bullets with speed that left afterimages on the retina, closing the fifty-foot distance in seconds. She didn't use weapons. She used her hands, her feet, her newly forged body.

Guards flew through the air like ragdolls, smashing through drywall. The sickening wet snap of breaking bones echoed over the screams.

Jon pushed Unity's wheelchair through the carnage, keeping his head down, shielding Unity from the spray of blood. Caterina was clearing a path straight to the throne.

She reached Mother Sophia. The guards around the Matriarch were broken heaps on the floor.

The Matriarch held her ceremonial axe, but she was slow. Old. Human.

Caterina didn't even break stride. She grabbed the axe handle mid-swing, wrenching it from her mother's grip with a sound like snapping dry wood. She slammed Mother against the wall, pinning her there with one black-eyed stare.

The silence that fell over the hallway was heavier than the gunfire had been.

"Do you know why I named you Caterina?" Mother gasped, blood trickling from her mouth, staring into the void of the monster she had engineered.

"I don't care," Caterina hissed.

"It means pure. After decades of work, you are my closest genetic match and soul replication."

Caterina raised the axe high. The overhead lights caught the steel blade.

"I said, *I don't care*. Rest in peace, Mother."

The blade fell.

Unity squeezed her eyes shut and looked away. She heard the wet thud. The collective gasp of the remaining clones.

Silence.

Caterina turned. She was drenched in crimson from chest to knees. She held the dripping axe loosely at her side. She stared at her terrified siblings huddled by the stairs. Chiara wasn't among them.

"Mother is dead," Caterina announced. Her voice rang with absolute, terrifying command, echoing off the blood-spattered walls. "Chiara has fled. I am the Matriarch now."

She pointed the axe toward the front door.

"Let them pass."

The sea of clones parted like terrified water.

Jon didn't wait for a second invitation. He abandoned the wheelchair, scooping Unity into his arms. Her legs dangled uselessly as he ran, adrenaline fueling his exhausted muscles. He carried her past the frozen, traumatized guards, over the body of the original Matriarch, and out the front door into the shocking cold of the Virginia night.

He threw her into the passenger seat of the transport van and scrambled behind the wheel, fumbling with the keys. The engine roared to life. Tires screeched on the asphalt as they tore out of the circular driveway, leaving the house of horrors receding in the rearview mirror.

Unity slumped against the dashboard, utterly hollowed out. Every nerve ending felt burned clean.

Mia, she thought, projecting the single word into the immense, dark void.

Unity! Mia's voice came back instantly, frantic, warm, and alive in her skull. *Oh my God, Unity. I felt... the rage. Are you okay?*

We're out, Unity whispered in her mind, watching the tree line blur past. *We're free, Mia.*

Where are you? Give me a landmark.

I don't know. Driving fast. North. But we're safe for now. Caterina... Caterina did it.

Unity closed her eyes, letting the heater blast against her

frozen face. She felt the hum of the engine beneath her and the distant, anchoring presence of her twin sister.

The war wasn't over. It had just escalated wildly. But for the first time in twenty years, her first battle was won.

SecDef

Mia

The Pentagon didn't just smell of floor wax and bureaucracy; it smelled of ancient coffee burned onto glass carafes, high-tension anxiety, and the scent of a thousand laser printers churning out classified secrets.

Mia Peers walked through the E Ring, her heels clicking with a sharp, military cadence on the polished linoleum that went on for miles. Every step sent a calcified jolt up her spine. Beside her, Chris held her hand, his grip tight enough to grind her rings together. He was still furious about the Livia disaster, the lie hidden in their basement, but here, in the heart of the American military machine, he wasn't letting go. Especially since Mia had lost all contact with Unity.

Mia wore a tailored red power suit, aggressive armor designed to hide her newest symptom. She was thirty-eight years old according to her birth certificate, but her cells felt eighty. Her muscles ached with a deep, structural fatigue that bone broth and sheer will couldn't fix. The Syndrome was accelerating, consuming her fuel faster than she could replenish it.

They passed the central courtyard—once Ground Zero for Cold War nuclear targeting, now hosting a banal hotdog stand.

The contrast between normal life and imminent apocalypse made Mia feel nauseous.

"Dr. Peers," a severe-looking aide said, opening a heavy mahogany door that looked bulletproof. "The Secretary will see you now."

Secretary of Defense Jack Asher sat at the head of an ebony conference table that probably cost more than Mia's entire graduate education. He was balding, aggressively overweight, and wore a ridiculous blue bowtie that made him look like a cranky physics professor rather than a man who commanded fleets.

"Sit," Asher said, not looking up from his secure tablet. His voice was a gravelly rumble. "Leave the phones in the box by the door."

Mia and Chris sat. The leather chairs were cold. The room was lined with moody oil paintings of 19th-century naval battles—ships burning on dark seas.

"Mr. Secretary," Mia said, fighting to keep the impatience out of her voice. "We were told this was urgent."

"It is." Asher finally glanced up. His eyes, usually magnified by reading glasses, were hard little flint stones. "We've found more bunkers. Intel is lighting up like a Christmas tree. Mexico. Southern Canada. The Midwest cell has gone active."

He gestured with a meaty hand to a wall-sized screen. A map of North America appeared, speckled with angry red markers.

"They're mobilizing," Asher said. "Not hiding. Moving. We think they're preparing for a coordinated strike. Or a mass exodus."

"Why tell us?" Chris asked, leaning forward, his lawyer mode engaging despite the tension. "We're not soldiers."

"Because you're the target, Mr. Holden. And frankly, I'm tired of your wife playing games with my security clearance." Asher glared at Mia, a look that withered generals. "Where is Livia?"

Mia kept her face perfectly still, though her insides were

churning. "She escaped," she said smoothly. "During the attack on the lab. We haven't seen her."

"Fantastic. A rogue supervillain roaming the countryside too." Asher held her gaze, then tapped the table. "We'll circle back to that. Look at this."

The screen changed. Satellite imagery, grainy and gray. A convoy of black SUVs and a single, nondescript tan van speeding away from a large estate tucked into the Virginia woods.

"Two days ago," Asher said. "Forensics confirms your sister, Unity, was in that tan van. Along with Jonathan Turner."

Mia's heart skipped a beat, then double-timed. Unity. She hadn't heard from her sister in the forty-eight hours since escaping. Mia had been airborne for hours ready for a rescue that never happened. The psychic silence was deafening, a void that terrified her more than Asher's sarcasm about Livia.

"Where did they go?" Mia whispered, leaning toward the screen as if she could see through the grain.

"We lost them. They scattered, switched vehicles under an overpass. Professional tradecraft. But we think they're heading for a port. They're probably trying to leave the country before we lock down the eastern seaboard."

The heavy mahogany door burst open. The aide rushed in, her face pale.

"Sir! You need to see this. It's CNN."

Asher swore, an inventive string of profanity. He grabbed a remote and flicked on the wall monitor, overlaying the map.

The screen filled with the breaking news banner, red and urgent. A woman sat in an undisclosed location, staring directly into the camera with patrician poise. She looked exactly like Sophia.

"My message to the United States is simple," Chiara said, her Italian accent sharp and clipped. "You are in danger. Dr. Mia Peers has betrayed you. She gave her volatile, weaponized serum to two of my sisters."

Mia stiffened, her fingernails digging into her palms.

"Their names are Caterina and Livia," Chiara continued, her face a mask of tragic resolve. "They are rogue. They are enhanced and dangerous. One has killed our mother and many of our innocent siblings in a fit of serum-induced rage. We are not with them. We are victims."

Mia stared at Chris, shock washing over her. *The Matriarch is dead?* The chessboard had just been overturned.

"We are leaving," Chiara said smoothly to the world. "We do not want war. We mourn our dead. Do not try to stop us. But be warned: Caterina and Livia are loose. They are monsters Dr. Peers created. And she is *your* problem now."

The feed cut to a stunned news anchor.

Absolute, suffocating silence filled the conference room.

"She's lying," Mia whispered, the words feeling inadequate.

"Which part?" Asher asked, his voice terrifyingly quiet. "The part about the rogue super-soldiers you unleashed on my country? The part about you giving them the serum?"

"I didn't give them anything! Sophia took some from my original lab, plus another vial when she tried to kill me at my house."

"It doesn't matter how they got it," Asher snapped, slamming his hand on the table. "It matters that there are enhanced, psychotic clones loose on American soil. And you're the reason."

He stood up, looming over the table. "I have to brief the President that we have not one but two potential superhuman domestic terrorists. Get out of my building, Dr. Peers. Take your husband and go back to your lab. And if you have any more secrets... bury them deep. Because I'm done protecting you. You're on your own."

On the helicopter ride back to the lab, the vibration of the rotors rattling her aching bones, Mia stared out the window at the Virginia landscape passing below in a blur of brown winter trees.

"They have her," Mia said softly, the realization settling like lead in her gut.

"Who?" Chris asked. "Caterina?"

"No. Unity. They have her again. That's why I haven't heard from her. Chiara's broadcast was a cover story. They captured Unity and Jon, and now they're smuggling them out of the country while everyone looks for Caterina and Livia."

"Why announce it on TV? Why draw attention?"

"It's another trap," Mia said, turning from the window. Her eyes were hard. "They want me to follow. They know I won't let them take her to Italy. They're baiting me."

"And Caterina?" Chris asked. "Is she really out there? Enhanced?"

"If Chiara said it, it's probably true, but twisted. Caterina helped Unity and Jon escape. It's all a distraction. A very dangerous loose end they want us to clean up for them."

Mia glanced down at her hands resting on her knees. The skin covering her fingers was drooping like silly puddy. With brute mental force, she willed it back into place.

"We need to evacuate the lab," Mia said suddenly. "Tonight. If I'm wrong about Caterina... she'll come for me. We're sitting ducks in that penthouse."

"Brian won't like packing up his toys," Chris said, though he didn't argue.

"Brian will understand. He's been up close with Sophia and now Livia. Caterina would be the nail in the coffin. He'll be happy to move."

Mia closed her eyes, leaning her head back against the seat. She reached out with her mind, pushing past the pain and the noise, searching desperately for that familiar hum, that golden thread connecting her to her twin.

Unity? Are you there? Please, just a signal. Anything.

Nothing. Just the cold mental static of the void and the physical roar of the helicopter blades.

Mia swallowed the hard lump of terror in her throat. Slowly, protectively, she placed a trembling hand on her flat stomach, feeling the impossible, tiny life growing inside her—a life she might not live long enough to meet.

Hang on, Unity, she thought, projecting the vow into the silence. *Hang on, little one. I'm coming for both of you.*

Rival Godmother

Jon

Jon Turner woke up in hell. Or maybe it was just a basement in suburban Virginia. In the pitch blackness, it was impossible to tell the difference, and the sensory experience was equally miserable.

He was hog-tied on a concrete floor that sucked the heat right out of his body through his thin clothes. His wrists and ankles burned where the coarse nylon rope dug into his skin, cutting off circulation. His mouth was taped shut with heavy-duty duct tape that tasted of adhesive and panic.

He squeezed his eyes shut, trying to piece together the fractured timeline. The escape. The adrenaline. The van speeding down the dark highway. Unity slumped in the passenger seat beside him, exhausted but free for the first time in twenty years. They had made it five miles. Maybe six.

Then the lights in the rearview mirror. The PIT maneuver that spun them off the road. The swarm of black, unmarked SUVs.

Mother Sophia might be dead, her head separated from her body by her own daughter, but her contingency plans were autonomous mechanisms, grinding forward without her.

Jon groaned, the sound muffled to a pathetic whimper by the

tape. His stomach cramped violently with hunger. How long had he been down here in the dark? Two days? Three? Time had lost all meaning, measured only by the cycles of shivering and the throbbing pain in his extremities.

A metal bolt slid back. The door creaked open with a groan of rusty hinges.

Light, blinding and sudden, flooded the room. Jon squeezed his eyes shut, tears streaming down his face at the assault.

Two shadows stepped into the light. They wore dark, ill-fitting suits. As his eyes adjusted, he saw their faces. Identical. Cesaro clones.

They didn't speak. They didn't need to. One of them produced a knife and cut the ropes around his ankles with practiced efficiency. The other reached down and ripped the duct tape from his face, taking a layer of skin and several days of stubble with it. Jon gasped, the air rushing into his dry throat.

"Get up," one of the clones said, his voice flat and devoid of inflection.

Jon tried to stand, but his legs, deprived of blood for days, were useless jelly. They buckled instantly. The clones didn't hesitate. They hauled him up by his armpits, dragging him out of the cell and down a long hallway.

They dumped him unceremoniously into a bedroom. It was furnished with bland, generic furniture, brightly lit, and scrupulously clean. A woman sat in an armchair by the window, calmly scrolling through her phone.

Jon blinked, his brain misfiring. It was Sophia.

No. Sophia was dead.

"Chiara," Jon croaked, his voice wrecked from dehydration. He sat up, rubbing his chafed wrists, trying to get blood flowing again.

"Please," she said without looking up from her screen, her voice cool and composed. "Show some respect. I am the Godmother now. Mother Sophia is... indisposed."

Jon sat on the edge of the bed, the room spinning slowly. "Where is Unity?"

"She's safe. Secure. Sedated for transport." Chiara finally looked up. Her dark eyes were cold, utterly devoid of the manic, theatrical energy that had fueled Mother Sophia. This was a different kind of evil. Pragmatic. Calculated. Efficient. "She was... disruptive when she woke up."

"And Caterina?" Jon asked, dreading the answer.

Chiara's lip curled in disgust. "She thinks she's a goddess now. But she's just another rogue element. Another Livia waiting to happen."

"You escaped her."

"She is not my problem now." Chiara stood up, smoothing the wrinkles from her designer skirt. "We are leaving, Jon. The family is returning home to Italy. We are done with this messy American experiment."

"Good luck," Jon said, finding a scrap of defiance. "I'm not going with you."

Chiara smiled, a slow, humorless curving of her lips. She held up her phone, turning the screen toward him.

It was a live video feed. A suburban street. A woman with curly dark hair was walking out of a grocery store in Baltimore, carrying two reusable bags. She was laughing at something on her cell phone, completely unaware she was being watched.

Zuri. Jon's baby sister.

The air left the room.

"You remember Zuri, don't you?" Chiara asked softly. "She looks happy. Ignorant. Safe."

Jon lunged, a pathetic, desperate movement. The two male clones stepped forward instantly, blocking his path, the cold metal of their gun barrels pressing hard into his chest.

"Touch me, and the order goes out," Chiara said, her voice bored. "We have a team on her. 24/7 surveillance. As long as you cooperate, Jon, she lives her happy little life. You step out of line, you try to be a hero... and she has an unfortunate accident. A car crash. A mugging gone wrong. Just like your parents."

Jon slumped back onto the bed, defeated, the fight draining out of him like water from a cracked glass. They had found the one lever he couldn't resist.

"What do you want?" he whispered.

"I want you to do your job," Chiara said, tucking the phone away. "We're taking Unity with us. You're going to keep her healthy during the transport. You're going to keep her calm. And most importantly... you're going to make sure she doesn't use any more of her little magic tricks. You're the only one she trusts. You control her."

Jon looked at her. He saw the cold calculation in her eyes, the arrogance of power. But underneath it, he saw something else, something that gave him a tiny flicker of hope.

Fear.

Chiara was terrified. She was young, she was new to the throne, and her empire was crumbling. She was running away back to the old country because she knew she couldn't win a war on two fronts against Mia and Caterina. She needed Unity as a bargaining chip, a nuclear deterrent. And she needed Jon to control the weapon she didn't understand and was secretly afraid of.

"I understand," Jon said slowly, lowering his eyes in feigned submission.

"Good." Chiara checked her watch and signaled the guards. "Clean yourself up. There are clothes in the closet. We leave for the airstrip as soon as the airplane can be readied."

She walked out without looking back, the guards following close behind. The heavy door locked with a resounding, final thud.

Jon went to the en suite bathroom and turned on the cold water, splashing it onto his burning face. He looked at himself in the mirror. Bruised. Battered. Trapped again.

But not broken. Not yet.

Chiara had made a critical tactical error. She thought fear was a leash that would hold him forever. She didn't realize that when you take everything from a man—his freedom, his dignity, his hope—you leave him with nothing to lose.

She was taking them to Italy. To the heart of the Romano power structure. Fine. That just meant the battlefield was moving to enemy territory.

Jon dried his face with a plush towel. He would put on the clean clothes. He would play the part of the beaten dog. He would protect Unity with his life. He would hope for Mia or Caterina to find them. And he would watch for the cracks in Chiara's armor.

And when the moment came... he would burn the Romano empire to the ground, even if he had to die in the flames.

Consent

Brian

T he bunker, buried beneath a nondescript horse farm in rural Virginia, was less of a government safehouse and more of a buried Ritz-Carlton. The air, filtered through military-grade scrubbers, smelled faintly of expensive cedarwood.

Brian Carter stood in the plush, thickly carpeted hallway, wiggling his toes against the familiar foam of his Crocs. He still wore thick wool socks underneath, a practical concession to the bitter Virginia winter raging above ground, but he refused to give up the shoes. They were his anchor, a bright, absurd touchstone of normalcy in a world that was rapidly sliding off its axis into a sci-fi horror movie.

The facility was obscene in its luxury. Ten bedrooms with attached baths, a gourmet kitchen stocked with stainless steel appliances, and enough dark mahogany furniture to furnish the West Wing of the White House. Major Washington claimed his Sentry Blade unit used it for "high-value asset protection scenarios," which Brian found highly suspect. The only scenario that warranted this level of opulence and isolation was the end of the world.

And judging by the data pulsing through Mia's bio-monitors,

the end was arriving ahead of schedule.

Brian headed into the makeshift lab he had set up in the largest spare room. The original four-poster bed had been dismantled to give him more space. Roger and Cynthia were already there, their faces lit by the cool blue glow of monitors, unpacking crates of salvaged Romano technology with hushed reverence.

The modified stasis pods sat in the center of the Persian rug, gleaming chrome sarcophaguses stripped of their insulated outer shells, their internal workings exposed like disemboweled robots. Wires and fiber optic cables snaked out of them like black veins, connecting to banks of servers and analyzers.

Brian ran a hand over the cold, polished metal. The probability of success for the consciousness transfer protocol was currently hovering at seventy-eight percent. A solid C-plus. Passing, but with a twenty-two percent margin for catastrophic brain death. He hated those odds.

"Hey, brother!"

Brian jumped, his heart rate spiking. Tony, the squad's chameleon, stood in the doorway. He was striking an exaggerated bodybuilder pose, flexing muscles that strained the seams of his black t-shirt, all while holding a delicate IV bag of saline solution.

"Where should I put this?" Tony asked, his voice dropping into a gravelly, theatrical roar that sounded like a chainsaw gargling rocks. "Whatcha gonna do when Hulkamania runs wild on you, brother?"

Brian blinked, his brain momentarily short-circuiting. He pointed vaguely to the corner. "Um. By the incubator units. Please."

"You got it! Say your prayers and take your vitamins!" Tony stomped over to the corner, flexing his biceps with every step, the floorboards groaning under his boots.

Peyton walked past the doorway a second later, carrying two heavy tactical duffel bags over her shoulders with practiced ease. She rolled her eyes at Tony's back. "Ignore him. Thunder Lips is extra edgy today. We're expecting a call from Command. Possible deployment."

"Thunder Lips?" Brian asked, horrified.

"Don't ask. It's a *Rocky* thing."

Brian turned back to his equipment, shaking his head. He had managed to synthesize a nutrient fluid that could work as a medium for both the adult stasis pods and the smaller, coffin-sized incubator units in the corner. Not that he needed the incubators—he wasn't planning on growing any clones—but redundancy was good engineering practice. You never knew when you might need a spare womb.

He checked his watch—a durable Casio, not a smartwatch that could be hacked. The doctor was late.

Dr. Anthony Fitzpatrick was one of the world's leading neurosurgeons, a man whose hands were insured for more than the GDP of some small nations. Getting him here, to a black site in the middle of nowhere, had required a significant chunk of Mia's dwindling fortune and a watertight NDA that threatened life in prison for any breach. But he was the only one Brian trusted to drill a hole in his skull and insert untested technology.

Brian hadn't told Roger or Cynthia the full extent of the plan. They thought he was building a better external interface, a way to translate the Romano neural code. They didn't know he was building a bridge.

A bridge between two souls—Mia's and Unity's. And he was going to be the pylon, the grounding wire that kept the current from burning them both out.

He walked out to the main living area, the thick carpet swallowing the sound of his Crocs. Mia sat on a velvet ottoman in front of the cold fireplace, her legs crossed, eyes closed in deep concentration. She wasn't meditating. She was holding herself together through sheer force of will.

Her skin looked loose, almost ill-fitting, like it was slowly detaching from the muscle underneath. A tremor ran through her body every few seconds, a visible seismic ripple of cellular failure that made her shoulders twitch.

She was dying. Her clone body was failing. The Syndrome was ten feet from the finish line.

Brian felt a sharp pang of sadness, a muted ache in his chest that he usually managed to suppress with logic. He wasn't good with emotions—they were inefficient variables—but he knew what loss felt like. He had lost Bianca to her own duplicity (correction, *almost* lost Bianca). He grinned at his latest secret. He wasn't going to lose Mia to bad biology. Considering Mia again, his grin disappeared as quickly as it had arrived.

Lethabo walked in from the garage entrance, shaking snow off his jacket, phone to his ear.

"Hey, Brian," the major said, lowering the phone. "Your visitors are at the checkpoint. They brought a lot of gear. It's taking a minute to sanitize everything."

"Thanks."

Ten minutes later, the heavy blast doors rolled open with a hydraulic hiss. A black SUV pulled into the underground bay. Dr. Fitzpatrick stepped out, looking calm and professional in a tailored wool coat, followed by three assistants carrying sleek, hard-sided medical cases.

The surgeon was taller than he looked on TV, with perfectly coiffed salt-and-pepper hair and eyes that seemed to x-ray everything they looked at, assessing structural integrity.

"Mr. Carter," Fitzpatrick said, his voice a smooth baritone, shaking Brian's hand. His grip was firm, precise, not a wasted nanogram of pressure. "Are you ready? Did you fast for twelve hours as instructed?"

"Yes, sir."

"And Dr. Peers? Does she know the specifics yet?"

"She trusts me," Brian said evasively, leading them toward the living area. "She doesn't need the engineering details just yet. She has enough on her plate."

"That's a dangerous game, son. Informed consent is a pillar of medicine. But it's your head."

They walked into the main room just as Mia and Chris were heading for the exit, bundled in winter gear. Lethabo and the squad were loading Pelican cases into a heavily armored Humvee, moving with urgent, silent speed.

"Mia!" Lethabo shouted over the engine noise. "Wheels up in ten! We have a thermal window on the target area."

"I'm coming," Mia said, adjusting her scarf. She stopped dead when she saw the entourage emerge from the hallway. Her jaw dropped slightly.

"Dr. Fitzpatrick?" she asked, her voice hoarse. She turned to Brian, her eyes narrowing with suspicion. "Brian, what is the chief of neurosurgery from Johns Hopkins doing in our secret bunker?"

Brian flinched, adjusting his glasses nervously. "He's... consulting. On the interface project."

"Consulting on what, exactly?" Mia crossed her arms, her gaze darting between them. The left side of her face sagged slightly, a terrifying reminder of the creeping paralysis of the Syndrome. "Brian, why is a man who charges fifty thousand dollars just to look at an MRI in my safehouse right now?"

Fitzpatrick stepped forward smoothly, smiling warmly. "It's an honor, Dr. Peers. I've followed your work for years. Big fan. And to answer your question... I'm here to install the hardware you paid for."

Mia stared at Brian, confusion warring with dread on her face. "Install it where? We don't have a subject."

Brian took a deep breath and pointed a trembling finger to his own temple.

Mia's face went deathly pale. "No. Absolutely not. You are not serious."

"It's the only way, Mia," Brian said, his voice flat, trying to sound rational. "The Romano interface is organic. It learns from experience. We can't just code a translator for it. We have to live it."

"You're not putting that thing in your brain," Mia snapped, her voice rising.

"This is necessary if you want to save yourself and Unity. I'll just be the buffer."

"It's too dangerous! The probability of rejection is huge!"

"So is dying," Dr. Fitzpatrick interjected gently. "Dr. Peers, Brian explained the situation. The Syndrome is accelerating rapidly. If we don't do this, you won't last the week. And neither will Unity, from what Brian tells me. You need to focus on rescuing your sister."

Mia glanced at the doctor, then back at Brian. Tears welled in her eyes, spilling over and pooling in the loose skin beneath her lashes.

"I can't let you do this," she whispered, reaching out to touch his arm. "Brian, please. I have enough blood on my hands already. Don't add yours."

"This isn't your choice," Brian said gently, covering her hand with his. "You saved me, Mia. When Sophia... when everything fell apart. Let me save you. Just promise me you'll get Unity back. She's the backup plan. I'll handle the rest."

"Mia!" Lethabo yelled from the garage doorway. "We have to go! Now!"

Mia wiped her face angrily with her sleeve. She stepped forward and grabbed Brian's face in both hands, resting her forehead against his. He could feel the tremor running through her.

"You stubborn, brilliant, reckless idiot," she choked out. "Be careful. Please don't die on me."

"I'm always careful," Brian lied. "I'm a minimalist. Only necessary risks."

Mia let him go with a shuddering breath and ran for the garage door. Lethabo ushered her into the back of the Humvee, and the armored vehicle roared away into the night.

Brian watched them go until the blast doors sealed again. He turned to Chris, who was standing by the couch, looking utterly lost and terrified.

"Come with me," Brian said.

Chris blinked, startled. "Where?"

"To my room. You need to see this." Brian gestured for the doctor and his team to follow him down the hall. "Mia is keeping secrets because she's trying to protect you from the ugliness of it all. But you're part of this equation, Chris. You're the constant. If we're going to fix Jeffrey's mistake and save your wife, I need you to understand exactly what we're doing."

Chris nodded slowly, swallowing hard. "Okay. Show me."

Brian led them into the brightly lit bedroom-turned-lab. One of the modified stasis pods gleamed under the surgical lamps.

"It's going to take about thirty minutes to prep," Dr. Fitzpatrick said, snapping on latex gloves with a sharp *thwack*. "Brian, take a seat in the chair. Let's get you hooked up."

Brian climbed into the cold metal chair. He felt suddenly, overwhelmingly tired. He hated explaining things. He hated emotions. He hated being the center of attention. But as the anesthesia mask was lowered over his face, smelling sickly sweet, he felt a strange, profound sense of peace settle over him.

He was finally fixing something that mattered.

He closed his eyes and let the darkness take him.

Family Intervention

Lethabo

The red brick mansion sat in the middle of the desolate West Virginia field like a malignancy. It was an architectural tumor, vastly out of place among the scrub brush and frozen dirt, guarded by ostentatious Roman columns that belonged in another century. A heavy, suffocating silence hung around it, a silence that felt thick and wrong, amplifying the sound of the wind rattling the dry stalks of dead corn.

Major Washington sat in the driver's seat of the tactical SUV, the engine idling quietly, vibrating through the soles of his boots. The cold of the window glass seeped through his gloves as he pressed binoculars to his eyes, scanning the house. It was dark, imposing, a fortress pretending to be a home.

In the back seat, the metallic *click-clack* of a weapon being disassembled filled the tense silence. Mia Peers was field-stripping a Sig Sauer P226 for the eleventh time in as many minutes.

Lethabo glanced in the rearview mirror. She was a wreck, a walking bundle of nerves and decay. She shook so violently that she kept dropping the slide release, fumbling with the small parts. Her skin was pasty, white in the fading winter light, loose around her jawline. The Syndrome was eating her alive from the inside out, but her eyes were two burning coals of pure, terrifying focus.

"Stop fidgeting with the hardware, Doctor," Lethabo muttered, keeping his eyes on the house. "You're going to lose a spring."

"Then stop telling me to wait, *Major*," Mia snapped, her voice tight. She slammed the magazine back into the weapon with unnecessary force. "She's in there. I can feel it. The connection is weak, like static, but it's there."

"Feeling isn't intel. We wait for confirmation."

"Alpha Leader," Kristin's voice crackled over the encrypted comms, sharp and clear. "Drone scanner confirms twenty-four distinct heat signatures spread throughout the ground and second floors. Plus a massive energy shield masking the basement level. It's a fortress, boss."

Lethabo sighed, his breath steaming in the cold cabin. He had a hundred National Guard troops shivering in the tree line half a mile back, itching for a fight they didn't understand. He had his elite Sentry Blade squad deployed in hide sites. And he had an enhanced, unstable scientist in his back seat who looked like she was about to melt into a puddle of goo before the first shot was fired.

And he had a profound bad feeling settling in his gut, a weight that had nothing to do with his tactical vest.

"Eyes on the target," he said softly into the mic. "Movement on the porch. Nine o'clock."

A heavy wooden door cracked open. A man stepped out into the twilight. He was Black, middle-aged, hunched inside a heavy wool coat. He looked up at the leaden sky for a moment, then nodded once, sharply, as if signaling someone in the distance.

"That's Jon," Mia said, leaning forward, pressing her face against the glass. "He's alive. He's signaling us."

"Or he's signaling a sniper on the roof," Lethabo said grimly.

"Stay down. Don't present a target."

"Alpha Three," Tony's voice came over the comms, his attempt at a Jim Carrey impression grating on Lethabo's last nerve. "Alrighty then. We got a bogey. Twelve o'clock high. Coming in hot."

Lethabo looked up from the binoculars. A dark, human-shaped object plummeted from the clouds, dropping straight down toward the house like a meteor, no parachute, no slowing.

BOOM.

The figure slammed into the frozen earth of the field between the SUV and the house with concussive force. The ground shook, rattling the SUV's frame. A cloud of frozen dirt and ice crystals billowed up.

As the dust settled, a figure stood up from the impact crater, shaking debris from her shoulders. She wore black tactical gear. A Romano.

"Caterina," Mia whispered, her breath fogging the glass.

"Hold fire!" Lethabo shouted into the radio, his voice echoing in his helmet. "Do not engage that target! I repeat, hold fire!"

Caterina turned slowly, scanning the field. She spotted the SUV and grinned, a terrifying baring of teeth. Then, without hesitation, she spun around and sprinted straight for the mansion, moving faster than any human.

"She's going in," Mia said. The SUV door flew open before Lethabo could stop her.

"Mia, wait! Stay in the vehicle!"

Mia was already running, her boots pounding the frozen ground. She was moving with a desperate, impossible speed that belied her trembling limbs, a blur against the dead grass.

"Damn it," Lethabo growled, slamming his fist on the steering wheel. "Alpha Squad, move up! Support fire only! Bravo Leader, hold position until my mark."

He grabbed his rifle, bailed out of the SUV, and started

sprinting after the scientist. His helmet HUD flared to life, painting green biometric tags over his team's positions in the tall grass.

Caterina reached the porch in seconds. She didn't bother with the handle. She hit the heavy front door at full speed, and it exploded inward in a shower of wood splinters and twisted metal.

Immediately, gunfire erupted from inside the house—the sharp crack of pistols, the deeper thud of rifles. Muzzle flashes lit up the darkened windows. Caterina took a hit to the chest, stumbling back a step, grunting, before racing inside.

Then a second figure appeared from the smoke-filled doorway. A woman with only one arm.

Livia.

"She's here," Lethabo breathed, skidding to a halt behind a stone garden gnome, sighting his rifle.

Livia raised a customized assault rifle with her single hand, bracing it against her hip, and opened fire with terrifying precision. She wasn't aiming at the approaching soldiers. She was pouring fire into the hallway where Caterina had just disappeared.

"Civil war," Lethabo realized, his mind racing to adjust tactics. "They're killing each other. It's a purge."

Scores of male clones—Cesaro copies in identical black uniforms—poured out of the house behind Livia, spreading out on the porch and lawn, firing wildly into the field.

"Sssssmokin'!" Tony yelled over the comms, opening fire from the flank, his machine gun chewing up the porch railing.

"Tony, shut up and just shoot!" Lethabo screamed, returning fire.

The field dissolved into chaos. Bullets zipped past, kicking up dirt. Mia reached the fray, ignoring the gunfire. She didn't have a weapon drawn, but she hit Livia like a freight train, tackling the one-armed clone off the porch and driving her into the frozen dirt.

"Alpha Five, report status!" Lethabo yelled, sprinting toward the melee.

"She's hostile!" Mia's voice crackled over the comms, breathless, grunting with effort. "Livia is protecting the house! She's with Chiara!"

Caterina burst back out onto the porch, fighting three male clones simultaneously with her bare hands. She moved like liquid violence. She snapped a neck with a sickening crunch, kicked a knee backward until it shattered, and grabbed the third man by the throat, lifting him off his feet.

"I let Unity out of her cell!" Caterina shouted over the noise of battle, tossing the man aside like refuse. Her voice bled through Mia's open mic. "I'm here for a family intervention!"

Livia threw Mia off with inhuman strength, scrambling to her feet. She was covered in dirt and blood, raising her rifle at Mia.

Lethabo dropped to a knee and fired three controlled rounds. His bullets caught Livia in the neck and chest. She stumbled, gargling blood, dropping her weapon. But she didn't go down. The wounds began to close immediately, skin knitting back together in seconds.

"Invincible," Lethabo muttered, a cold dread washing over him. "They're freaking invincible."

"Go around back!" Caterina yelled to Mia, grabbing a dropped rifle. "Unity is on the top floor, east wing! I'll hold Livia off!"

Mia nodded once, but stood there as if paralyzed with indecision.

"I'm hit!" Peyton's voice screamed over the comms, tight with pain. "Leg! Femoral artery! I'm down, Major!"

Lethabo's heart hammered. "Kristin, pop smoke and cover her! Get a tourniquet on that! Bravo Leader! Green light! Get your people in here now!"

The tree line erupted as a hundred National Guard soldiers charged the field, a wave of green and gray moving toward the house.

Lethabo reloaded his rifle.

The only thing standing between victory and a total massacre was a dying scientist trying to save her sister, and a rogue clone trying to uproot the family tree.

Reunion

Mia

The front lawn was a killing field, a tableau of snow and blood illuminated by the strobe light of muzzle flashes.

Mia Peers stood frozen for a heartbeat, her breath catching in a throat raw with cold air. She watched as Livia and Caterina became a blur of violence—two enhanced sisters tearing each other apart in a proxy war for a dead mother. Livia, despite the grotesque absence of her left arm, moved with a feral, unpredictable speed, her body a weapon honed by rage. She fired her rifle in short, controlled bursts, the brass casings arcing through the air like sparks. Caterina absorbed the hits that would have killed a human, her skin knitting back together even as she fought. She used her body as a battering ram, slamming into her sister, the sound of their impact sickeningly wet.

"Go!" Lethabo shouted, grabbing Mia's shoulder and shoving her toward the side of the house. His voice was raw, fighting to be heard over the roar of gunfire. "Get Unity! We'll hold the line!"

Mia didn't hesitate. She couldn't afford to.

She holstered her pistols—her hands were shaking too badly from the accelerating Syndrome to aim effectively anyway.

They were just weight now. She sprinted for the rear of the mansion, her boots slipping on the frozen grass, her breath burning in her lungs.

Her body felt heavy, sluggish, as if she were running through wet cement. The Syndrome was dragging at her muscles, a deep fatigue that pulled her skin down like melting wax. Every step was a battle against her own biology. She focused on the second-story window Caterina had indicated, a beacon in the chaos.

Hold on, Unity. I'm coming. Don't you dare give up.

She rounded the corner of the massive house, the noise of the battle fading slightly. A male clone—another interchangeable Cesaro face—burst out of the back door, leveling a rifle at her chest.

Mia didn't slow down. She couldn't fight him; in this state, she'd lose before she threw the first punch. She had one advantage left: sheer, desperate momentum.

She channeled every ounce of her remaining strength, every drop of adrenaline, into her legs. She didn't stop running. She accelerated.

She leaped.

It was a desperate, enhanced jump that defied gravity. She soared through the air, above the clone by fifteen feet, his rifle tracking too slowly. She smashed through the second-story window in a shower of glass, wood, and torn curtains.

She hit the floor hard, rolling instinctively to absorb the impact, ignoring the shards of glass that sliced into her tac-suit. She scrambled to her feet, pistols drawn again, her heart hammering against her ribs.

The room was dim, lit only by the moonlight filtering through the broken window. In the corner, a figure stood frozen—Jon Turner. He looked terrified, his clothes rumpled, his eyes wide and darting like a cornered rat. He held a medical bag clutched to his chest like a shield.

But Mia only had eyes for the bed.

A figure lay under a white sheet, perfectly still, hands folded over her chest like an effigy. Mia's breath caught.

It was Unity.

She looked peaceful, almost ethereal in the gloom. Her hair, once blonde like Mia's, was short and dyed a severe black, framing a face that was no longer gaunt. The hollows of the twenty-year coma were gone, filled out by months of therapy and proper food, and perhaps by their strange psychic connection. Her skin, even in the low light, glowed with a terrifying health. She didn't look sick. She looked perfect. Too perfect.

Mia rushed to the bedside, falling to her knees. Her tremors were violent now, a full-body seizure that made her teeth chatter uncontrollably. She reached out with a shaking hand and touched Unity's cheek.

The moment skin met skin, the world stopped.

The shaking ceased instantly. A wave of profound, impossible calm washed over Mia, a stabilizing current that flowed from Unity's body into hers. It felt like plugging into a high-voltage charger. The cellular decay, the pain, the exhaustion—it all receded, held at bay by the sheer power emanating from her twin.

Mia let out a sob of relief, slumping against the mattress.

"Jon," Mia rasped, her voice thick with emotion, not looking away from her sister's face. "Wake her up. Now."

"Mia," Jon stammered, stepping out of the shadows. He looked wretched, guilt oozing from every pore. "I... I'm so sorry. For everything. I didn't have a choice."

"Not now," Mia snapped, her voice hard, the scientist taking over. "Do you have a stimulant? Adrenaline? Anything?"

"Yes. Epinephrine. It's in the kit. Standard protocol."

"Get it. Don't talk, just get it."

Jon fumbled with the bag.

Mia kept her hand on Unity's face, anchoring herself to the calm, drawing strength from the connection. Outside, the battle raged. She heard explosions that shook the floor, screams of pain and rage, the relentless, rhythmic *thwack-thwack-thwack* of the National Guard helicopters finally arriving.

"Argh! God!"

Lethabo's scream cut through her earpiece, sharp and sudden. It wasn't a combat shout. It was a sound of pure, agonizing pain.

"Lethabo?" Mia touched her comms, her heart lurching. "Status! Talk to me!"

"Kitchen," Lethabo gasped, his voice tight with shock. "Eye. My eye. Shrapnel."

"Hang on, Alpha Leader! I'm coming!" Tony's voice broke in, the fake Jim Carrey act dropped, replaced by raw panic.

Mia's heart clenched. She couldn't help him. She was the only one who could help Unity. She had to finish this.

Jon held out a syringe. "Here. It's prepped."

Mia snatched it from him. The moment she let go of Unity's skin to take the needle, the tremors returned with a vengeance, violent and punishing. Her knees buckled under the sudden weight of her own body.

Jon caught her. He held her up, his arms trembling, guiding her hand back toward Unity's arm.

"I've got you," he whispered, his voice rough. "I've got you, Mia."

Mia glanced at him then, *really* looked at him. She saw the guilt in his eyes, the weight of years and years of lies. But she also saw the fear, and underneath it, a desperate love for the woman in the bed. He was a traitor, a coward, but he was also the only person who had cared for Unity when Mia couldn't.

"Forgive yourself later," Mia said, her voice steadying as she found the vein in Unity's arm. "Right now, save her."

She plunged the needle in and depressed the plunger,

emptying the stimulant into Unity's system.

"Come on, U," she whispered, leaning close. "Come back to me. It's time."

For a second, nothing happened. The room held its breath.

Then, Unity's eyes snapped open.

It wasn't a waking. It was a detonation.

A shockwave of invisible, raw force blasted outward from the bed. The remaining glass in the windows shattered outwards. The heavy oak dresser was lifted and slammed against the far wall. Mia and Jon were thrown backward violently, skidding across the carpeted floor.

Mia scrambled up onto her hands and knees, gasping, staring at the bed.

Unity sat up. She didn't move like a coma patient; she rose with fluid, terrifying grace. Her eyes were glowing—not with light, but with raw, uncontained psionic power that distorted the air around her.

She stared at Mia, and for a terrifying second, she didn't look like a sister. She didn't look human. She looked like a god waking from a long slumber, and she was furious.

Mia, Unity's voice echoed inside Mia's skull, deafeningly loud, drowning out the battle outside. *You came.*

Commands

Unity

The world was a nauseating blur of noise and violence, a sensory overload that assaulted Unity from every angle.

She lay cradled in Mia's arms, her body a dead weight, bouncing jarringly with every step as her sister sprinted through the darkened, smoke-filled house. Her head lolled against Mia's chest, her ear pressed over her sister's heart, which was hammering a frantic, terrified rhythm. The epinephrine injection Jon had administered was coursing through her veins, waking her mind with the force of a chemical slap, but of course it hadn't fixed her legs. Nothing could fix them. They dangled uselessly, and always would.

She was a passenger in her own rescue, baggage being hauled through a warzone.

But her mind... her mind was awake.

It felt like she had plugged her consciousness directly into a high-voltage line. The air didn't just smell of cordite and blood; it crackled with raw, uncontained intent. She could feel the psychic footprints of the soldiers outside, their fear a sharp needle prick, their aggression a low, throbbing bass note painting the night in jagged strokes of red and blue on the canvas of her mind. It was overwhelming, a cacophony of other people's emotions threatening to drown out her own.

"Keep my body in front," Unity commanded, the thought slamming into Mia's brain with the force of a physical shove.

"I'm not using you as a shield, not even for my child!" Mia shouted aloud, her voice raw over the roar of gunfire from the yard.

DO IT, Unity projected. It wasn't a request. It was a compulsion, a psychic override of her sister's motor functions.

Mia's spine straightened involuntarily. Against her will, she shifted Unity's weight, angling her sister's body forward so that Unity was leading, her chest a shield for Mia's core. Mia's eyes went wide with shock at the loss of control, but her body obeyed the silent command.

They burst out the back door into the chaotic freezer of the yard.

Flashes of automatic weapon fire lit up the night. Bodies littered the frozen grass—clones in plain clothes and soldiers in tactical gear tangled in death. The air was thick with smoke and the screams of the dying.

Behind them, Tony carried Lethabo, whose face was a ruin of blood. Jon brought up the rear, stumbling, looking like he was about to vomit from the sheer terror of it all.

"I can see them," Unity whispered in Mia's mind, the connection clearer now than speech. "The red shapes. The ones burning with hate. Those are the enemies."

Mia nodded, her face grim, sweat freezing on her brow. "Guide me. Tell me where to go."

Unity closed her physical eyes. The battlefield resolved in her mind into a thermal heatmap of intent. Friendly forces were cool, steady blue. Hostiles were burning, chaotic red.

A red shape lunged from the shadows to their left, a clone with a knife.

SLEEP, Unity thought, focusing her will like a laser, pouring all her fear and new-found power into the single command.

The clone collapsed mid-stride as if his strings had been cut, hitting the dirt with a heavy thud, unconscious before he landed.

It was intoxicating. For twenty years, Unity had been the ultimate victim, helpless and silent in a bed. Now, she was a god, dispensing consciousness with a thought.

Two more red shapes appeared on the right, raising rifles.

Left is friendly, Mia thought frantically. *Right is foe. Take him down.*

Unity separated the mental signatures. She pushed against the hostile consciousnesses, a psychic shove. *SLEEP.*

The clone fell, his weapon clattering on the frozen ground.

Gunshots cracked behind them. Jon was firing his pistol wildly, his hands shaking so badly he was more likely to hit a tree than a target. Unity felt a sharp pang of sadness for him. He was a healer at heart, a man who read Dickens, not a killer.

But tonight, everyone was a killer.

"Contact front!" Tony yelled, his voice ragged.

A male clone stepped out from behind a large oak tree directly in their path. He raised a military-grade rifle, sighting in on Mia.

Unity reached for his mind, commanding him to *SLEEP.*

He resisted.

His mind wasn't open like the others. It was a fortress, shielded by intense training or perhaps just sheer fanaticism. The command bounced off his mental armor. He didn't waver. He raised the weapon, the barrel steady, aiming at Mia's chest.

He's going to shoot, Mia thought, raw panic spiking through the link.

Unity felt the threat like a physical blow. Panic flared hot and bright in her own mind, burning away the restraint. She didn't want to just stop him anymore. She wanted to end him.

DIE! she screamed in her mind, a psychic shriek of pure, unfiltered rage.

She pushed with everything she had, pouring every ounce of

her twenty years of isolation and anger into the attack.

The clone's head exploded.

It wasn't a metaphor. The psychic pressure was too great for the physical structure of his brain to contain. His skull detonated from the inside out in a grotesque spray of bone and mist. His body crumpled backward, headless.

Unity gagged, the psychic backlash hitting her hard. She buried her face in Mia's shoulder, trembling. *I didn't mean to... I just wanted him to stop...*

Get used to it, Mia projected back fiercely. Her mental voice was a cool, steadying blanket over Unity's panic. *We survive. That's the only rule tonight. Don't apologize.*

They kept moving, stepping over the body. The extraction point was close now. Unity could feel the rhythmic *thump-thump-thump* of the heavy lift helicopter rotors vibrating in her teeth.

A figure emerged from the smoke ahead, illuminated by the chopper's searchlight. Covered in blood from head to toe. Holding a woodsman's axe.

Mia raised her pistol.

"Friend or foe?" Mia asked aloud, her voice tight with exhaustion.

Unity opened her eyes. The figure was Caterina. She looked like a nightmare, her clothes shredded, her skin slick with gore. But her mind... her mind was clear. The red rage was gone, replaced by cold determination.

"Friend," Unity said, the word heavy.

"How can you be sure?"

"Because I *know*."

Caterina saw them emerge from the smoke. She immediately dropped the axe and raised her blood-streaked hands in surrender.

"Don't shoot!" she shouted over the rotor noise. "I'm with you! Don't shoot!"

"Hold fire!" Tony yelled to the advancing soldiers. "She's with us!"

Soldiers swarmed them, forming a protective ring of rifles. Medics rushed to take Lethabo from Tony. Someone tried to take Unity from Mia's arms, but Mia snarled like a wounded animal and refused to let go.

"I've got her," Mia snapped. "Back off."

They reached the helicopter, the massive bird squatting in the field. The wash from the rotors was immense, whipping Unity's short hair across her face, stinging her eyes with ice crystals. They scrambled inside the troop compartment, strapping in as the bird lifted off with a lurch.

We did it, Mia thought, tears streaming down her grimy face. *We're out. We're free.*

Unity looked at her sister in the dim red light of the cabin. She saw the gray pallor of Mia's skin beneath the dirt, the way her muscles sagged with exhaustion when she wasn't focused.

We're not safe, Unity projected back, her voice somber in Mia's head. *I can feel you fading, Mia. The connection... it's weak. Your light is dimming. You're dying.*

Mia nodded slowly. *I know. I used to win at everything. Now I'm failing. But we have a plan. There's someone you need to meet.*

Who?

Brian. He's... brilliant. And crazy. He thinks he can save us. But we have to hurry.

Unity leaned her head back against the seat, exhaustion dragging her down into the darkness. Even still, she held onto Mia's hand like a lifeline.

Then let's go, Unity thought, closing her eyes. *Before we both disappear.*

For All to Hear

Mia

Mia carried Unity through the heavy blast doors of the bunker, her arms trembling with exhaustion. She refused to let go. Skin-to-skin contact was the only thing keeping the Syndrome at bay, a fragile circuit that held her dissolving biology together. The moment she broke that connection, she knew the tremors would return, the weakness would spread, and she would begin to melt.

Chris stood in the foyer, arms crossed tight over his chest as if holding himself together. He looked wrecked. His face was drawn, his eyes red-rimmed and shadowed with sleeplessness and worry. He watched them approach, his gaze fixing on the bundle in Mia's arms.

He saw Unity—frail, impossibly small, her hair dyed black that contrasted sharply with her pale skin. Yet, even in exhaustion, she was glowing with a strange, internal vitality, a psychic resonance that seemed to vibrate in the air around her.

Chris's expression softened, the anger and fear bleeding out of him, leaving only relief.

"You got her," he whispered, his voice thick.

"I got her," Mia said, her voice trembling not just from physical strain but from the sheer emotional weight of the moment. She stopped in front of him, shifting Unity's weight. "Chris... I'm so sorry. For everything. For the lies."

Chris didn't smile, but he stepped forward, closing the distance. He leaned in and kissed Mia's forehead, his lips cool against her feverish skin. "We'll talk later. Get her inside. You look like you're about to collapse."

Mia carried Unity past him into the expansive main living area. The Persian rugs muted her footsteps. Brian was waiting by the fireplace. He wore a fresh lab coat over his pajamas. A small, neat square bandage sat on his left temple, covering the fresh surgical site. He was smiling—a genuine, uncharacteristically bright smile that reached his intense eyes. It made Mia deeply nervous.

Dr. Fitzpatrick stood by the hearth, looking grave and out of place in his expensive suit. And in the far corner, shifting her weight from foot to foot like a cornered cat, was a young woman with dark, curly hair and a terrifyingly familiar face.

Bianca.

Mia stiffened, her grip on Unity tightening involuntarily. The traitor. The Mafia operative. "What the hell is she doing here?"

"I found her," Brian said.

His lips didn't move.

The voice didn't travel through the air. It echoed directly inside Mia's skull, clear and resonant, bypassing her ears entirely.

Mia gasped, nearly dropping Unity. Unity's eyes widened, her head snapping toward Brian.

"Telepathy?" Mia asked aloud, her voice shrill. "Brian, what did you do to yourself?"

"I bridged the gap," Brian said aloud, tapping the bandage on his temple. His voice was calm, clinical. "The Romano implant plus Cynthia's AI plus a synthetic version of your DNA. I'm part of the network now. A hub. And I needed Bianca. Despite her... previous allegiances, she's the only one who understands the core code as well as I do."

"Take it easy, Mia," Unity whispered against Mia's chest, her voice weak but clear in Mia's mind. *His thoughts are clear. No deception. He means well. And so does Bianca.*

Mia carried Unity to a plush velvet armchair near the fire and set her down gently. She sat on the ottoman beside her, immediately gripping Unity's hand again, re-establishing the lifeline.

"Fine," Mia said, glaring at the corner. "But if she tries anything, if she so much as looks at a comms device, I'll throw her through a wall. Do you understand me, Bianca?"

Bianca flinched visibly but didn't speak. She glanced at Brian with a complex mixture of awe, fear, and something that looked uncomfortably like devotion.

"Everyone, sit," Brian commanded, his voice—both internal and external—brooking no argument. "We're out of time for pleasantries."

Chris pulled up a dining chair. Dr. Fitzpatrick and his two assistants gathered around the large mahogany coffee table. The room felt heavy.

"First things first," Brian said, turning his intense gaze on Mia. "We need to clear the air. Unity is holding your physical structure together right now, but she's draining fast. You're both running on fumes. If we don't start the procedure in the next hour, you both die. Your systems will crash."

Mia glanced at Chris. She squeezed Unity's hand, drawing strength from the connection, feeling the hum of her sister's presence in her mind.

"Chris," she said, her voice shaking. "Before we do this, I have to tell you something. And I need you to promise me you won't freak out."

Chris reached out and took her free hand. His grip was solid. "I'm past freaking out, Mia. I'm running on pure adrenaline and terror. Just tell me."

Mia took a deep breath. "I'm pregnant."

The room went dead silent. The crackle of the fire sounded like gunshots. Chris froze. His eyes dropped to her stomach, then snapped back to her face, wide with disbelief.

"Pregnant?" he whispered.

"Twins," Mia choked out, the tears finally spilling over. "Heard the second heartbeat yesterday. I'm so sorry. I didn't tell you because I knew you'd stop me. You would have locked me in this bunker and I never would have saved Unity."

Chris just stared at her. Then, slowly, he leaned forward, resting his forehead against hers. His shoulders began to shake. He started to cry—silent, racking sobs that shook his whole body.

"We're having babies," he murmured into her hair.

"About that," Brian interrupted, his voice cutting through the emotional moment like a scalpel. "The procedure I'm about to perform... it's highly invasive. It involves massive neural and biological restructuring. It is absolutely not compatible with pregnancy. The biological stress will kill the fetuses within minutes."

Chris's head snapped up, his tears drying instantly. "What?"

"We have a solution," Brian said quickly, holding up a hand. He gestured toward the hallway leading to the lab. "The Romano incubators. We've modified them. They are fully functional artificial wombs. Dr. Fitzpatrick's team is ready to perform an emergency transfer. We can move the babies into the pods right now. They'll be safe."

Mia stared at the neurosurgeon, terror warring with hope. "Is that even possible? They're so small."

"It's risky," Dr. Fitzpatrick said, his voice grave. "Extremely risky. But compared to leaving them in a body that is actively dissolving? It's their only chance, Dr. Peers."

Mia looked at Chris. He nodded slowly, his face pale but resolute. He squeezed her hand.

"Do it," Chris said. "Save them."

"Okay," Brian said, clapping his hands together once. "Step one: save the babies. Step two: save the mother."

He glanced at Mia, then at Unity. His bright smile faded, replaced by a solemn, terrifying clarity that chilled Mia to the bone.

"This next part," Brian said, his telepathic voice echoing in their minds, "is the price. To fix the Syndrome, to stop the cellular decay... we can't just patch the code. It's too corrupted. We have to rewrite the entire operating system."

He stared directly at Unity.

"Your body works. It's healthy, it's recovering, it's... human. Your mind works, and it's powerful. But Mia's body is failing catastrophically. And her mind... her mind is half a soul trying to run a full system. It's burning out."

Unity tightened her grip on Mia's hand, her mental presence flaring with protective instinct. "What are you saying, Brian?"

"I'm saying there's only one vessel strong enough to survive this," Brian said softly. "I can't save both bodies. The math doesn't work. I can only save the soul."

He took a deep breath, the silence in the room absolute. Then, for all in the room to hear, he said, "To save Mia... I have to merge you. Permanently. Into one body."

United

Brian

The underground safehouse hummed with the quiet, desperate energy of a hospital waiting room at 2:00 AM, where hope and dread were balanced on a razor's edge.

Brian Carter stood over the complex control console, his face lit by the cool blue glow of a dozen monitors. His eyes darted between the scrolling code and the two modified stasis pods that dominated the room. The biometric implant in his own brain felt like a low-grade fever, a constant, humming connection to the AI network they had built from scrap and genius. Sweat beaded on his forehead, despite the chill in the subterranean room.

In Pod One lay Mia Peers. Her body was a ruin. The Syndrome had accelerated drastically, consuming her faster than Brian could synthesize stabilizing agents. Her skin, once vibrant, was now a dull white, sagging loose over bones that seemed too sharp. Her muscles, enhanced by the serum, were atrophied, devoured by her own hyper-active metabolism. She was sedated deep, a fading signal on the bio-monitors, her chest barely rising.

In Pod Two lay Unity. She was asleep, induced by a mild sedative to keep her calm. Her dyed black hair was stark against the white sterile pillow, framing a face that had finally lost the gauntness of a twenty-year coma. Her body was frail, unenhanced, but it was healthy—a pristine human vessel waiting to be filled.

And although the sisters were separated, each had one arm stretched toward the other, their hands placed together for constant physical contact. It seemed the only failsafe to keeping Mia from dying.

In the corner, tucked away like precious cargo, the twin incubator units glowed with a soft, steady amber light. Inside, bathed in nutrient fluid, two tiny, impossible heartbeats fluttered rhythmically on digital displays—Chris and Mia's children, safe from the biological storm raging in their mother's body.

Chris stood by the heavy blast door, his back against the cold metal. His face was pale, his eyes red-rimmed and hollow. He looked at the ruin of his wife in Pod One, then at the sleeping stranger in Pod Two who bore her likeness. His former high school girlfriend. The silence stretched, heavy and suffocating.

"Do it," Chris whispered, the words scraping his throat. "Save them."

Brian nodded once, a jerky motion. He didn't trust his voice. He closed his eyes, reaching out with his mind, interfacing directly with the machine through his implant. *Initiate transfer sequence. Authorization: Carter Central Four Five.*

The hum of the pods deepened instantly to a resonant thrum that vibrated through the floorplates. Lights flickered overhead as the power draw spiked.

It wasn't a surgery. It was a download. A massive data migration. Thirty-eight years of memories, instincts, fears, loves, and scientific brilliance were being streamed from a dying hard drive to a stable one.

Brian felt the data move through him—a roaring, chaotic river of pure consciousness using his mind as a conduit. It was overwhelming. He felt Mia's terror of death, her fierce determination to protect her family, her deep, abiding love for Chris that felt like warm sunlight. He felt Unity's quiet strength, her deep-seated rage at her stolen life, her terrified acceptance of this final sacrifice. The two streams swirled, clashed, and then began to merge, flowing into the receiver.

Then, with a sharp psychic snap, the connection severed. The hum died down.

In Pod One, Mia's body shuddered violently. A high-pitched alarm began to shriek on her monitor—*CRITICAL FAILURE. SYSTEM COLLAPSE.*

Then, it began to dissolve.

It was a horrific, rapid acceleration of the Syndrome's endgame. The flesh lost cohesion, the cellular bonds snapping apart. Skin sloughed off bone, muscle turned to liquid. In seconds, the woman in the pod was gone, replaced by a pool of steaming gray sludge.

Chris turned away, retching dryly, unable to watch his wife disintegrate.

But in Pod Two, the bio-monitors spiked with activity. Heart rate normalized. Brain waves shifted from delta sleep to swift, active beta.

Unity's eyes snapped open. They were clear, sharp, and utterly aware.

A Future

Mia

The first week was a blur of vertigo and identity dissonance. The woman who woke up in the safehouse bedroom didn't know who she was.

The woman's mind was a kaleidoscope of fragmented memories that didn't fit together. She remembered winning a regional karate tournament at sixteen, the sweat and the glory. She remembered defending her PhD dissertation on advanced genetics in a cold lecture hall. She remembered the darkness of a twenty-year coma, a silent void. And she remembered the terrifying, weightless sensation of falling from a private jet before hitting trees.

She looked in the bathroom mirror for hours. Short black hair framed the face of a person she hadn't known since she was a teenager, but it wasn't the face she expected. The eyes were different—harder, older.

But when she spoke, the voice that came out of her throat was unmistakably Mia's—confident, articulate, resonant.

"Chris?"

Chris was there, sitting in a chair by the bed, holding her hand tightly. He stared at her, searching desperately for his wife in the eyes of her sister, terrified of what he might find.

"I'm here," he said, his voice thick with emotion.

"It's me," she whispered, squeezing his hand with surprising strength. "And it's her. We're... us. We're both here."

Mia and Unity decided to keep the name Mia. It was the pragmatic choice—it was the name on the degrees, on the bank accounts, on the marriage license. Unity, the part of the new consciousness that remembered the coma, didn't mind. She was tired of being the invalid, the tragic victim in the story. She was happy to finally be part of the strength.

The recovery was miraculous, defying all medical expectations. With Mia's enhanced memories of movement and muscle control merging with Unity's overall healthy physiology—and perhaps a lingering trace of the serum's residual energy carried over by the soul—her atrophied legs regained strength in days, not months. She walked with a cane on Tuesday. By Friday, she was running on the treadmill in the bunker gym, sweat dripping off her face, laughing with the sheer joy of movement.

It was a new life. A second chance for two broken souls.

A month later, the snow had melted, and the loose ends of the war were being tied up.

Caterina stood at the reinforced gate of a secure government facility in rural Maryland, dressed in an orange prison-issue jumpsuit. She seemed relaxed, leaning against the concrete wall, watching the convoy of black armored SUVs that would take her to her new home. Mia stood beside her, the wind whipping her black hair across her face.

"They wanted to keep you active, you know," Mia said. "As an asset. Lethabo had to threaten to resign. I told them if they tried to weaponize you, you'd break out in a week and level D.C. just out of spite."

Caterina smirked, a flash of the old, violent clone. "I might have. I don't like cages."

"You're going into deep stasis," Mia reminded her. "Secure

cryo. It's the only way to stop the Syndrome from advancing in your enhanced body. You'll sleep until Brian and I find a cure. It could be years. Decades."

"I can wait," Caterina said with a shrug. "I've been awake too long anyway. Better to sleep than to melt like so many of my siblings."

She offered her hand. Mia took it. The grip was strong, enhanced, a reminder of the power coiled beneath the skin.

"Thank you, *sister*," Caterina said softly. "For the chance."

She released Mia's hand and climbed into the back of the armored transport van without looking back.

The hardest goodbye was Jon.

He stood by his modest sedan in the driveway, a single duffel bag at his feet. He looked older than his years, worn down by years of living a double life, his shoulders slumped with the weight of his choices.

"You're sure about this?" Mia asked, stepping off the porch. "We have room at the new lab. You're a skilled technician. You could start over, help us with the research."

"I can't," Jon said, shaking his head. "I need to find my sister. I need to make sure she's really safe. And... I need to not be here. Too many ghosts in this house. Too many reminders of what I did."

He looked up at her. Really looked at her, past the surface.

And in that split second, something shifted in the air. The sunlight seemed to catch Mia differently.

Mia felt a distinct tug in the center of her chest, a warmth spreading outward. The short black hair on her head seemed to shimmer, the roots darkening instantly to an even deeper, obsidian black. Her posture softened, the tension draining from her shoulders.

"Jon," she said. But the voice that emerged wasn't Mia's confident alto. It was softer, tinged with a deep, melancholy gratitude. It was Unity's.

Jon's eyes went wide, his breath catching. "Unity?"

She stepped forward and hugged him fiercely. It wasn't the polite hug of a sister bidding farewell to an employee. It was the desperate, clinging embrace of a woman saying goodbye to the only man who had seen her when she was invisible, the man she had come to love and admire since waking.

"Thank you," Unity whispered in his ear, her voice thick with tears. "For reading to me. For protecting me. For seeing me when no one else did."

She pulled back, wiping her eyes. She slipped a sleek black bank card into his hand. "It's untraceable. Unlimited funds. Go find Zuri. Buy her a house. Go live a real life, Jon Turner."

Jon stared at her, tears spilling down his weathered cheeks. He nodded. He squeezed her hand one last time, got into his car, and drove away down the long driveway.

As the taillights faded around the bend, the shimmer passed. Mia took a deep, shuddering breath, rolling her shoulders as if resetting them. She was back in control.

Lethabo was the last to leave the safehouse.

He stood in the driveway next to his personal truck, wearing civilian clothes—jeans and a flannel shirt—that looked strange on him. A black leather eyepatch covered the left side of his face, a permanent souvenir from the Romanos. He looked like a pirate who had retired to the suburbs and wasn't happy about it.

"Lieutenant Colonel," Mia said, walking down the steps and snapping a crisp salute.

Lethabo laughed, a deep, rumbling sound. "Don't do that, Doctor. You look ridiculous. You're not military."

"So do you. A desk job? Really? I thought you'd hate it."

"Someone has to keep the Pentagon honest about the clone situation. Make sure they don't try to start a program." He touched the eyepatch self-consciously. "Besides, I'm done with field work. I have a family in Maryland I haven't seen enough of. It's time to go home."

"What about Tony and the squad?"

"They're staying in Sentry Blade. Tony's running the unit now. Says he needs to keep perfecting his Schwarzenegger impression for the rookies."

They shook hands, a firm grip of mutual respect forged in fire. "Watch your back, Mia," Lethabo said seriously. "The Romanos are scattered, but Chiara is out there. She has resources, and she holds a grudge. She won't forget what you took from her."

"Let her come," Mia said, instinctively touching her flat stomach, where two tiny heartbeats used to be. "I have a family to protect now. And I'm not the same woman she thinks I am."

That evening, Mia and Chris stood on the balcony of the newly secured lab penthouse, watching the sun set over the valley in a blaze of orange and purple.

It was finally quiet. The soldiers were gone. The clones were gone. The noise of the last few months had faded to a hum.

"So," Chris said, wrapping his arm around her shoulders, pulling her close against the evening chill. "Here we are. We have a state-of-the-art lab. We have two babies growing in incubators downstairs. And we have... you. Both of you."

Mia leaned into him, resting her head on his shoulder. For the first time in her life, she felt truly whole. Strong. Balanced.

"We have a future," she corrected softly. "A real one."

"What about the Romanos?" Chris asked, looking out over the field. "Chiara said on the news they were leaving the country. But you know them. They'll be back. They need a cure."

Mia smiled. It wasn't a gentle smile. It was a dangerous, calculated look that belonged to a woman who had died and come back stronger.

"They do," she said, her voice hard. "But I don't intend to be waiting here when they come knocking on our door."

She gazed past the horizon, toward the east, across the Atlantic Ocean toward Italy.

"Someday," Mia whispered, the promise hanging in the air between them, "the future will come to them."

Epilogue

Mia

The lab buzzed with a new kind of energy. It wasn't the frenetic panic of impending doom anymore; it was the steady, productive hum of a facility changing the world. And occasionally, the cry of hungry infants.

Mia Peers walked through the main research floor, bouncing her daughter, Unity, on her shoulder. The baby smelled of milk and baby powder, a scent that grounded Mia in a way no serum ever could.

She stopped at a workstation where Arjun Kasudia was hunched over a microscope evaluating the lastest spinal muscular atrophy work. He looked older, his hair thinner, but his eyes were bright with focus. Mia had forgiven him for his role in her parents' death. Forgiveness was part of the new Mia—part of the Chris and Unity influence.

"How's it going?" Mia asked, patting the baby's back.

Arjun glanced up, blinking. "Close. I can feel it. The new viral vector is promising."

"How's Natasha?"

"Stronger," he said, a smile touching his lips. "She sat up on her own yesterday."

"Good. Don't work too late, Arjun. Go home to them."

Chris approached from the break room, looking harried. He held their son, Milo, in one arm and a bottle in the other. His tie was askew, and he had a spit-up stain on his shoulder.

"He won't eat," Chris said, sounding desperate. "He just screams."

"You're tense," Mia said. "He can feel it. Relax your shoulders."

"Relax? I'm holding a tiny, angry human who hates me."

"Here," Arjun said, holding out his hands. He took Milo and the bottle with practiced ease. He tickled the baby's cheek, and Milo latched onto the bottle instantly, silence descending on the lab.

"Traitor," Chris muttered at his son.

"Go see if Ginger wants him for a bit," Mia said, taking Milo back from a reluctant Arjun. "Arjun has actual work to do."

They walked over to the corner of the lab where Ginger had set up an easel. She was painting a landscape—rolling hills and a bright blue sky. It was good, but not as good as Mia's new work. Unity's talent had survived the merge, enhancing Mia's stick figures into masterpieces.

"Hey," Ginger said, putting down her brush. "Give me the boy. You two look like you need a nap."

"We need a miracle," Chris said, handing Milo over. "Or a nanny."

"I'm free," Ginger said, cuddling the baby. "Best job I ever had."

Mia watched them, a warmth spreading through her chest that had nothing to do with biology. This was her family. Not the one she was born into, but the one she had built from the wreckage.

But the peace was fragile. She knew that.

That morning, she had felt it. A tug in her chest. A whisper in the back of her mind that didn't belong to her.

It's time.

It wasn't a voice, exactly. It was an intuition, sharp and clear. Unity was still in there, woven into the fabric of Mia's consciousness. And she was right.

"Chris," Mia said. "I have to go."

He glanced at her, his smile fading. "Go where? It's almost dinner."

"I have an errand to run."

"An errand," Chris repeated flatly. "Does this errand involve passports?"

Mia stepped closer, cupping his face. "It involves finishing what we started."

Chris sighed, leaning into her touch. "I knew this domestic bliss was too good to last. You're going to Italy."

Mia grinned, then shrugged one shoulder. "Guilty as charged? Sometimes I wonder what I was thinking when I married a lawyer."

"Fine," Chris said. "Go. Do what you have to do. Just... come back."

Mia kissed him—a deep, lingering kiss that tasted of coffee and trust.

"Always," she whispered.

She kissed Unity's forehead, then Milo's. She grabbed her coat and headed for the elevator.

The evening air on the rooftop helipad was crisp, biting deep in her lungs with the sharp promise of autumn. Below, the Shenandoah Valley was going to sleep, a patchwork of river fog and turning leaves, vibrant reds and oranges bleeding into the lingering green.

She looked east. Toward the ocean. Toward the old country.

The Romanos thought they had escaped. They thought they were safe in their villas and vineyards. They thought they were rid of the Peers.

Mia smiled, and it was a smile that belonged to two women. She stood at the very edge of the roof, her toes over the concrete lip, looking out at the world she was about to leave behind.

She wasn't wearing a white lab coat stained with chemical reagents. She wasn't wearing heavy tactical gear weighing her down with ceramic plates and Kevlar. She wore simple black yoga pants that hugged her legs and a sleeveless shirt, the fabric cool against her skin. Her hair, no longer the natural blonde of her past life but now a rich, deep brunette, fell loose across her shoulders and whipped in the wind.

She closed her eyes, shutting out the stunning view, turning her focus entirely inward. She needed to feel the machine before she turned it on.

Since the procedure—since Brian had cracked the genetic code and merged two souls into one stable vessel—her body was no longer just a biological creation subject to decay. It was a canvas, and she was finally the artist, holding the brush.

She took a deep breath, centering herself. She felt the change begin in her marrow. It was a sensation of effervescence, like champagne bubbles rising in her blood. She felt the density of her bones shift, the calcium lattice rearranging itself at a molecular level, becoming porous and hollow like a bird's, shifting pounds of misplaced weight in seconds. She felt the mass in her muscles redistribute, sliding under her skin like mercury, optimizing her center of gravity for lift and balance, preparing her shoulders for a stress load no human joint should be able to bear.

It wasn't magic. It was high-speed, conscious chemistry. Her atoms burned, recycling energy in a way that standard physics said was impossible, but biology—her enhanced, perfected, unique biology—allowed. The hum of it rejoiced in her chest, a powerful, silent engine idling.

She opened her eyes. The sky was a brilliant, orange and red blend. She didn't need a helicopter anymore. She *was* the aircraft.

She glanced back at the lab one last time, her gaze penetrating the concrete walls in her mind's eye. Inside the penthouse, one floor down, Chris was probably feeding Milo his dinner bottle, the baby's small hands gripping his finger. Ginger was likely holding Unity in one hand while painting with the other. Brian was undoubtedly in the basement, arguing with a machine that wasn't processing data fast enough for his liking.

They were safe. They were whole. And to keep them that way, to draw the fire away from the home they had built, she had to leave. As Brian might say, this was the final variable in the equation.

Mia took one last breath of Virginia air, tasting the pine and the damp earth. She raised her chin to the sky, and with a calm, deliberate movement, stepped off the ledge into the void.

Gravity, ancient and jealous, reached up to claim her, pulling at her ankles. But she refused its call.

Instead of falling, she soared.

It was a violent, exhilarating rush. The wind screamed past her ears as she shot upward, a black streak against the sunset, leaving the lab far below. She banked east, turning her face toward the vast expanse of the Atlantic Ocean. Toward Italy. Toward the source of the rot.

Mia landed silently on the cobblestone driveway of a secluded villa deep in the hills of northern Italy. The air here was warmer, thicker, smelling of sun-baked dust, cypress trees, and distant olive groves.

As her feet touched the ancient stones, she commanded her bones to re-densify. The bubbling sensation reversed, and she felt the comforting, solid weight of her own humanity settle back onto her frame. She was just a woman in workout gear again.

The estate was silent, bathed in the golden afternoon light. It was guarded by high walls covered in climbing roses and a network of sophisticated cameras that tracked her every movement as she approached. Yet, no alarm sounded. No dogs barked. It was the silence of a held breath.

She walked to the massive front doors of the villa. They were dark, ancient oak, reinforced with bands of iron and studded with steel bolts. They were locked tight, a physical barrier meant to keep the world out.

Mia didn't knock. She didn't bother with lockpicks. She stopped in front of the wood, closed her eyes, and reached out with her mind. She felt the complex mechanism inside the wood—the heavy brass tumblers, the tension springs, the steel deadbolt buried deep in the doorframe. It was a puzzle made of metal.

She grasped it psychically and twisted with a sharp, brutal mental shove.

CRUNCH.

The sound was loud in the quiet afternoon. Metal sheared against metal. Springs snapped. The heavy deadbolt sheared right through the doorframe, splintering the wood. The doors groaned and swung inward, revealing the darkness inside.

Mia stepped over the threshold into the foyer. It was a cathedral built to worship wealth—tapestries of deep red velvet hung from the two-story walls, a crystal chandelier the size of a small car suspended from a frescoed ceiling, catching the light in a thousand prisms. A spiral staircase carved from Carrara marble dominated the center of the room, looking like a helix of pure money ascending to heaven.

"Hello?" Mia called out. Her voice wasn't a shout, but she tweaked her vocal cords, adding a subsonic resonance that vibrated the glass in the window frames and rattled the crystal drops of the chandelier. "Is anybody home? It's Mia Peers. I was in the neighborhood and thought I'd drop in."

The silence shattered instantly. Footsteps thundered from the upper floors, a stampede of heavy boots on wood and stone. The distinct *click-clack* of weapons being readied, safeties clicking off, echoed off the marble walls.

A figure appeared at the top of the stairs, emerging from the shadows of the landing.

An old man in an impeccably tailored black suit. He leaned heavily on a silver-handled cane, his posture slightly stooped with age. But his face, framed by shock-white hair, was unlined by frailty. His eyes, dark as obsidian, were sharp, intelligent, and infinitely cruel.

Mia knew him instantly. Not from photos, but from the blood singing in her veins. Her enhanced senses read his genetics like a barcode from fifty feet away—the source code, the original template.

Cesaro Romano. The Patriarch.

He wasn't dead. He hadn't graciously passed the torch to his wife. The true story flooded Mia's mind, pulled from the psychic ether that permeated the house like a scent: Mother Sophia hadn't inherited the empire; she had stolen it in a coup. She had knocked her own husband unconscious decades ago and shoved him into a stasis pod in the deepest sub-basement to rot while she played queen.

But now Mother Sophia was dead, her head severed by her own creation. And the king had returned to his throne.

A woman stepped up beside him, clutching the banister. Chiara. She looked pale, her beautiful face distorted by terror and rage. Her eyes were wide with hate as she saw Mia standing below.

"Kill her!" Chiara screamed, her voice cracking, pointing a trembling finger down at Mia. "Don't let her speak! Kill the abomination!"

Dozens of clones poured onto the landing and down the

stairs, filling the foyer. Men and women, all beautiful, all deadly, armed with automatic assault rifles. They surrounded Mia in a tight semicircle of death, weapons raised, fingers tense on triggers. The air was thick with the smell of gun oil and fear.

"Drop your weapons," Mia said.

She didn't shout. She didn't have to. She injected the Command directly into the syllable. It was a psychic shockwave that rolled out from her, hitting every Romano in the room in the deepest part of their conditioned brains.

Clatter. Thud. Clang.

It was instantaneous. Every rifle, every pistol in the room hit the marble floor, sounding like a cascade of falling metal. The clones stared at their own empty hands in horror, bewilderment washing over their identical, perfect faces as their bodies betrayed them.

"I'm glad you're all here," Mia said calmly, stepping over a discarded rifle. "Saves me some time."

She walked toward the stairs. The crowd of armed clones parted for her like the Red Sea, their bodies moving against their conscious will to clear a path, pressing back against the tapestries. "Stay put."

She climbed the marble steps slowly, deliberately, her shoes silent on the cold stone. She stopped three steps below the landing, looking up at the Patriarch, meeting his gaze.

"Cesaro Romano," Mia said, her voice level. "Why don't you invite me in for tea? We have much to discuss."

Cesaro chuckled. It was a dry, dusty sound, like old parchment crumbling. "You have spirit, girl. I'll give you that. Sophia always said your line was too willful."

"Grandfather!" Chiara hissed, grabbing his arm, her nails digging into his suit jacket. "Don't listen to her! She's dangerous! She has mind control! We need to kill her now before she—"

Cesaro turned slowly to his granddaughter. His face twisted

with profound disgust. "You prattle, girl. You let the Americans find us. You lost the serum to a rogue. You are no longer useful to this family."

He reached out with shocking speed for a man his age. His hand, gnarled but powerful, snapped around Chiara's delicate throat. He squeezed. Chiara gagged, clawing at his hand, her face turning red.

"Release her," Mia commanded softly.

Cesaro froze. His hand opened involuntarily, as if stung. Chiara stumbled back, gasping for air, clutching her bruised neck, staring at Mia in terror.

Mia walked up the final three steps, standing eye-to-level with the old man.

"I'm not like you, Cesaro," Mia said, her voice cold. "I don't kill family just because they fail. That's lazy."

She turned her back on him, a calculated insult, looking out over the sea of clones filling the foyer below and the landing around her. Hundreds of faces, all variations on a theme, all looking up at her with a mix of terror, awe, and a dawning, desperate hope.

"Listen to me," Mia said, her voice ringing like a clear bell through the cavernous space, reaching every ear. "This ends today. The selling of your brothers and sisters is over. The training for war is finished. You are a family now, not a factory product."

"Yes," the crowd murmured in unintentional unison. A hive mind of obedience shifting its allegiance.

"You will live normal lives," Mia continued, laying out the new law. "You will use your vast wealth to hide, to survive, to integrate. And you will wait."

She paused, letting the promise hang in the air, letting them taste the possibility of a future that didn't end in a puddle.

"My team is working on a cure," she said. "For the Syndrome that kills us. We will find it. And when we do, I will send

Caterina back to you with it. She will be your leader, not your owner. Until then... you sleep in stasis if you must to survive. But you do not kill."

Cesaro stared at her back, his face a mask of disbelief. "You would save us? After everything we did to you? To your sister?"

Mia turned her head slightly to look at him over her shoulder. "I'm not saving you, old man. I'm saving the world from you."

She leaned in close to him, her voice a whisper that only he could hear, heavy with psychic weight.

"The Romanos will never come after me or my family again," she commanded, embedding the order deep in his psyche.

"Never," Cesaro repeated dully, his eyes glazing over as the compulsion took hold.

"Never," the crowd echoed below, the word rolling like thunder through the villa.

Mia nodded. It was done. The loop was closed.

She walked back down the stairs, moving through the crowd. The clones bowed their heads as she passed, a ripple of submission. Some wept silently. Some glared with impotent rage. But none of them moved a muscle to stop her.

Mia walked out the front door, past the broken lock, into the bright Italian sunlight. The air tasted sweet.

She walked down the long driveway, leaving the villa and its ghosts behind her. She walked until she reached the small town at the bottom of the hill, the smell of strong espresso and freshly baked bread filling the air.

It was a beautiful country. Peaceful. Ancient.

But it wasn't home.

Mia stopped in the center of a quiet, sun-drenched piazza. She gazed up at the endless blue sky, clear and inviting.

She felt light. Lighter than air. The weight of the past—the twenty-year coma, the secrets, the guilt, the split soul—was finally gone. She was whole. She was one. She was free.

And somehow, despite her *choice*, Mia had saved herself and

Unity both, enabling Unity to have a genuine, meaningful, and fully healthy life and body.

Mia smiled, a true, deep smile that reached her eyes. She bent her knees and pushed off the ancient cobblestones.

With a silent rush of air, she soared upward into the clouds, banking sharply to the west. Heading across the ocean. Heading to her family. Heading home.

Acknowledgments

I will forever start by thanking my wife, Michelle. You, you are my rock and soulmate. Thank you, babe.

My son, Connor Baldwin, for introducing me to *Save The Cat! Writes a Novel* by Jessica Brody.

My daughter, Sydney Baldwin, for her encouragement and support.

My son, Tyler Baldwin, for his technical expertise to market this novel.

My book designer, Adam Hay, for my incredible cover and logo. You can find Adam on Reedsy.

About the author

Paul Baldwin is a minimalist and retired Airman living in Virginia who navigated a C-130 and rocked life as a public affairs officer from the Pentagon. As a second lieutenant, Paul stared at a heavy 1990s computer monitor attempting to craft a novel about adventures in the Air Force. After waiting over twenty-five years, his writing dream finally took flight. When he's not authoring, editing, rewriting, and then crying (you get the picture), Paul contemplates hiking more and eating fewer Biscoff Cookies topped with their oh-so-incredible cookie butter. Paul is a former owner of two 1981 DMC DeLoreans who treasures his wife and three adult children more than time machines.

By Paul Baldwin

Serum
Syndrome

www.ingramcontent.com/pod-product-compliance
Lightning Source LLC
Chambersburg PA
CBHW050728180626
46814CB00002B/653